THE
IMMORTAL
HEART

The Immortal Bound Series

EVERBOUND
PRESS

A LOVE SO POWERFUL, IT CAN'T BE DENIED

THE
IMMORTAL
HEART

CHRISTINA FARLEY

Published by Everbound Press

Library of Congress Control Number: 2024920347

www.ChristinaFarley.com

Cover and Interior Artwork: Trif Book Designs

Map Artwork: Veronika Wunder

ASIN: B0D52K38VF

ISBN (hardcover): 979-8-9864624-6-2

ISBN (paperback): 979-8-9864624-5-5

ALSO BY CHRISTINA FARLEY

For Andrea Mack, critique partner and friend

1
BEING AN ESCAPE ARTIST IS HARDER THAN IT LOOKS
ESTRELLA

Florida

Ever since I first stepped out of the hospital three weeks ago my goal has been to survive.

I woke up at Nadia's Home for Girls and showered, brushed my teeth, and shrugged into my hand-me-down clothes. Stared at myself in the mirror, wondering who this blonde-haired girl with the strange tattoo on her shoulder blade is.

Endured the flashing pains in my head, desperately wishing for my memories to return.

But today is not that day.

Today I'm going to escape this life.

The dagger I stole from our headmistress's secret room

last night is tucked deep in my backpack. The magic of its blade still tingles across my skin from when I slipped it between my school books this morning. After battling that horrible Wraith monster last night, I can't stand the thought of parting with its sharp-tipped protection.

Besides, my gut warns me my time here is ticking down minute by minute. I need to be ready for whatever I face.

The thick, muggy Floridian heat greets me as I step outside where my best friends, Lexi, Mara, and Tiffany are waiting for me. It's our morning ritual to walk the sandy path together to the bus stop.

But when I go to leave, I find Nadia standing by the doorway, arms crossed. My body stiffens. Behind her hangs the sign: *Let go of your past and seize your future!*

The frown on her face deepens, and her thin lips pinch tight as her gaze narrows on me. Her brown hair is pinned tightly in a bun and her shirt and pants are pressed crisp against her frame like a uniform of war.

My feet hurry past her to join my friends on the porch. Every nerve in my body is wound tight as a knot just waiting for her to announce that she knows it was my friends and me who snuck into her office and stole the files and dagger. It will only take a snap of her fingers to send those Wraiths that lurk around the grounds to kill us.

"Come home directly after school," Nadia calls to our backs.

Lexi spins around. Her bright red hair flutters in the morning sea breeze, sparks escaping a fire. "But what about play practice?"

"What about play practice?" Nadia asks.

"I've got the lead role. If I don't show up, the principal might call here looking for me."

"The principal?" Nadia lifts her eyebrows. "Looking for you?"

There's no way the principal gives a hoot if we don't attend play practice, but Lexi's right. Based on the plan the two of us laid out in the early morning darkness, I may need extra time after school to talk to Tristan, which is why "going to play practice" is essential.

"The principal is a patron of the arts," I add, jumping to her defense. "If he were to find out the key actors and crew members were missing, it could cause a stir."

Nadia shakes her head as if she's not buying our excuse, so I quickly interject, "Don't worry. We'll be back with plenty of time for me to do all the dishes."

The reminder of my punishment for coming home late last night with Dion seems to console her because she nods, saying, "I'll have Val pick you up after your precious play practice."

Then she waves us off with her hand. The four of us clatter down the wooden steps and onto the sandy path. My pack seems to burn against my back as if screaming that I'm carrying away one of her stolen treasures.

I peek over my shoulder, expecting Nadia to somehow know it's tucked inside, clattering around with my books and peanut butter and jelly sandwich. But she merely settles into one of the rocking chairs beneath the Chimes of Forgetting. I take a final look at the old Floridan home, sprawling beneath moss-laden oaks, and the lighthouse spearing up into a dawn-streaked sky of pink and purple ribbons.

The memory of the four of us scrambling up the old

wrought-iron staircase to the top of the lighthouse still burns strong in my mind, and my steps quicken.

Tonight we're going to escape. Nothing is going to stop me.

"She suspects something," Mara whispers as we scurry down the path.

"But she can't prove anything," Lexi adds.

"She will if she goes looking," Mara points out.

"Just keep walking," I say through clenched teeth.

"What are you all talking about?" Tiffany asks.

"We'll explain on the bus," I say.

Tiffany didn't join us last night in our break-in of Nadia's office and discovery of the secret room. I didn't want to implicate her in our criminal activity in case things went sour.

My whole body chills colder than ice as I slip through the gates. The Wraiths—or should I say monsters?—leer down at us as we exit the iron gate of Nadia's Home. I desperately keep my eyes focused straight in front of me, knowing if I give any hint that I can see or hear them, they'll know my memories are returning.

Because apparently, that's worthy of death.

The bigger question that rattles in my mind is if the creatures know it was me who stabbed one of their own. I clench my fist tighter, remembering how I thrust the dagger into the Wraith's dark heart and watched its form crumble to dust at my feet.

The gate slams shut behind us, and I jerk at the sudden noise. Thankfully, the bus barrels up to our stop. I can't climb the steps fast enough. Once I slip into a vinyl seat, I dare glance out my window. The creatures sit still as stone as if they are merely gargoyles decorating the gate. They may suspect something, but the proof of what my friends and I have done has yet to be discovered.

It's now a battle against time. I just need to find a way to escape before it's too late.

2

STALKING MISHAPS AND MISADVENTURES

ESTRELLA

Florida

"Tell us everything about your date last night," Tiffany demands, settling beside me while Mara and Lexi sit behind us. "I've been dying to hear how it went."

The bus takes off. Its sway usually lulls me to sleep. Today of all days it should since after our encounter with the Wraith and sneaking in Nadia's secret room, I stayed up the rest of the night creating the beginnings of an escape plan.

I should be tired, but instead, I feel wired and restless. I finally have a purpose.

"Did he take you to a fancy restaurant?" Lexi asks.

"He better have with that dress she was wearing," Mara adds.

"It was amazing." I hug my backpack, glad to talk about anything other than death and monsters. "We went on a helicopter ride."

"Girl!" Lexi gasps while Tiffany squeals.

I share the details. Just the memory of my time with Dion makes me miss him already, and my heart aches. I wish our date hadn't ended with me freaking out. Is he upset about how things ended? Since he's visiting his family, will there be a way to get in touch with him when he returns?

Then a new thought hits me. Will I even be around when he does?

"So what were you all talking about on the walk to the bus?" Tiffany asks. "What might Nadia suspect?"

I peer over my shoulder at Lexi and Mara to see if they think I should tell her. Mara shakes her head in a no while Lexi shrugs.

"What is it?" Tiffany looks at the three of us. "Tell me! We don't keep secrets from each other."

I sigh and relent. "Last night I broke into Nadia's office," I admit, deciding to keep the other girls out of this.

"What?" Tiffany gasps, her dark brown eyes wide. "It was you who set off the alarm? Nadia and her orderlies went on a witch hunt to find out who it was."

I nod, biting my lips, trying to decide how much to tell her. "She doesn't know it was me. At least, not yet."

Tiffany sits straighter, eyes widening. "You found something, didn't you?"

"Files on each of us," I say.

"What did they say?" she asks, breathlessly. "Did you find anything useful? Anything that can help us know about our pasts?"

"Based on what I found, I think we need to escape Nadia's as soon as possible." I hate not telling her the whole truth, but the less she knows, the safer she'll be. "There's someone I think can help us. I'm going to try to talk to him today."

Lexi snorts and mutters, "It's a bad idea."

"Can we even trust this mystery guy?" Mara asks.

"I don't know," I say, "but he's the best option we have."

"Wow." Tiffany leans back against her seat. "You better take me with you when you go. Promise? And no more secrets."

The bus pulls up to the front of the school and screeches to a halt. I squeeze her hand. "Absolutely."

The moment I get off the bus, I bolt to the office.

"Excuse me," I greet the receptionist. "I forgot my school project. Can I use your phone to call home?"

"Of course, sweetie," the receptionist says, setting the phone on the counter in front of me.

I quickly dial Tristan's number I memorized at the mall. He picks up on the first ring.

"You're still alive," he says.

"That's how you answer your phone calls? What if it wasn't me?"

"You and Katka are the only ones who have this number."

"Who's Katka?" I shake my head. "You know, never mind. I need to meet today after school."

"Not a problem. Everything alright?"

"Last night my friends and I broke into Nadia's office." I glance around and switch to a whisper. "I may have killed a Wraith."

"You what?" he yells. "How is that possible?"

"Long story." I stiffen when I see Chandra breeze into the office, her long black hair fluttering in her wake. "Let's just say I don't have much more time. Meet me after school at the auditorium."

Chandra slides up to the counter right beside me, leaning over its edge to ask the receptionist a question. I slam the phone onto the receiver before Tristan can even agree. She doesn't bother to glance my way, which puts me on edge even more. She's up to something and a niggle on my stomach warns me that something is me. Why can't she just mind her own business?

"Thanks so much for letting me use your phone," I tell the receptionist. "Nadia said she's going to bring my school project later today."

"Have a lovely day, dear," the receptionist says.

I switch my backpack so it rests on my stomach rather than my back, needing the dagger as close to me as possible. Then I rush out of the room as far away from Chandra as possible.

Except it's like she's becoming a ghost desperate to haunt me. All day long I can't escape her. She's everywhere I am, stifling me like she's sucking out the air I'm breathing.

Sashaying in her tight red dress by my locker. Sitting at the lunch table next to us along with her entourage of guys, laughing way too loud. She was even in the bathroom at the same time as me. That girl spends way too much time putting on lipstick. But when she suddenly joins my art class, I just can't take it anymore. I march to her workstation, clutching my paintbrush as if it were a weapon.

"Excuse me," I demand. "Why are you taking this class now?"

"Oh, hi, there," Chandra says blandly, not bothering to even glance my way. "Estrella, right?"

She dips her brush into the red and sweeps it across the canvas. The girl definitely does not know how to paint. But that's beside the point. The point is I need to get her out of my life today. If she follows me to play practice, I might lose it.

I try a different tactic.

"Dion and I had such an amazing time last night," I say, putting on a dreamy look as I gaze off in the distance. Not that it's hard to look dreamy just thinking about him. "Helicopter ride and dinner in an aquarium. It was simply amazing!"

Chandra's brush falters, and she clears her throat. "He really shouldn't be doing that sort of thing. You know, he has a girlfriend."

My heart stutters at her words, and all my bravado slips away like ice on hot pavement. "What? No, he doesn't."

"That's why he had to go back to Brazil," she continues smoothly.

I nearly drop my paintbrush. She's lying. "No, his father sent for him."

"His girlfriend had an accident and apparently is in the hospital." She shrugs, finally turning to face me. Her eyes are shining in victory. I think I hate her. A lot. "They're so cute together. In fact, his parents have been desperate for them to *marry*."

"Marry? Aren't they a little young to be getting married?"

"I tried to warn you not to get involved with him. Besides, he's only here for a few weeks before he has to go back for good. I guess you were his spring fling or something."

"Spring fling?" I choke the words out, backing up. *Impossible.* He seemed so into me, or maybe that was just my stupid messed-up brain telling me that.

At the same time, I did always feel like he was holding back from telling me something. Like he was too afraid to tell me the truth. Suddenly, I don't know anymore. Is that his secret, and he didn't have the heart to tell me? A slow smile curls on Chandra's lips. *Ugh.* I refuse to let her think she's got to me.

Even if she has.

"I suppose when Dion gets back," I say, "we can ask him if I'm a spring fling or not."

"Yes." She nods thoughtfully. "I'm sure he'll tell you the *truth*."

It's like she stabbed me in the chest. I can't explain why her words hit me so hard, but the part of my brain that refuses to work properly is screaming at me that she's right.

And it terrifies me.

For the rest of class, I make sure to ignore her, instead focusing completely on my painting and Lexi. When the bell rings, I put away my art supplies.

"I'll meet you at play practice," I tell Lexi. "I just need to drop some books off at the media center."

I wave goodbye and bolt out the door. As I weave my way through the hallways, I try to lose Chandra, but the girl is annoyingly stubborn. It's like she's following me. *Wait. Is she following me?* After what happened at the mall, all my senses are in overdrive.

Biting my lip, I switch tactics and board my bus. Once I'm settled in the seat, I pretend to read a book, but really I'm watching Chandra through the window from the corner of my eye. She pauses outside the bus door, scans the windows until she finds me, and then pulls out a tube of lipstick from her bag. More and more students board the bus, and worry kicks in. If she doesn't move soon, the bus is going to leave with me on it. I'll miss play practice and meeting Tristan.

How long does it take to put on lipstick?

She smacks her lips a few times, staring at herself in a handheld mirror before glancing around and then taking off toward the parking lot. I let out a breath of relief, and crouching down so she doesn't see me, I scurry down the aisle and step off the bus.

"You not riding today?" the driver calls after me.

Shaking my head, I say, "Changed my mind. Thanks!"

I glance at the parking lot to make sure Chandra hasn't turned to check on me, but the coast is clear. I hurry back into the school, weaving through the halls until I reach the auditorium.

But as I grab the door handle, my skin prickles with the sensation that someone is watching me. I freeze, taking in my surroundings, but all I see are students headed home or to their school activities.

It's just my imagination. After surviving that Wraith attack last night, I think I might be on edge for the rest of my life. Letting out a deep breath, I tug open the door. It's time to meet up with my friends and plan out our escape.

3
YOU'VE BEEN AWAY FOR TOO LONG
DION

São Paolo, Brazil

The cool water of the Traveling Pool shivers across my skin as I step out of the water into my family's home. My mind flickers back to the first time I traveled with Estrella through the magical Water Channels that carry immortals from one location of the earth to the next in a blink of an eye.

She'd clung to me as we zipped through the channels to New York City because she'd been afraid of the channels. Not that I can blame her. Some get lost in them, wandering from place to place. It takes concentrated focus on your end location to make sure you end up where you want to go. Tonight, as I walk up the stone steps out of the pool, the memory sears me with pain. She will never remember our first moments together.

How we first met.

Our first kiss.

It's all gone.

I shake free of my tortured thoughts and focus on my surroundings.

The ceiling arches above, the painted frescos of my family members from hundreds of years ago painted on its surface. It's almost as if they're watching me, making sure I do my part to keep the family name immortalized.

The walls sprinkled with flecks of gold shimmer against the pool's magical blue light, illuminating the room even more. One step back into my ancestral home and instantly I'm reminded of my place and duties. I shift uncomfortably.

A servant steps forward with a towel in his hand. "Greetings, Master Dion. Welcome home."

I take the towel with a nod, wondering how long he's been waiting for my return. I was expected hours ago. "Thank you."

"A set of clothes is prepared for you in the dressing room," he continues. "Your father awaits your presence in the library."

I grimace. "Of course he does."

The towel is soft and smells of lavender as I dry myself off. I slog my way to the dressing room, eager to get out of these wet clothes. A fresh pair of dress pants and a long-sleeved, black button-down shirt hang on the rack. I lift my eyebrows.

"So we're going formal tonight," I mutter. "Interesting."

My mother is all about appearances, and the fact that

she's laid out formal wear is an indicator that my father has something big to tell me. Usually, I know exactly what he's going to say, but I've been spending too much time away from home lately. First living in the Midnight Kingdom in Antarctica to be near Estrella and now in Florida. He hasn't requested my presence in years.

But when my father calls, I come. No questions asked.

Except this trip will have more than one purpose. Guilt rears up inside of me, but I push it away with a focused determination.

Once changed, I clip my way down the brightly colored tiled corridor, desperation to find out what my father wants from me nipping at my mind. Pillars line either side, holding decorative arches, while ornate lanterns spill warm fractured light across the sprawling mansion. The large marble staircase stretches up before me, and I take the stairs two at a time. I'm trying to stay calm, but my heart drums against my ribcage.

What if he knows about my secret plans? Could that be why he sent for me?

If he even suspected I was planning on running away with Estrella and abandoning the family, he'd lock me away until I "grew up" as he would say. It's a huge risk even coming here with things being so volatile with Estrella.

Or perhaps this is about my secret mission with the Empress. He knows I'm working for her, but he doesn't know what I'm doing or why. Then again, even *I'm* not sure why the Empress has me watching over Estrella. Especially when Quadril is so desperate to have her killed. The games those two play always confound me.

I clip down the hallway until the library's wooden doors

stand before me. They're carved with ornate florals and geometric designs. I take a deep breath, clutching the iron handle and pulling the door open.

Our family library is one of the largest in South America. The walls stretch up two stories high with books packed into the shelves in precise order. A large chandelier of oval glass bulbs hangs from the fresco ceiling, and at the far end, by floor-to-ceiling arched stained glass windows, sits my father's massive mahogany desk.

But he's not sitting at his desk tonight. Instead, he's settled in his favorite leather chair in the sitting area of his library. A fire crackles and snaps brightly from the fireplace behind him. He's holding a glass filled with amber liquid, studying me intently.

Many people say I'm his spitting image with his midnight, swooping hair, bronze skin, and dark eyes. I get it. Sometimes it's like I'm looking in the mirror.

Though we immortals stop aging around thirty-five, he still has this ancient look and feel about him. As if he's been around longer than his one hundred and seventy-five years.

Maybe it's the fact that he's been so intent on continuing the Cabral family as one of the most powerful names in all of immortal history. Or perhaps it's the worry that after waiting over a hundred years trying to sire a son, I've failed to become everything he's hoped me to be.

Immortals don't have many children. Some never have offspring at all. My mother told me that when I was born, my father wept a thousand tears of joy.

I've never seen my father shed a single tear, so I seriously doubt her words.

"Dion," my father greets me in Portuguese, his voice

smooth as silk. It's a little jolting after living in Florida and speaking English for so long. "You are late."

"I had some issues to attend to." I stand before him, hands behind my back. Every muscle in my body is tightly coiled, ready to spring free.

"Ah, there's my little boy." It's my mother's sweet voice, filling the strained silence. She glides over to me, wearing a sunshine-yellow chiffon dress that trails across the tiled floor behind her. Her long, dark, curly hair is half-swept up with a jeweled clip while the rest cascades down her back. "You have been away from us too long."

"It's good to see you, Mother," I say, and I mean it. I kiss her forehead as she greets me.

"Please tell me you're here to stay." Her forehead crinkles with worry.

"I'm afraid not. The Empress has been keeping me busy."

"Speaking of the Empress, sit." Father waves at the leather chair across from him. "We have things to discuss."

My mother nods while I drop obediently in the chair, my back ramrod straight.

"I heard you've been assigned a task to work with the Empress," he continues, swirling the amber liquid round and round in his glass.

"I am. A specialized project she's asked me to oversee. I'm not allowed to discuss it."

"We don't keep secrets in the Cabral family," Father snaps. "I will not have the Empress ruling over my own home. She's overstretched her boundaries beyond what I ever imagined she would take, and I won't have her power seep into these walls."

"Haven't they already?" I push back, unable to ignore the anger rising up in my chest.

It was the Empress's decision to allow Estrella to be mortalized, and I will never forgive her for that. But at the same time, my father and the other Nazco lords have allowed her power to grow over the years instead of keeping her in check. I'm not sure if it was because they were lazy, blind, or too busy with their own affairs.

"Stop playing coy."

"Fine," I acquiesce, because he does have a point. "I'm watching over Estrella, making sure her mortalization process runs smoothly."

"Estrella?" Mother asks. "The girl who passed the Conduit trial but was cast out?"

I nod, staring bleakly off at the rows of bookshelves, hating how sharp the memory of that moment still stabs at my heart. I had been reaching for her hand, ready to dance with her to celebrate her success when the guards ripped her away from me.

"You cared for the girl, right?" Mother presses, but I won't answer that question. It's too dangerous.

"It doesn't matter now, does it?" I say instead.

Father mutters under his breath then sips at his drink. "This reeks of the Empress's meddling. Something isn't right about all of this. She always has a reason for what she does. There's a reason she has you watching over the ex-Conduit rather than someone else."

Perhaps she just likes to torture people.

"But that isn't why I called you home," Father continues. "Something has come to my attention, and I believe you've been keeping information from me."

I squirm in my chair. He knows about my plan to abandon the family and disappear with Estrella. And why wouldn't he? He's got a whole crew whose number one job is to seek and find out information. My mouth dries up like it's been stuffed with sandpaper.

A servant enters with a tray of drinks and a plate of cheeses, olives, and slices of bread. He sets it on the small table between my parents and me before leaving. My stomach twists at the thought of food, but I take the glass of fresh-squeezed orange juice, needing something to parch the dryness of my mouth.

"A few months back you went on a field trip with your old school," Father begins. "And don't deny it because I've already had my men interview your professor at Shadowland Academy."

Relief cools my hot skin. So he doesn't know about my plans. But what would he care about my old school?

"Interview my professors?" I chuckle, which only darkens my father's face. "More like force the truth out."

"When you are master of the Cabral family, you will understand."

I decide now isn't the time to share my disappointing news of leaving the family. "What about the field trip?"

"It has come to my attention that this trip was created under the guise of a deeper investigation of a certain exhibit."

I lean forward at this news. "A deeper investigation?"

"Why were you on that trip anyway?"

He already knows the answer if he's interviewed Professor Calenta. "I was tasked with keeping Estrella safe. She had been tapped to possibly become our next Conduit and since it was a graduation test for the seniors, she needed to go to pass. But it was also a risk for them to bring her out of the Midnight Lands."

Father nods and rubs his chin thoughtfully. "Apparently the Sabians showed up at the same time and stole a clay tablet from this exhibit."

I frown, remembering the incident. I'd not thought anything of it after everything that had happened, but Estrella had been adamant about the importance of the tablet.

"Professor Calmat said a group of girls chased after the Sabians, including Estrella. And when they found the girls, you were with them."

"I had been tasked to protect Estrella." Which was far harder than it should've been.

"Do you know what was on this tablet?" Mother asks. "What the writing said?"

"It was shattered into pieces," I say, rubbing my chin. "But the Sabians managed to salvage what they could and escape."

Now I've caught my father's attention. He sets down his drink and his eyebrows knit almost as one, clinging to every word I say.

"One of the girls exposed her powers to the mortals. Estrella had hoped by getting the tablet back, it would clear her friend's name. Thinking back to it, Estrella had been certain there was something important about that tablet."

A flash of clarity hits me. Lexi had been one of Estrella's friends implicated in this event. And now she's also at Nadia's Home. It can't be a coincidence that both girls were sent to the same Removal Facility, could it?

"Did Estrella tell you why she thought it was important?" Mother asks.

"It was an eventful day," I say vaguely. "I was just trying to keep Estrella alive. Beyond that, I don't remember much."

Not mentioning the fact that I'd been utterly captivated by her. Except after Lexi had been excommunicated, Estrella had been relentless in not just finding Lexi, but she had also been spending hours a day researching ancient texts. And then the night of her testing she'd told me she'd found something.

A secret that has either been forgotten or purposely hidden, she had said. *Tonight after I pass my test, I'll show you.*

But she never got that chance.

"Interesting," Father says. "Well, the Empress seems to think this tablet is important as well. She's sent a secret undercover team to retrieve it from the Sabians. So far with no success, but based on what my people have gathered, she's sparing no expense—or lives—to get it."

"We need to get our hands on that tablet before she does," Mother says. "For a woman as obsessed with power as the Empress is, something tells me this tablet could be our demise. She's been looking for some power source to destroy our family"

"Or it could give her more power," Father muses.

"So you called me all the way to Brazil for this?" I ask, annoyance filling me. "You could've asked me on the phone."

I hate the fact that I had to leave Estrella.

"Hardly," Father scoffs. "Tomorrow morning I need you to talk to my Truth Seeker. Perhaps he can help you remember events of that day better."

My instincts warn me Estrella is in danger. I hadn't planned on being gone for another day. Just make my appearance, grab the item I need, and leave. Every second I'm away from Estrella puts her in greater danger.

"I'm not staying here until tomorrow," I say. "I need to get back to Estrella. Quadril has sent his assassins after her, and it's my job to keep her safe."

"If Quadril has sent in his assassins," Father says, "you should stand down and let them do their work."

"Not according to the Empress," I counter.

"Is your job sanctioned by the Council?" Mother asks, her eyes narrowing. "Or is this a pet project of the Empress?"

"It's her pet project," I grudgingly admit.

"She picked you because you're in love with this girl." Mother sucks in a breath in realization. "Oh, the Empress is smarter than I'd given her credit for."

"You're not wasting your time or talents watching over a mindless girl that is being mortalized," Father says. "You're staying until I say you can leave, and that's final."

"Unless there's something else we should know," Mother points out, eyebrows lifting.

My insides grow cold. I can't have them suspect my plans when I'm so close to executing them. Especially with Father's Truth Seeker here, eager to pry into matters that I can't have him revealing. I just need to answer the Truth Seeker's questions about the field trip and act like the perfect son.

"No, there isn't anything else." I swallow my worries. "I'll talk to your Truth Seeker."

Besides, Chandra is watching over Estrella. What could go wrong?

4

THE DRAMA QUEEN MEETS BLOODY MARY

ESTRELLA

Florida

Darkness greets me as I open the side door to the auditorium. I usually don't come in the back way, but I didn't want to risk walking near the front of the school in case Chandra changed her mind. Fear grips my limbs as the door slams shut behind me. I never thought of myself as someone afraid of the dark, but after everything that's happened, my nerves are always on edge.

I hug my arms around my chest as I wait for my eyes to adjust from the bright Florida sun to this darkened corridor. A long hallway stretches before me and I quickly hurry toward the door at the end, eager to find my friends. When I enter the backstage area, I search for Tristan.

Beams of light pool over the stage, illuminating all the students sitting in a circle. The drama teacher stands in the center, talking. The rest of the lights in the auditorium have been turned off except those on the stage.

Lexi spots me as I step out of the wings and waves. Seeing that Tristan isn't here, I figure I can play my part as a set crew member. Quickly, I scoot down into the circle between her and Mara.

"You made it!" she whispers. "I was getting worried there."

"Chandra was annoying as ever," I huff. "It was like she was following me or something. Where's Tiffany?"

"I haven't seen her yet." Lexi frowns briefly. "I'm sure she'll come soon."

After the drama coach explains where to find the materials and what needs to be done, I head backstage. A paint wagon filled with brushes and paints is ready for me to use. I wheel it to a group of wooden chairs and tables stacked against the wall of the backstage area.

Still, other than the muted voices on the other side of the curtain, the auditorium feels too large, too quiet, and too dark. I'm oddly grateful for the low rumble of the wagon's wheels echoing backstage. I even begin humming, only a little off tune. Anything but this awful silence.

Where is Tristan? He should be here by now. Worry niggles at my stomach.

I start painting the red cross that will hang over the medical clinic when I hear a clopping sound.

Footsteps.

The noise jerks me to standing, splashing my perfect set

piece with a smear of crimson. My head whips to the door, and I hold out my paintbrush in front of me.

"Nice pose." Lexi lifts her eyebrows, waltzing across to where I'm standing. "So dramatic. Do you dance as you paint? Because that might actually be pretty vogue."

"Right." I attempt a smile as my heart returns to its regular beat. I'm like a spooked animal, jumping at the slightest noise. I try to steady my shaking hand.

"You okay?" Lexi frowns. "You look a little red."

She points to my hand. Paint has splashed all over my skin and is dripping on my sneakers. Quickly, I drop the paintbrush back into the can, but the damage has been done.

I grimace. "I look like I'm bleeding."

"Come on." Lexi nods to the hallway. "Follow me. I'll show you where the bathroom is. You can wash up there."

I trail after her. "All day, I've been having a hard time concentrating. Dion's gone and when I was talking to Chandra, she dropped the bomb that he has a girlfriend back home."

"Wait, what? Are you sure? He seems so into you."

"That was my first thought, but honestly, how well do I know him? We've only gone out on one date and hung out at school. I don't even know where he lives!"

I stop abruptly when I spot Tiffany standing by the bathroom door, arms crossed.

"Hey, Tiff," I say. "We were looking for you earlier."

She smiles, but her eyes are hard and steel cold. "I had to get some backups and permission."

"Backups and permission?" Lexi giggles. "What are you talking about?"

"Come on in." Tiffany pushes open the door and waves for us to follow her. "I'll show you."

The two of us follow her, but the moment we step inside my heart seizes. Cold terror shudders through me, and my knees nearly buckle beneath me. This was a big mistake.

How could I have been so blind?

5
NOTHING STINKS WORSE THAN TOILET TREACHERY
ESTRELLA

Florida

Not one.

Not two.

But three Wraiths loom before us. Their cloaks shift about in the non-existent wind. They stand still as stone, heads covered with black hoods. Fear claws at my heart as one lifts its blood-red eyes to meet mine.

"Shalik," it says.

I grab Lexi's arm and turn to run, but Tiffany has stepped in front of the door, blocking our escape.

"Tiffany?" I choke. "What are you doing?"

She pulls out a thin, iridescent green wand. "The Wraiths want their vengeance. You killed one of their own. Not to mention broke the most important rule."

"How do you know all of this?" I choke.

"What have you done?" Lexi whispers.

"I've never wanted things to come to this," she says in her typical sweet voice, except today it's sickly sweet. "I've been keeping a close eye on you, Estrella, playing along, but last night, you went too far."

"I trusted you." Her words slice my heart. "I thought you were my friend."

"Some things are greater than friendships."

"You are despicable," Lexi spits out.

"No, you are. Because you're traitors." Tiffany clucks her tongue. "Traitors must die a traitor's death."

A cawing sound startles the silence. I spin and recoil against the bathroom sink as the center Wraith's clawed hands lift back its hood.

Ashen face, blue veins popping out under his skin, and a long crooked nose that looks more like a bird's beak.

Lexi and I scream and dive for the door, but Tiffany swipes that green bar through the air and we both slam into some sort of shield she's created. I stumble backward from the impact, my vision swirling.

"What did you do?" Lexi asks. "It's like a wall."

"I can create barriers," she says, twirling her wand like she's in a parade. "Keep people where they need to stay. Keep noises from escaping."

Lexi's body is jerked back as one of the creatures grabs her. Its clawed palm slaps over her mouth and pins her against its body.

"No!" I scream, and fumble for the zipper of my backpack. My hands shake.

I'm not fast enough because the second creature

29

reaches out and wraps its hand against my neck, knocking my head against the mirror. The glass splinters. The world spins.

Tiffany steps to its side. "How did you do it?" she asks.

I try to speak, but the creature's blocking the air from my lungs. It's like a cork is stuck in my throat.

"She can't talk." Tiffany rolls her eyes. "Loosen your hold on her throat."

It eases its grip, and I gasp for air.

"Don't hurt her," I beg.

Tiffany's eyebrows lift and she turns to Lexi and tells her captor, "Make her bleed."

"No!" I scream.

The third creature swipes a claw across Lexi's neck. Blood trickles down her throat, and her scream cuts my soul. Tears stream down her face, and her whole body shudders.

Seeing her like that sends my pulse hammering against my temples. My mind is whisked back to another time and place.

An ice palace with glittering snowflakes falling like tears.

Lexi and Jamie pressed to their knees on a cold, unforgiving floor.

And two of these creatures standing over them.

Something deep inside me, buried in a forgotten place, rears up. This has happened before. A forgotten memory.

"Beautiful," the Wraith holding her says in a gargled voice, snapping me back to reality. "They always are right before I rip their hearts out."

"No!" I beg. "Please let her go. She's innocent. She doesn't know anything."

"Don't lie!" Tiffany says. "Why were you in Nadia's office?"

"To find the truth."

"Who else is involved?"

My gut squeezes as I think of Mara, Jamie, and Zayla who helped.

"It was just me," I say.

"LIES!" Tiffany's eyes bug out. "I heard you on the bus. Lexi and Mara are both involved."

"They just suspected something was up."

"Get your filthy claws off me," Lexi half-growls, but the creature presses a jagged blade against her neck.

A dark red stain blooms on her shirt. She suddenly goes rigid, whimpering.

The room sways a little as panic swarms through me.

"She will die first," Tiffany says. "You will watch, and then we'll find Mara and repeat this whole conversation until you tell me who is involved, what you know, and what your plan is. Is that how it's going to be, Estrella?"

Her words wake me. I can't let Lexi or Mara die. I won't. My fingers rip back the zipper of my backpack. The dagger inside leaps into my palm like it was waiting for me.

"Wield my power," a woman's voice speaks to my mind just like the last time I touched the dagger. A burst of energy crashes into me like a tidal wave.

Roaring.

Sea and salt, swelling into a crest.

Ready to crash.

Something warns me that there isn't as much energy flowing from it as last time, and the blue isn't as deep as before. But I don't hesitate. I slice its sharp edge along the

Wraith's arm. It screeches and pulls its hand back, releasing me.

"What is that?" Tiffany stares at my dagger. "Where did you get that weapon?"

Just like last night, I aim for the creature's heart. With a cry, it goes to knock the weapon from my grasp. But the dagger is like the waves crashing on the beach. I follow its call and move with its force. I twist and bend, arching my back so only the flutter of the monster's sleeve finds my face.

I dive forward. A flash of storm blue.

And plunge.

The scent of brine consumes the air. The Wraith gasps and then crumbles into a pile of dust before vanishing before our eyes.

"What did you do?" Tiffany screams, pointing at me. "Kill her!"

The Wraith not holding Lexi tosses back his cloak, revealing a half-man, half-vulture body. His face and bald head contrast against his black-feathered form. Wings stretch out as he arches his body. Claws from one hand draw up in attack while another lifts a dagger.

It opens its mouth filled with long, sharp teeth. A screech like a death cry fills the bathroom. A cry announcing a kill. The sound shudders against my bones and rips at my ears.

Sucking in a terrifying breath, I rush at the creature. But Tiffany waves her green wand, and I crash into an invisible barrier. I'm unable to reach it.

Lexi screams at the top of her lungs. The Wraith holding her flings her to the ground like garbage, its knife crimson.

Blood gushes from her neck. This isn't a little cut. She's going to bleed to death, and fast.

"Lexi!" I cry out. "Press on the wound."

Her eyes widen as she sags against the wall, but she clutches her neck.

"As if that will help." Tiffany snorts. "She'll bleed out in less than five minutes."

I growl in fury. I come at the Wraith again, but Tiffany's barrier holds.

"Why are you doing this, Tiffany?" I ask. "You were our friend. We were a team."

"It's nothing personal." She shrugs. "Nadia's Home was your second chance, and you blew it. The safety of the Nazco nation is more important than either of you."

As if to prove her point, she whips her wand downward. Instantly, the Wraith snakes its clawed hand around the wrist I'm holding the dagger with. The quickness surprises me. I don't have time to respond.

My hand numbs from its grip, and the dagger clatters to the floor. She kicks the dagger to the far end of the room and swipes another barrier to keep me from reaching it.

"There," Tiffany says, shaking her arms. "Now we're back in business."

I tried to be careful over the past week, but just like Mara warned, I was not careful enough. The worst part is I put my best friend in the center of this madness. Lexi and I are nothing more than some twisted game of Barbie dolls.

The Wraith pins me to the wall. Darkness oozes out from its dark shrouds. It hefts its dagger into the air.

I'm going to die.

6

ABOUT TIME YOU
SHOWED UP
ESTRELLA

Florida

The bathroom door smashes open.

Light blazes through the room, piercing the darkness surrounding the creatures and filling every crevice with blinding light. I blink against the glow to spot its source. It's Tristan, his feet spread apart with his silver sword in hand. His hair flames like the sun.

Tiffany screams and goes to wave her wand in front of him.

But someone else rushes in next. He slams his sword against her wand, and it tumbles to the ground.

"Sabians!" she exclaims in horror.

I frown, wondering why she's calling them that.

Their presence consumes the place. Both point long

swords at the creatures and Tiffany. But Tristan's blade burns red, flames licking out of the end like a hundred serpents' tongues.

"Take your filthy claws off her," Tristan tells the Wraith holding me. His voice is fierce, commanding.

"Same goes with you," the other guy says, stepping toward the Wraith that moved back to hover over Lexi.

The creature's creepy eyes lift up from where he stabbed Lexi. It caws a barking sound.

The pressure against my chest vanishes. I drop into a heap on the ground, gasping for air.

Tristan leaps at the Wraith once holding me, aiming his flaming sword at its chest. The creature blocks it with the jagged knife, but Tristan's partner stabs its wing. The creature cries out.

Tristan parries again, coming at the beast with a swooping, arcing blow. It hits against the Wraith but a clang fills the air, warning that the creature's skin is hard as armor. Fire blooms out of Tristan's sword, burning the creature's cloak to ashes.

Meanwhile, the other warrior battles against the Wraith hovering over Lexi. He cuts at its wings, slicing it into ribbons.

Tristan and his friend work in tandem as if they have fought together in a similar situation many times. Arching swoops of swords clash against the creatures' steel blades. Ash billows about the room. The stench of burnt flesh burns my nostrils.

Tristan's shirt pulls against his muscular frame, and his hair flies across his face as he twists and ducks with the grace of a dancer.

Not only is he a warrior, but he's well-trained.

Who is he really?

Tiffany scrambles for her wand, pulling me back to the moment. I dive for my dagger at the same time and scoop it up, the hilt now more of a sky blue. I point it at her. "I don't want to hurt you."

She waves her wand, blocking me from her. Then she backtracks toward the door.

"That's the Estrella I was counting on." She smiles. "Because I need to alert Nadia that not only was it you who broke in, but that you're working with the Sabians."

I don't know who the Sabians are, but I can't let her get away and tell Nadia our secret. Before I can react, she spins and runs for the door.

To my right, Tristan shoves the Wraith against the stalls. The doors crumble. The creature screeches, and the mirrors splinter. The other Wraith whips around as if responding to its partner's cry. Seeing Tristan's back exposed, it lifts its dagger above him.

Do I save Tristan or stop Tiffany?

Tristan's friend spears him with his sword, but the Wraith is undaunted and hurls its blade through the air, aiming for Tristan's back.

"Duck!" I warn.

He drops to the ground with a roll. The Wraith's dagger continues to fly through the air only to stab Tiffany in the back as she turns the door handle. She slumps to the floor, lifeless.

Undaunted, the Wraith pulls out another dagger from its belt with a snarl. With the last ounce of energy I have, I leap across the distance, throwing myself at the creature, my dagger hefted above my head.

I aim for its back, and as I fall, I plunge the blade through its hard armor skin. It sinks straight to the heart.

The creature's body starts to disintegrate but not as quickly as last time. It bats me away mid-fall, and I smash against the air dryer. My dagger clatters onto the tile floor. Pain sears my back, and tears spring to my eyes. I sink to the ground in agony. Tristan's friend shoves the spear deeper into the monster's core, and finally it crumbles to dust.

"Are you alright?" Tristan rushes to me, lightly touching my back. "You should never have put yourself in jeopardy like that."

"Are you upset at me for saving your life?" My voice is shaky as I scramble for my dagger. It's suddenly become my most prized possession.

"Where did you get that?" His eyes narrow as he studies the dagger. "That is a powerful weapon."

Before I can answer, the final Wraith rises up off the broken stall door, black blood dripping from its side. It growls. Tristan and his warrior friend turn away and as one, they rise up and attack the creature.

But my eyes focus on Lexi.

She's lying on the floor, still as the concrete walls entombing us.

With a horrified cry, I crawl to her side while the others continue to battle. Her eyes are closed. I hate how peaceful she looks.

As if she's left me and escaped to a better place.

"No!" I take her hands in mine. "You can't leave me!"

I search for her pulse. It's there, but weak.

Then I feel something else under her skin. A flicker of heat. A tiny, sputtering flame crying to be saved. I clench my hands around hers, willing that flame to spark and grow, tears streaming down my face.

Something inside me rushes into her. I don't really understand what is happening, but Lexi's skin looks a little less pale and her eyelids flutter.

A piercing cry, echoing across the tiled floor, startles my focus. A quick glance over my shoulder tells me all I need to know. The creature is dead. Its grotesque limbs lie sprawled in a pool of blood before it too vanishes.

Tristan scowls. "That last cry was a call for help."

"You sure?" the other warrior asks. "It sounded like it was in pain."

"Positive. We don't have much time." Tristan wipes the blood from his sword using paper towels. The blood is black as coal. "More Wraiths and probably Nazco will be here in no time."

"Call 911," I beg as I clutch Lexi's palm. "And hurry!"

The other guy rushes to my side, his eyes assessing her quickly. "Move," he orders.

"No." I squeeze Lexi's hand tighter. "Not until you call 911."

"This is my best friend, Conrad," Tristan explains. "He's a Healer. He can help your friend far faster and more effectively than mere mortal doctors."

"Mortal doctors?" I scoff, hovering over her even more protectively. "I don't know what you're talking about, but it's not reassuring. What's he going to do? Some weird voodoo thing?"

"Estrella," Conrad says softly. "Please. Let me help your friend."

I study this Conrad guy. Tall, broad shoulders with a toned body. Not as muscular as Tristan's but definitely athletic and lean. His brown hair is cut fairly short as if he doesn't want it to get in his way, and his face is clean-shaven.

But it's his kind, rich brown eyes begging me to let him help along with his calmness that finally win me over. Slowly, I release Lexi's hand and shift so he can reach her. He flings aside the blood-soaked cloth at her neck and instead cups his hands over the wound.

He closes his eyes and starts muttering.

"You're not hurting her, are you?" I ask, panic making my vision swim. When he doesn't respond, I look at Tristan. "What's he doing?"

Tristan's eyes flicker between Lexi and Tiffany lying lifeless on the ground. His body tenses. He adjusts his grip on his sword as if he's preparing to use it.

"We need to leave," he says. "Neither girl is safe."

"Where will we go?" I ask.

"You need to come with me."

I cross my arms. "I'm not going anywhere without Lexi."

He turns to Conrad. "Can you move her?"

"Maybe." Conrad grimaces but swoops her up into his arms.

"Good, let's go." Tristan cracks open the door, peeking into the hall.

We dart outside and rush down the corridor outside the auditorium. Halfway down, a cawing sound vibrates across the hall. I glance over my shoulder to see the outline of a robed form, its tattered ends fluttering about in a non-existent breeze.

My skin turns cold.

"One found us!" I half-screech.

Tristan takes off running. Conrad and I race to keep up. Another caw echoes through the empty corridor, this time much closer. Once we reach an outer door, Tristan shoves his arm into it just as the beast careens around the corner at the end of the hall. Seeing us, it starts running.

A scream jams in my throat. Terrified, I turn back and continue running. The creature advances toward us, bounding down the hallway all too fast. Heart pounding, I bolt out of the open door and stumble into the bright Florida sun. Looking over my shoulder, I watch it leap into the air, sailing toward us almost as if it's flying.

Once Conrad is through, Tristan slams the door shut and presses his body against it. The monster smashes against the door, indenting the center.

A shudder shakes my body. I clench my dagger tighter.

"We have to jam the doors," Tristan says. "Grab that chair over there."

Once I do, he shoves the legs of the chair through the two door handles. The Wraith keeps pounding on the doors, but the chair holds. Tristan and Conrad slip their swords into a strap on their backs hidden under their shirts. If I hadn't found Nadia's case of weapons in her secret room and used this dagger, I'd never have believed what I saw was possible.

"That should slow the creature down." He takes off down the sidewalk at a jog. "At least until it finds another exit."

"We need to take Lexi to a hospital," I say, eying her long red hair swaying back and forth under Conrad's arms. Her skin is far too pale. "And then you're going to tell me exactly who you are and what's going on."

"The hospital is too dangerous," Tristan says. "Either the Wraiths will track her down there or the hospital will call your headmistress. And the less your headmistress knows about what happened, the better."

This sobers me because I know he's right. But I also know that Mara is still potentially in danger, as are the rest of the girls.

"I've stopped her bleeding," Conrad says. "But she's lost too much blood. If she's going to live, we need to take her to the hospital right now."

"See?" I say. "We need to take her to the hospital. We have to try to save her."

He pauses behind a set of trees near the parking lot, scanning the area. "We need to split up."

"No," I counter. "I'm staying with Lexi."

Tristan groans and rubs his forehead before turning to me. "If you care about your friend, you'll get as far away from her as possible."

I swallow, thick dread clotting my veins. "You think she might die because of me?"

"She's not going to die," Conrad says.

"Which is why we need to split up," Tristan continues. "Conrad, you take care of Lexi. Estrella, you come with me. It's the only way we all get out of this."

My eyes trail from Lexi back to the auditorium as I debate what to do.

"Or," Tristan adds, a bit harshly if you ask me, "you can

trot back in there and ask the other Wraiths for a ride back to Nadia's."

I glare at him. "Fine. We split up. But only if Conrad promises to help Lexi."

"He's an excellent Healer, and I trust him with my life," Tristan says. "Your friend will survive."

"I promise." Conrad flashes me a reassuring look. "I will do everything in my power to help your friend."

Conrad's calming demeanor and the fierce way he clutches Lexi in his arm tell me he's telling the truth. Plus, from what I saw back there, it looks like he can hold his own in a fight, too.

I step closer to find the cut on her neck has healed. She's no longer bleeding, but her breathing is shallow.

"Okay," I agree, desperately hoping I'm making the right decision. "We split up."

I'm about to turn away to follow Tristan when something tugs at my mind. It's hard to explain the sensation, but it's like I'm having some sort of déjà vu. Like I've had a moment like this before, which is silly.

I lightly touch her on the arm.

"Stay safe," I whisper into her ear. "I'll be back as soon as I can. I promise."

And then I take off after Tristan, hoping I, too, can keep my word.

7
GHOSTING: THE BEST 'OUT OF SIGHT, OUT OF MIND' STRATEGY
DION

São Paulo, Brazil

I wait in the darkness, fully clothed, lying in my bed. The mahogany wood of the four posters holding up the canopy frame stand alert like sentinels on guard as moonlight pours through the paned windows. What would life have been like if Estrella could have stayed immortal?

Would she have come and met my family? Would we have wed in the family chapel under the stained glass colors of my ancestors?

Spoken the prayer of eternal love and sealed it with a kiss?

I'd have brought her back to this very bed and made the

lifelong bond with her. We'd have been happy together. I'm sure of it.

But that is all lost now. With each day, as her memories slip away, her powers fade, too. A pang of loss, of what could've been—should've been—clouds my thoughts and squeezes at my heart.

So tight. Too tight.

No, I won't let my thoughts stay there. Her becoming mortal changes nothing. I will still love her. More even because of what she sacrificed despite having no knowledge of that.

Only when my clock reads 4 a.m. do I stir, sliding off the silk sheets and touching the old, wooden floor. This room has been the only place I've called my own. I know the path across the floorboards to my door where I can avoid every creak and groan.

I crack open my door and peer down the hall. Once I'm satisfied that the whole house is sleeping, I creep down the massive stone stairway and head along the corridor surrounding our main courtyard. Arched stone beams swoop over my head and moonlight slips through the large floor-to-ceiling windows, illuminating the frescos painted on the walls. But my eyes remain focused on my destination and my muscles tighten as I head down a narrow staircase into the basement. My steps are quick and sure as I work my way to the family treasure room.

The entrance is small and unassuming. Simple, uncarved wood with an unlocked doorknob. A stranger or even a guest would never guess how purposeful and calculated this entrance was. I turn the knob and slide inside.

Racks of cleaning supplies along with a plentiful supply of brooms and mops greet me.

To an intruder, it would look like nothing more than a broom closet. But I know better.

I push aside a stack of sponges and flick the switch on the back wall. Instantly, the shelf swings inward to reveal another wall, this one with a single needle and a stone plate beneath it.

The blood test.

The only way for anyone to enter this next section is if they carry the blood of the Cabral family. I prick my finger and let a drop of blood plop onto the stone. The crimson liquid seeps into its surface and runs along the tiny divots etched toward the lock. The moment it hits the metal, the lock clicks.

I take a deep breath and push the door open, stepping inside. The air is slightly musty as if it hasn't been breathed in decades. Our family treasure room is large by immortal standards, encompassing a warren of small rooms. Every wall hosts a glass shelf where artifacts are stored in neat precision. There are pirate treasures stored in chests and priceless books kept in airtight cases. Jewels gleam under the can lights, and crowns glisten as if begging to be worn.

The artifact I'm seeking should be in the second room against the far wall. I pass through the weaponry room and enter the artifact chamber. There are so many boxes, glass domes, and stands holding relics of immortal powers that it's a little overwhelming. But I'm only here for one in particular. My fingers hover over the air as I skim along the shelf, not daring to disturb the film of dust that has accumulated over the years.

Finally, I find what I'm looking for. The box is a navy-blue rectangle. I pick it off the shelf and pull back the lid.

The Ghost pendant.

The cloudy-crimson gem clutched in an iron clasp hangs from a silver chain. Its surface swirls in a murky glow, always moving, always cloaking the wearer in a shrouded mist.

I suck in a deep breath and close my eyes, imagining placing it on Estrella's neck where it would nestle against her chest and keep her hidden from a Tracker's searching power. Not only will it cloak her from a Tracker, but it will burn bright red when she's in danger.

This heirloom has been with the family for centuries, far longer than even my parents' memory. Mother once told me that a family member had imparted their Ghosting power into the pendant moments before he'd been beheaded. He may have died, but his gift lived on.

Now, anyone who wears this pendant carries a fragment of his power.

I clench the necklace tight and tuck it into my pocket before setting the box back on the shelf exactly where it had been resting. This pendant will make all the difference. It will allow Estrella to slip away and never be found again. It will keep her safe until her mortalization process is complete and she's fully human.

Now I merely need to survive the Truth Seeker's probing without him discovering my plans, and then I'll be able to get back to Estrella before another night passes.

8
THE TRUTH FINDS ITS WAY
DION

São Paolo, Brazil

Every meal at my family's home is a grand event. Which is why instead of throwing on shorts and a T-shirt like I would do in Florida, I'm dressed in dark dress pants and a button-down shirt. As I head down to breakfast, I'm trying to prepare my mind to push Estrella as far from my thoughts as possible. Which is honestly maddening.

I hardly slept last night. Between waiting up to get the pendant from the treasury and then pacing my room until dawn, dark circles now ring my eyes.

The windows and doors to the courtyard have been thrown open to allow the morning breeze inside. The air smells sweet like roses and blossoms along with the scent of coffee and Nana's famous tapioca crepes. I smile. She knows I love her crepes and must have made them for me when she found out I was here.

For a moment, I'm pulled back to my childhood. I grew up here until I had to leave for Shadowland Academy. Those had been the days of innocence—before I knew how greatly our family was feared or how much the Empress despised my father for his position among the Nazco.

I'm about to step inside the dining room when my phone rings. Frowning, I glance down to see who the call was from. BJ. That could be good or bad news.

"Olá," I say in greeting.

"Thought you'd want to know she made it safely to school and Chandra is keeping an eye on her," BJ says. "I'm headed back home but wanted to give you an update."

Relief crashes through me. I'd been expecting the worse. "Excellent. Thank you. I needed to hear that."

He hangs up, and my step is lighter as I head into the dining room for breakfast. My parents sit at either end of the dining table, Father skimming through the daily reports his scouts give him while Mother reads the gossip column from her phone.

"Bom dia, dear," she greets me in Portuguese as I settle into the lone chair on the side. "You slept well?"

"Like a baby," I lie. "It's good to be home."

Stay positive. Keep them happy. Let this day be one of good memories. After all, this might be the last time I see them for a while.

Father grunts, looking over at me with a sharp gaze. "I've decided it's time you start working for me rather than the Empress."

I shift uncomfortably and load my plate with crepes. "I think this assignment will be done soon," I say.

"I'd like you to start working at the office with me," he continues. "It's time you learn the job of finance."

Father runs the most successful financial company in South America, one he's built from the ground up over the last fifty years. It's his newest pet project, which basically funds his art collection and Mother's shoe obsession. Plus he says it keeps him grounded, but really I know it's an excuse to escape his daily oversight of the immortals in São Paolo.

But I'm not an idiot. This is his first attempt to start bringing me back closer to the family. I've avoided being a part of things since I graduated from the academy last year. I've always known it was a matter of time before I'd have to face the music and get serious or get out.

He has no idea that I plan on getting out. I plaster on a sincere smile and shovel another forkful of my crepe into my mouth to hide the growing worry swelling inside me. When word gets out that I've disappeared, they will both be destroyed.

It will gut them. That thought alone makes the crepes in my mouth sour.

"That sounds great," I say, finally uttering my lie. "It will be good to learn what you do."

His face lights up and he nods happily. He opens his mouth to say something else, when a servant enters announcing, "Dominic, The Truth Seeker, is here. I've left him in the Green Room."

My stomach flips, and suddenly I wish I hadn't eaten those crepes.

"Excellent," Father says. "Tell him he'll be there momentarily."

"Yes, sir." She bows and darts out of the room.

Father turns back to me. "The Truth Seeker can help you remember what you didn't realize you knew. Don't let him stress you out. Later, we will talk about getting out of the Empress's clutches and here at my side where you belong."

I nod, dread pooling in the pit of my stomach. No longer hungry, I push my chair away from the table and stiffly stride into the Green Room. My emotions are at war. One part of me yearns for my father's acceptance and approval. The other part—the part where my heart rules—can't imagine life without Estrella.

When I thought I'd lost her before, it nearly killed me. I won't let that happen again.

The Green Room is aptly named. The panels in the ceiling are painted emerald with gold ribbon edges boxing each section in. Evergreen wallpaper fills the upper half of the walls while the lower half is painted shell white. Candles illuminated by a Fire Wielder flicker from the twisted chandelier above, washing the room in a warm glow.

Arched bookshelves packed with medical journals are tucked neatly into the wall between an ancient armoire filled with collected animal bone specimens and bottles. The Truth Seeker sits primly at the oak desk beneath the paned window while I settle in the corner of the room on the green leather couch beneath a hanging dinosaur skeleton.

"Greetings," Dominic says, eyeing me under thick, bushy eyebrows as if I've got something to hide.

I nod and try not to grimace. I know my parents have the

best intentions using a Truth Seeker, and Father trusts the man, but over the past year, I've learned to trust no one.

He steps closer and touches my temple, strengthening the bond between his power and my memories. When a Truth Seeker questions you, it's impossible to not answer with the truth. Some powerful Truth Seekers, like Dominic, can even see glimpses of a person's memories.

"The day of the field trip to the Metropolitan Museum of Art," the Truth Seeker begins unceremoniously, startling me with his abruptness. "Why did you go after the Channeler, Estrella?"

"I was assigned to watch over her. Protect her."

"But you failed, didn't you? She was injured by an Ice Wielder."

The clarity of the memory washes over me as Dominic's power slides through my mind. I shiver, knowing his power will force me to speak about it.

Maybe this is a bad idea.

"We got separated at the museum when I was fighting off a Sabian," I say. "When she went chasing after the Sabians, I followed her, but I wasn't fast enough."

"Seems rather rash," he snorts. "Chasing after experienced Sabian warriors."

I shrug. "Desperation makes you do desperate things." My fingers dig into my pocket where the Ghost pendant lies hidden away.

"Do you know why the Sabians were at this exhibit?"

"No. But Estrella..." I frown as the memory solidifies in my mind. "She was picking up the pieces of the broken tablet. Cut herself and passed out."

"You think the tablet had powers infused into it in some

way?"

"No."

And then another memory bursts into my mind brighter and clearer than ever with the Truth Seeker's clarity as if it's happening before my eyes. Her hands wrapping around my body, taking my powers from me, and then giving them back but stronger this time. Amplifying them beyond anything I could do on my own. The bond we created was intoxicating. The thought that we would never have that again sends a tidal wave of sadness through me.

I push him away and bury my head into my hands, overwhelmed by the sudden surge of emotions tied to that memory, but also fighting to now share them with Dominic.

"Are you okay, Master Dion?" Dominic asks. "Tell me what happened."

I lift my head, shoving my emotions into a compartment of myself that must never be seen. Must never be opened again if I don't want to lose my mind.

"There was chaos everywhere at the museum," I say. "Alarms were going off, gates were being shut, but Estrella was determinedly packing the tablet pieces into her backpack. I had to fight off a guy from attacking her and when I turned back around, she was lying passed out on the floor, bleeding from one of the sharp ends of a tablet piece she touched."

Dominic nods thoughtfully. "We believe the Sabians had come that day for the tablet. Had risked exposure of their powers to get it because they were that desperate. Estrella and her friends." He looks at his notes. "Jamie and Lexi, I believe their names are, were willing to risk their lives to retrieve that backpack. Why?"

"Estrella said she needed it to show the Empress. A bargaining chip for Lexi for displaying her powers to the mortals."

"Do you think Estrella or her friends know anything about what this tablet holds?"

Anger erupts from me like a volcano. "They remember *nothing*. The Empress shipped them off to a Rehabilitation Center and stripped them of their memories so their visik powers would slowly die. So no, they won't be of help. I'm done here."

I rise out of my seat and storm out of the room. Electricity races up and down my arms and legs, spiking across the floor and leaving scorch marks in my wake.

Those memories haunt me, scream at me, warn me of things to come.

A desperate need to get back to her claws at my throat.

"Dion!" Mother calls to my back, but I don't stop moving.

I can't stay here another second. I've been away from Estrella for too long. It was foolish to leave her. Clenching the pendant in my palm, I burst into the Traveling Pool room. I don't bother changing out of my clothes or wearing a wetsuit but march to the water's edge.

"Master Dion," the attendant says cheerfully. "I hadn't expected you to travel back so soon. Would you care for a wetsuit or some boots to keep your feet dry?"

Ignoring him, I jump into the pool like a sharp knife, plunging through the water and entering the magical channels.

My thoughts focus on Estrella.

Willing myself to return to her again because something

warns me I'm too late.

9
BABY, LET'S GET OUT OF HERE
TRISTAN

Florida

I can't believe I actually managed to get Estrella to come with me. I should be feeling victorious in this moment, but worry jams itself into my chest like a two-edged sword.

Not only did I kill two Wraiths—the Nazco's sacred creatures they created to protect them—but Estrella's friend is severely injured and now involved, too. Not to mention the other girl, Tiffany, who was killed. That could cause real problems.

My feet pound the hard pavement of the parking lot as I race up to my little Kia Soul. I swear under my breath. This is why I needed a better car. A faster car. I'm sure Dion would never be caught dead in this sandbox toy, much less use it for one of his missions.

I throw open the passenger door, ordering Estrella to get inside.

She hesitates a moment as I race to the driver's side and rev up the engine. Her hair flutters in the wind, long golden strands floating as if escaping with the sea breeze. I dart a glance in my rearview mirror, half-expecting Dion to show up and stop us, but he's nowhere to be found. It feels too good to be true. Then reality slaps against my face like the cold truth that it is.

A strong wind sweeps through the parking lot, tugging at the air like it owns it. A damp, cold wetness comes alongside. Frustration brews within my chest as Estrella clings to the open door, squinting at three figures warily approaching the vehicle.

I lower her window.

"We've got company," I tell her. "Unless you want to face off against three trained assassins, I suggest you hurry."

Rain splatters against her face, but still she remains frozen in place, her mouth parted as if she was planning on saying something but the words died on her lips. I twist in my seat, following her gaze.

Her eyes are riveted on a man, dressed in a pin-striped suit that hangs to his thighs. I'm startled by his shockingly white hair. I know of only a handful of immortals who have white hair, the Empress one of them.

"Excuse me," she calls out. "Do I know you?"

"Perhaps," the strange guy says. "It depends on if you remember."

The man's words twist and worm their way into my

chest. This is bad. Very, very bad. Two others slip in beside him. The dark-haired girl I recall seeing around school begins waving her hands about.

Brilliant.

She's a Wind Weaver. What's her name? Chan or was it Shandra? If I don't get Estrella out of here, my little Kia is going to be riding a tornado like a Ferris wheel.

"Chandra?" Estrella says. "Why are you here?"

Her words yank me out of my daze and shove me into action. "Estrella!" I reach across the tiny car and tug at her arm.

She jerks at the sound of her name, or perhaps it's from my touch. It revs her to life, and she ducks into the car. Instantly, I take off, not bothering to wait for her to close the door.

She screams as the car screeches across the parking lot. With a heave, she manages to shut the car door.

"Put on your seatbelt," I order.

She fumbles with it until it clicks.

Sheets of rain pelt the windshield so hard it's impossible to see where I'm going. I slam on the gas, hoping I'm not going to crash into a car or fence. The back of the car lifts up as the wind catches its rear like a giant's hand getting ready to toss it into the air. I grit my teeth and clench the steering wheel, fighting to keep the car from veering left or right.

We swerve out of the parking lot. The back of the car bumps up and down, our heads smashing against the ceiling. Estrella screams and grips the sides of the seat, eyes wide.

The car spins in a three-sixty spiral, tires screeching in resistance. The centrifugal force slams my body against the door as I fight for control. With a twist and a break, I finally get the tiny engine moving again in the right direction.

Then we're zipping down the road as fast as this sputtering engine can manage. We burst out of the storm cloud, and the wind and rain stop. It's like we entered a cruise advertisement—the kind where the palms wave gently under a blue Caribbean sky.

Now that we're free from the Nazcos' reach, I'm able to relax. Somewhat.

"You saved my life," she rasps.

"I've been trying to since we first met. That said, you saved my life back there, too."

"Chandra. My boyfriend's friend was back there. I don't...I don't understand. Who was that other guy?"

She's starting to hyperventilate. "Relax. Take slow, easy breaths."

Will her mind be able to handle what I'm about to tell her? We don't really know exactly how the Nazco's mortalization process works.

"Listen," I continue. "I need to make a call so we can get a better car. We're not out of the clear yet."

"How can you be so calm after that?" Her voice pitches higher, her breathing coming out in gasps.

I shift the car into the highest gear it can go. "I'm anything but calm."

"She's part of all of this, isn't she?" Estrella chokes out, confusion knitting her brow. "Does that mean Dion is, too?"

I try to give her my best 'I'm sorry' look, but honestly, it's hard, knowing those people were trying to kill her. "Was she a close friend?"

She barks out a sobbing laugh and shakes her head.

"Hardly. In fact, I think she's hated me since we first crossed paths."

"I guess her trying to stop us tracks with your suspicions."

"I can't believe this is happening." She leans back in her seat as tears stream down her cheeks. "I hope Lexi is going to be okay."

"I'll have Conrad help her make up a story when she goes back to Nadia's. That's the best way to keep her safe."

She rubs her forehead and nods mutely while I call Katka.

"Please tell me you have the girl," Katka barks.

"You're on speaker. Estrella is here with me." I glance over at Estrella, whose whole body has stiffened at Katka's words. *Fantastic.* "Katka, I'd like to introduce you to Estrella."

There's silence on the other end of the line. I can only imagine Katka's lifted brow as she calculates what I'm trying to do.

"And Estrella, this is Katka," I continue. "She's been trying to assist me in extracting you from Nadia's and has been instrumental in this escape plan."

"I appreciate whatever it is you've done," Estrella says. "Especially helping us escape from those horrible creatures and people."

"What horrible people?" Katka cuts in.

"We left behind a bit of carnage at the school and met up with a few of the unfriendly variety. Nothing I couldn't handle."

"You forgot I did rescue you," Estrella adds.

"Rescue him?" Katka practically yells. "This sounds like

a disaster. Please tell me the mortals aren't going to find dead bodies lying around the school."

"You'll need to send in a crew and move the dead body of a girl somewhere else so Nadia won't realize that we had anything to do with her death."

Estrella blanches and grips the side of the car. "When do you think we can go to the hospital and check on Lexi? I want to make sure she's okay."

"Wait a second," Katka says. "There's another girl involved? Please tell me I'm wrong."

"But I thought you didn't like to be wrong?" I grin at the road. Katka doesn't bite. "We have an issue. I need a new car. And sooner than later because we're going to have company very, very soon. This Barbie car you booked me is going to be flattened by our new angry friends."

"Unbelievable," she says. "Fine. I'm messaging you with the closest Traveling Pool to your location. I'll tell your father you'll be here within the hour."

"Like I said before," Estrella interrupts. "I'm not going anywhere with you until I know why you're helping me. No one risks their lives just because they want to be nice."

"Really?" I say. "You need to get out more. Not everyone in this world is as awful as the Nazco."

"Nazco? Traveling Pool? Who are you and what's going on?" She holds up her hand. "You know what? Forget it. Right now I just need you to take me to the hospital to see Lexi."

In my rearview mirror, a car zooms into view. Its speed tells me we don't have much time.

"Forget the Traveling Pool. We won't make it there before company shows up." Frustration pulls at me, ready to snap like a cord. "I need a faster car so I can outrun these guys or the only traveling we'll be doing is into the next life. Besides, I don't want a battle at the Traveling Pool or they could follow us through the Water Channels."

"You always make things so complicated." Katka huffs. "I've accessed your GPS. Follow those instructions. The car should be ready for you in thirty minutes."

"Thirty minutes?" I yell. "I don't have thirty minutes!"

"Well, I guess you'll have to get creative then," she says.

"I'm requesting a new handler next time I'm sent out on a mission," I say, but she's already hung up on me.

"You really need to work on your charm." Estrella glances over her shoulder at the oncoming car. "You might have gotten a better outcome. Because honestly, things aren't looking so great for us right now."

I grunt because she's not wrong. "Hang on tight. I've got to lose this guy or we're both going to die in the next few minutes."

10

YOU REALLY NEED TO WORK ON YOUR DRIVING SKILLS

ESTRELLA

Florida

The car weaves in and out of traffic, screeching its tires like it's begging for Tristan to slam on the brakes and walk far away. I double-check my seat-belt and cling to the edge of my seat.

"With your driving skills," I say, "whoever is following us isn't going to need to kill us. You'll take care of that for them."

Tristan flashes me a wide grin, showing off perfect white teeth. "I suppose this isn't a good time to tell you I never got my American license."

"No, it's really not."

The light in front of us turns red, but Tristan makes no

move to slow down. Instead, he slams on the accelerator and flies across the intersection. One car's tires screech while another car swerves, stopping in the middle of the intersection and barely missing us. The driver blares his horn, which only widens Tristan's grin.

"Well, that was invigorating," he says.

"Did you not see the red light?" I yell. "You almost got us killed."

"We've almost got killed like twenty times in the last hour," he says. "Nothing new. Besides, did you not see what I did?"

"Other than breaking a bunch of traffic laws and nearly sending us to the hospital?"

"That car blocked the intersection so the guy who was following us couldn't get through."

I let out a long breath and lean against the seat, closing my eyes. My heart has been racing on full adrenaline ever since my eyes first landed on those horrible Wraiths. I shudder at the memory. Sure, Tristan obviously saved my life on more than one occasion, but that doesn't mean I can trust him. In fact, I don't trust anyone.

I thought Tiffany was my friend. And Chandra was just an annoying girl at school.

I frown. What was Chandra doing with those two other people? It was obvious that one of them caused a rainstorm and another caused a windstorm. I've been chalking up all of these strange events to my own personal issues, but now I'm beginning to realize somehow I'm involved in something bigger than I possibly could imagine.

Tristan turns, driving into a tiny road, and then takes

another right. He's hoping to lose them, and I'm glad for it. But at the same time, I've no idea where I am or what I've gotten myself into with this guy who can wield fire and battle with swords.

My body trembles and I wrap my arms around myself, but I'm not shaking from the cold. What I experienced today and last night was darker and more terrible than any rainstorm could be. Tristan leans into the backseat and grabs a jacket, holding it out to me.

"Might help," he says.

I take it gratefully, tucking it close to my body as if this small layer of material can protect me from the horrible experiences I just had.

It smells like him, sandalwood and pine.

I check the side mirror. "Looks like we lost whoever was following us." I tuck the edge of the blanket under my chin. "Last night, my friends and I snuck into Nadia's secret room. I took out files about each of us and I also stole this."

I hold up the dagger. Its brightness has faded into a stormy gray.

"This is all starting to make a lot of sense. That weapon you have has been fused with an immortal's power. They must have had high powers for its blade to be able to kill a Wraith."

I gulp. "High powers? Is that what the flaming thing is that you do with your sword?"

He chuckles. "Yeah. No one's ever called it a flaming thing though. Kind of like it."

"So this is worth killing me for?" I point to the dagger in my lap.

"That's valuable, but you are far more valuable than that."

"If I'm so valuable, why kill me?"

"That's the million-dollar question." His phone pings. "Can you check that for me? I haven't quite mastered the art of driving and texting."

"I don't think you're supposed to do both," I point out.

He cocks an eyebrow with a shrug. "You may be right."

I sigh but look at his phone. "It's a text from Katka. She says the car is ready at this location."

I click on the link provided and it switches me to the GPS. I press GO.

"You will arrive at your destination in five minutes," the GPS voice intones.

"Excellent." Tristan blows out a long breath. "I'll be glad to get into a car that actually works."

He turns off at the next exit. Soon we're pulling into an old lot packed full of beat-up cars. Some are missing tires. Others are rusted out.

"This doesn't look very promising," I say.

"You've got to be kidding me," he mutters. "How is this any better? Text Katka back and ask her if she's trying to kill me."

I send off the text and she replies. "She says, 'Don't tempt me. Drive to the back of the lot. Your chariot awaits. You're welcome.' I get the feeling she doesn't really like you."

"Yeah." His face sobers. "That is likely true."

Tristan drives to the back where a black, hulking Range Rover sits, waiting expectantly for us. Its midnight paint glistens under the hot Florida sun. Tristan zips the tiny Kia Soul into a parking spot and leaps out.

"Now that is a beauty." He pops open the Kia's trunk and gathers up a bag and an umbrella.

I climb out of the car, following him. "Well, at least you're prepared for the weather."

"This thing?" He holds up the umbrella, eyes twinkling. "Oh, most definitely. All sorts of weather in fact."

The doors to the new SUV are unlocked so we slip inside. The key rests in the center console. Tristan pushes the start button, and the engine rumbles to life.

"Are we going to meet up with Conrad and Lexi now?" I press as he peels out of the parking lot.

"That's a bad idea. Right now, you need to give Lexi time to heal. In that glove box, there is an assortment of medical supplies, but nothing powerful enough to mend the damage the Wraith did. And sure, we might be safe for the moment, but that can change at any second. Lexi can't handle another attack. I know this is hard to understand, but it's you that's the bigger threat to them, not Lexi."

"It's not safe for me at Nadia's anymore, is it?"

He shakes his head. "I'm sorry. Nadia's house is guarded by the Wraiths. Now that they know we've killed their own, they will kill you at first sight. The only good news is everyone that knew Lexi was a part of this is dead, so she's safe for now."

I need to pull myself together and get out of this mess. Freaking out isn't going to help. I glance out my window, taking in the landscape while breathing in deep breaths. Swampland stretches out as far as my eye can see. Nobody lives out here. We could be flying toward the edge of the world for all I know. Maybe we are.

I recheck the security of my seatbelt and peek at the speedometer. The car is speeding down the highway at one hundred miles per hour.

"Where are we going?" I ask. "You need to give me answers before I agree to go anywhere with you."

He exits the ramp and we pass by an old gas station cluttered with weeds and fallen palm branches.

"You're right," he says, annoyingly unfazed. "We need to talk before I take you through the Traveling Pool. I want to find a place where we won't be interrupted by assassins or Wraiths."

I dig my nails into my palms. "We can talk anywhere. Like right now. In the car."

The car makes two quick turns before rumbling along a sand road and into a parking lot. My hand is already pushing open the door as the car slows into park. A massive sand drift blocks my view, but I can smell and heart the roar of the ocean on the other side.

I leap out of the car, desperately wanting to hear what Tristan has to say, but also wanting to run away from him as fast as I can. I scamper across the parking lot and climb up the dune, hot sand pooling into my sneakers. As I crest the top, a breeze sweeps over me. It lashes at my hair and wipes the sweat off my face. The air smells and tastes like salt, fresh air, and sun.

Stretched out before me lies the endless blue ocean. It rushes at the beach and then curls up in a crown of frothy whiteness before crashing down at the shoreline, spraying up a final mist. Looking in either direction, the beach is barren. Not a person, house, or boat for miles.

If Tristan wanted to hurt or kill me, this would be the perfect place to do it.

I spin on my heels to face him, holding out the dagger between us.

"It's time to come clean," I announce. "What is it that you want from me?"

11

NOTHING A LITTLE SALTWATER THERAPY CAN FIX

ESTRELLA

Florida

"That weapon won't work as well as before." He grimaces. "It needs a recharge of power. There aren't any sources nearby. To recharge an artifact, we'd have to take it to a place that has sacred ground or is an original power source."

I glance at the dagger. Sure enough, the cerulean blue has turned into a murky gray. Even now as I touch it, only a trickle of its power glimmers against my palms.

"So they're disposable?" I ask.

"What?" His eyes widen. "No. Definitely not. Objects like these are very rare, very sought after. My sister had a weapon such as that one." He swallows and his eyes become stormy blue. "Because of her abilities, she was able to wield it with more power than others. If I'm right, you're a lot like her."

"I saw what this did when I used it." I run my fingers along the blade. "But I don't really understand how it works."

"If my memory is correct, this artifact is called Tide-breaker."

"Tidebreaker," I whisper the word, and as I do, the dagger warms in my palms like it's answering to its name. "I think you're right. It's a perfect name for it, too."

"I've read about it. And according to our records, it's said its power is like that of one who can command the ebb and flow of the ocean's strength. Obviously, it's bonded to you and has served you well."

I blink, trying to process everything.

"How about we start back at the beginning?" he offers. "Like how your car wreck was set up and made to look like you're a mortal."

"Set up?" I frown and tuck the dagger into the waist of my jeans. "A mortal? What are you talking about?"

He sighs and rakes his hand through his hair. "Come on. Let's sit down and talk."

He sits on the soft sand, resting his forearms on his knees. The breeze cuts through his thick blond hair. Swallowing hard, I slip off my shoes, letting my feet sink into the hot sand. I join him, sitting crossed-legged.

"Why did you bring me here?" I ask.

"It's a calming place. Hard to get upset with a view like this. We don't have beaches or oceans where I'm from."

He has a point. I mean, it was already calming my screaming nerves. "Where are you from?"

"A kingdom deep in the mountains and hidden from mortals. A place I think you'd come to love if you'd give it a chance."

He turns to me then with a look I can't quite read. Is it pity that makes his forehead crease? Sadness?

I don't want either.

"Tell me everything," I whisper.

Facing the ocean again, he begins, "Dion and Chandra are Nazco. Their nation is one of the four immortal races."

The roar of the ocean crashing against the shore matches the roaring in my ears. "Immortals? As in people who don't die?"

"To a point. Their capital is in Antarctica, but they also rule South and North America where they live alongside mortals. Many of them have been breaking the unbreakable rule of sapping the strength from humans so they can be more powerful."

He spits out those last words like he tasted something bitter.

"Did you drive me all the way out here to tell me some kind of fairytale? What does this all have to do with me?"

"You're one of them."

12

YOU'RE SAYING I'M LIKE IMMORTAL?

ESTRELLA

Florida

I snort. "Very funny. So you're saying I'm like immortal?"

"Yes." Then he shrugs. "Well, you were. Now, I really don't know where you stand in the process."

"None of that makes sense. Why don't I know this?" I give him a pointed look. "You'd think I'd know if I was immortal."

He stares at his hands. "If a Nazco citizen has displeased the Overlords or the Empress or broken sacred rules, it's either death or excommunication. If a Nazco is cast out, they're given an implanted memory like a mortal's. Once the brain has accepted the mortal mind, they are unable to use their powers and will die of old age just like a human."

I open my mouth, close it, and then laugh.

"You know," I shake my head, "it's great to find someone else as crazy as I am."

"Deep down your heart tells you I speak the truth."

My pulse kicks up and my hands grow clammy, even though it must be in the eighties. His words hit a chord.

"Last night, I stole some of the files on myself and other girls in the house. My file said I was from Antarctica, which I thought was strange, but here you are confirming it. The file also said I was excommunicated due to foreseen betrayal."

"Betrayal?" His eyebrows lift. "Interesting."

"Let's back up a little. You said implant. Are you saying I have an implanted memory?"

"Sometimes the implanted memories don't work properly. If this happens, an executioner, a Wraith, is sent to exterminate them. That could be why the creatures attacked you in the bathroom."

"Lexi did warn me to pretend I didn't remember things." A new thought crosses my mind. "The mall and the parking lot. Those people aren't Wraiths. Who are they?"

"Assassins. They work for the Empress and the Nazco Overlords."

"Empress? Overlords?"

My sweaty palms turn into blocks of ice. I jump to my feet and take off down the beach. Deep down, I know there's truth to his words, far more truth than Mrs. Blaire's story about a fire, dead relatives, and a bump on my head.

My hand reaches for the necklace Zayla found for me. This locket is real. I know that deep down. Not those pictures my caseworker gave me. Tears stream down my cheeks as I try to process what Tristan just said.

Immortal.

Not wanted as my own.

Somehow the implanted memory of losing my family in a fire is so much more palatable than knowing my own people don't want me. So much so that they are willing to kill me. I kick at the sand as anger and resentment build up inside me, roaring like waves. Tristan jogs to catch up.

"You okay?" he asks.

"I just...I don't know what to believe anymore."

"If you need proof, I can give it to you."

"I don't want your proof." But didn't I? Hadn't I been crying every night for the memories that had vanished?

"Remember when I said your tattoo was actually a birthmark?"

I stopped, mid-stride. Now he's caught my attention. "Yes."

"Every immortal is born with that mark. Except yours is fading, isn't it?"

"How did you know?" I whisper.

"It's a sign that you're losing your immortality and powers."

I hold up my hand as if to stop all the words. It's too much. "I can't. I can't handle all of this."

My knees tremble, the world spinning around me. My stomach heaves and I stumble off to the side. I fall to my knees in the sand and throw up.

I can't stop shaking. The world won't stop spinning.

Tristan touches my shoulder but I shove his hands off me and leap away, pressing my own shaking hands against my jeans.

"It's okay." He holds up his hands as if to calm me. "This

is why I didn't want to tell you this at your school. I was worried about the side effects of being told the truth. The implant they put in your brain is created to make your body want to reject the information. So it can be very dangerous to tell an immortal going through the mortalization process the truth of who they are."

I hate that he's right. My whole body screams at me to run away from him and escape. To plant my hands over my ears.

"Maybe it will help to focus on me rather than you," he offers. "As I said, all immortals have a birthmark."

He doesn't move closer to me. Instead, he pulls off his shirt, exposing a rippled chest. "As you can see, I have one, too."

Slowly, he turns around. A jagged scar runs diagonally across his muscular back, but that's not where my eyes are drawn to. It's to the mark on the top left corner. A bunch of twisted knots bound together, just like the leather necklace he wears.

Just like mine.

What are the odds that we both have the same mark on our bodies? I step to him and reach out. When I touch his skin, my fingers trail the curves of the knot. It's a symbol that never ends, just like mine. Heat sinks into my fingers, soaking deep into my core.

I don't know how to explain it, but as I touch him, it's like I don't want to stop. He's fire. A burning sensation that seeps through me all the way to my toes. My vision clears a little and the queasiness in my stomach settles. Flushed, I quickly snatch my hand away as if I've been burned. He turns around and stares intently at me.

"You okay?" he asks.

"Maybe?" More questions hit me. "Back to you. Why are you helping me?"

He hesitates and then says, "I'm a Sabian, one of the other four immortal groups."

"You make it sound like that's a big deal."

"The Sabians and Nazco don't get along."

"So you're like my enemy?"

"To put it mildly." He chuckles and stares back at the ocean. "I've been commissioned by the Sabian King to help you recover your memories and keep you safe."

"A king wants you to help me? Why would he even care if I exist?"

He opens his mouth as if he's about to tell me something, but then he grimaces and rubs the scruff on his chin. "If you were able to recover your memories, we were hoping you could help us out."

"I don't have anything to offer a king." I dig my toe through the soft sand. "I mean, the Nazco obviously thought I was worthless."

"I'd like to believe they underestimated you. And if you are able to recover your immortal mind, you'll be able to recover your powers."

"You think I have powers?"

"Every immortal has been gifted with some sort of power. Some have high powers, while others have minor abilities."

Water laps at my feet. It's hard to understand everything he's saying—and not saying—but I need all the information I can get. "Tell me more about these immortals."

He hesitates. "You've had a lot of information at one time. I don't want to push the memory implant too much."

"It's okay," I say. "I'm feeling better now. I'll let you know when to stop."

We begin to stroll down the beach, the sand sparkling under a deep blue sky.

"About 2,000 years ago, a civil war broke out among the immortals. Sects formed into nations and our great race broke apart. The Nazco left for Antarctica and South America, Caladrians moved to Africa, the Eien remained in Asia, and we Sabians migrated to Europe. Since then, each nation hasn't always gotten along, but the Nazco causes the most trouble. Especially with their new ruler."

My head whirls and that sick sensation rises up in my stomach. "Okay, so that's a lot to process. I'm guessing you're hoping I'll remember something your king wants to know. What if I can't recover my memories?"

"Then you can go and live with the mortals with our blessing." He studies me for a moment as if weighing his next words. "But we believe it takes time for the implant to set in."

"My file said my treatment period was six months. Do you think that's what it meant?"

"Maybe. We do know there's a correlation between the birthmark and your memory. When your birthmark disappears, your immortality is lost."

A giant wave crashes in front of us, foaming until it becomes a gentle rush of water that licks my toes and disappears. Is my life like that? Like a great wave dissolved into nothing?

"A part of me can't stand not remembering. But some-

77

times I get these dreams or visions. I've always wondered if they're memories." I frown, my heartbeat kicking up. Dion had been in those dreams. What does that mean? "But some of them aren't good. More like nightmares. And if that's what my old life was like, I'm not so sure I want to remember it."

He touches my arm, and a spark flutters across my skin. "But if we can help you, you could start a new life. This is your chance to stop the corrupted Nazco leaders."

"What I really want is to help my friends. What they are doing to us at Nadia's is wrong."

"So will you join us?"

13
THE ODDS OF SURVIVAL ARE ONE IN TEN
TRISTAN

Florida

I hold my breath, hoping she'll say yes. The odds of keeping her alive here are slim to none. Especially now that the Nazco saw her run off with me.

She stares at me, then the ocean. "Yes. On one condition. You agree to help me rescue my friends."

"I can't promise that. At least not until you have fully recovered your immortal powers."

"What will happen to my friends when I leave? Lexi is literally fighting for her life because I dragged her into this. I can't abandon any of them."

"If you want to help your friends," I nod toward the parking lot and we start heading back to the car, "you need to get yourself healed and regain your powers. This situation we are in is very delicate. One misstep could cause another war between the Sabians and Nazco."

"Can you call Conrad and find out where he is? I want to see Lexi. I can't just leave her behind without talking to her."

I nod, but I worry this is a bad idea. Katka would say I'm making too many concessions. Father would be furious I'm letting this girl call the shots. But I have a gut feeling that if we are to truly gain her confidence, she needs to leave here on her own terms.

Once we're back in the car, I dial Conrad's number, listening to it ring and ring. Finally, he answers.

"Everything alright?" he asks.

"I was going to ask you the same question."

"Lexi and I are safe. She's resting right now. I'm planning on taking her to the hospital soon."

"Estrella wants to see her."

"You sure that's a good idea?" he asks.

"No, but I don't know what else to do."

"Alright. In twenty minutes, meet me outside of the ice cream shop at the location I'm sending you. Then I'll take you to her."

I hang up and look over at Estrella. Her head is pressed against the back of the seat, eyes closed, but she must have overheard our conversation because she says, "Thank you."

"I hope you like ice cream."

She opens her eyes and considers this for a moment. "I really don't know actually."

"You don't know if you like ice cream? Now that is a problem we must rectify."

~

Once I pull into the parking lot of the ice cream shop, I step out of the car and assess the area. Conrad has sent us to a quaint downtown with brick buildings and paved sidewalks. The center of the two-lane road holds a miniature park peppered with flowers and a gazebo.

"Looks like all is clear," I tell Estrella as she climbs out of the car. Her head whips back and forth, eyes wide like a scared rabbit. I don't blame her.

I flip open the trunk and open my bag of supplies. My eyes scan the array of weapons. Swords, knives, a bow, and arrows along with a time releaser.

"Wow." Estrella gasps as she rounds the car and takes in the spread. "That is..."

"Decent." I shrug and snatch up a small sword that will hide well across my back.

"I wouldn't exactly call this decent," she says. "More like intense."

I slide the sword into the sheath under my shirt and hold out a small knife to her. She lifts her very scary, very powerful dagger up. Based on how it disintegrated the Wraiths, I don't want that accidentally stabbing me.

"I have mine," she says.

"Be careful with that thing. It's not a toy. There are plenty of immortals who will kill for that weapon alone. I recommend keeping both. Two is always better than one." I dig around in the back for a belt with knife sheaths. "Here. Put this around your waist. You can store your knives inside it."

"You know we're not even allowed to have forks at Nadia's. Knives? Strictly forbidden."

"Look at you. Such a rebel."

She rolls her eyes as she wraps the belt around her waist but struggles with the clip.

"Here." I step closer. "Let me help."

With her body so close to mine, I can't help but smell her lavender shampoo and feel her presence. My fingers fumble a little on the belt.

"There." I step safely away. There's something about her that seems to call to me, and it's unnerving. Maybe it's her powers. That would make the most sense. "Now pull your shirt over the knife so it remains hidden."

I close the trunk and squint my eyes, taking in the area one last time before we continue.

"Try to stay calm," I tell her. "Act like you're just here to get ice cream."

We stroll as casually as possible down the walkway toward the ice cream shop. I check my watch.

"We have a few minutes before Conrad's supposed to meet us," I say. "Let's get ice cream. Might help us blend in."

"You think there are assassins here?" she whispers. "How would they know to look for us here?"

"They could have a Tracker."

"You think they put a tracker inside of me?"

He chuckles. "No. An immortal with the power to track down people."

"Oh." She frowns, and her forehead knits as if she's processing this information.

A red and white striped awning stretches over small round tables, and the smell of waffle cones reels us through the doorway. Inside, a glassed-in freezer runs along the counter where big tubs of ice cream are tucked in neat rows.

"So what's your favorite?" I ask her.

"I can't even remember if I've ever eaten ice cream before," she says. "I've no idea. Vanilla?"

"Let's find out."

The ice cream attendant scoops out vanilla for her with a little pink spoon. I lean against the counter, watching her and unable to keep the smile off my face. Her long blonde hair is windblown and her cheeks have a bright glow to them from our hike along the beach. I had worried about her completely losing it after I told her everything, but she's taken it surprisingly well.

Could it be because I let her touch me? Except she doesn't even know how her powers work, does she? Who knows? She might not even have powers for that matter. She puts the spoon in her mouth and closes her eyes briefly.

"It's good," she says. "Very good."

My attention is drawn to her pink lips, and all I can think about is what it would be like to kiss them. I swallow hard, quickly looking away. What is the matter with me? This mission is entirely about getting a Conduit back for our people, not me messing around with her romantically or even as a friend.

"Try another," I say, forcing myself to focus on the flavors.

She points to the chocolate. After tasting five more flavors, she waves her pink spoon into the air.

"Vanilla is not my favorite." She grins like this is a game. The ice cream worker leans over the counter, having as much fun as we are. "Mint chocolate chip is my favorite. It tastes like ice-cold winters with a kick."

I try to smile, but I can't help but wonder if she's unconsciously missing her homeland. "Load up a bowl of that."

"Actually," she says, "I'll have one of those waffle cones."

"You know, I can't remember the last time I had this much fun."

I realize I've never had a moment like this with someone. Back home, it's always about training, protecting, following the rules, and preparing to be my people's next ruler. I'm the prince, the honored one, the revered one.

But for a few moments, I'm just a kid from high school eating ice cream with a pretty girl. Feels a little too good to be true. Armed with a waffle cone each, we head outside and settle at a table under an umbrella. I scan the area, but all seems safe and I allow my muscles to relax.

At the beach, I almost told her I was the king's son, but I stopped myself. It just hadn't seemed like the right moment. Will she be upset at me when she finds out?

I also still haven't told her the whole truth about how powerful she could be. How important she is. And how she could change everything for our people.

"Was it strange knowing your first guess wasn't true?" I ask.

She licks her ice cream. "I guess it's more like now I know why I like ice cream. It's creamy and soft and sweet."

"You should try this out on everything. You need to find out who you are, not who *they* want you to believe you are with the implanted memory they've given you."

She nods, but her smile flutters away. A part of me wishes we could go back to being normal teens with our biggest worry being what flavor of ice cream to eat.

But this isn't a game. This is real, and I can't fail her or my people.

"I've been thinking a lot about what you said at the

beach." She licks her cone and scrunches up her nose, twisting her mouth as if she tasted something awful. "Is that a cockroach in my ice cream?"

"A what?"

She screams and throws the cone onto the table. A swarm of black bugs scatters across the ice cream. I leap to my feet.

"Those aren't chocolate chips," she yells. "They're bugs!"

My eyes widen as I realize my chocolate chips have also transformed into cockroaches. I toss the cone aside and leap over the table, brushing off the roaches biting Estella's arm.

"I think I swallowed one," she croaks, holding her throat.

Fear clenches at my chest in a vice grip as I scan the area. There's a Nazco assassin nearby, and these deadly cockroaches are his trademark.

14

MINT CHOCOLATE CHIP IS OFF THE LIST

ESTRELLA

Florida

"He's got to be here somewhere." Tristan whips his head around as if searching for something, and then wraps his arm protectively around me.

"Who?" My throat tightens like it's swelling. Tears spring to my eyes, and it's becoming hard to breathe.

"Roach." Tristan stops short and stares ahead of us at a man dressed in a shiny black suit standing in the shadows by a fountain. Under a baseball cap, his beady black eyes glimmer and his mouth twitches almost like he was laughing. Tristan tugs me toward the guy.

"Hello," I say. "Shouldn't we be racing in the opposite direction of that twitching creep?"

Especially since as we grow closer, I realize this man's

suit has shiny black cockroaches creeping over the material. But everyone is too busy going about their day to stop and notice.

"Nope. That guy is too creepy." I go to turn around when pain stabs my stomach and I double over, leaning into Tristan's side. He holds me up, strong and unmovable.

Roach snickers. "I love watching them die from the bites," he hisses.

"Hand over the antidote," Tristan growls.

"And miss my moment of glory? Never!"

"Now or die!"

I jerk back up at Tristan's words. "Please," I say, tugging on his elbow. "Take me to the hospital."

"You'd kill me in a public place?" Roach's eyes widen. "You bluff. You cannot kill me without drawing the mortals' attention. How would that look to your Sabian weak-minded king?"

Tristan stretches his hand behind his back and pulls out his sword. "Try me."

With a screech, Roach scampers off with surprisingly fast speed. Tristan breaks into a run after him, towing me along, but the pain in my stomach sends another spasm through my core. I hunch over, barely able to breathe.

Tristan picks me up, cradles me in his arms, and takes off into a sprint. He nearly plows over a lady as she cries out in surprise, but he steps sideways just in time.

"Halloween isn't until next week," someone else yells out.

When we hit the parking lot, I spy Roach sliding into a van across from our car.

"There!" I point.

Roach peels out of the parking lot as Tristan helps me into the car and then practically throws himself into the driver's seat. Roach's van swerves into traffic. Tristan backs out of the parking lot and races after him, tires screeching.

The stoplight is red. Tristan ignores it, slicing through a gap in the intersection. My body smashes against the door. I fumble with the seatbelt, but the pain in my stomach makes even the smallest motion difficult. Tristan's arm stretches over my body, pulls the seatbelt across for me, and clips it in.

Tristan pushes a button on the console and the glove compartment pops open. The bottom slides back and a tray filled with maybe twenty glass vials ejects from a hidden sub-compartment.

I gape at the sparkling liquid. "This doesn't look like a med kit."

"Drink the pink one." Tristan says, swinging into the oncoming traffic lane to avoid the bumper-to-bumper traffic.

Cars honk as they swerve around us to avoid a head-on collision.

"We're going to crash!" I scream.

"Now!"

I focus on the tray, but my vision blurs and my breathing comes out wispy. With a shaking hand, I pull out the pink one and fumble with the cork. Finally, I pop it open, but I hesitate. What if this stuff will actually kill me rather than help? But if Tristan wanted to kill me, he would've done it a long time ago.

My throat tightens even more. If I don't drink it now, I'm not sure I'll be able to breathe. I put the glass edge to my lips and tip it back, letting the cool liquid stream into my mouth.

It tastes like a mix of grass and the watermelon I had in the cafeteria.

My throat relaxes.

The burning in my stomach dulls.

"It worked," I announce, setting the empty vial back into the trap.

"Thank Katka when you see her." He punches the button again, and the tray slips back into the glove compartment. The flap closes shut with a click. "She's the one that remembered the med kit."

With a jerk, Roach whips around the car in front of us, scraping the highway guardrail. Tristan accelerates. I clutch the sides of my seat, bracing for impact. Sure enough, we smash into Roach's bumper.

My body jerks forward and then snaps back against the seatbelt, and I let out a moan.

"Shouldn't we be running from this guy instead of chasing him?" I ask. "After all, I feel much better."

"I don't think Conrad has the antidote," he says. "And he's the closest Healer I know of in this region. We must get it from Roach before the bites poison your system. The antiqual you drank is temporary. An adrenaline kick."

"Antiqual?"

"It's like medicine but created with immortal powers."

Sirens break through the screeching tires. I peer over my shoulder. "Police!"

"Great. I'll try to lose them."

The van cuts across two lanes of traffic, causing a semi-truck to slam on its brakes. The car behind it crashes into the semi. I gasp, hoping the driver in the car is okay. Roach whips right and enters a narrow street. Tristan follows.

We spin into an abandoned parking lot as the van screeches to a stop. Roach jumps out, disappearing into the ground. Tristan bounds out of the car.

"Where did he go?" I open my door, hurrying after Tristan.

He points to a manhole. "There." He tosses off the thick metal lid as if it were made of plastic. Air, smelling like sewage, escapes from the deep darkness below. A metal ladder trails down into the emptiness.

"Yuck!" I exclaim as I step away.

"I hate to say this," Tristan says, "but you're going to have to come with me. Once I get the antidote, you'll need to drink it ASAP."

"What if I don't?"

"You die."

"I feel so reassured."

"Glad somebody is," he says and jumps in.

I hover over the edge until I catch a beam of light about ten feet below. Tristan is holding a pale blue glowing crystal. Gingerly, I scale down the ladder rungs, wrinkling my nose. Sensing Tristan's urgency, I hop down the last two feet, my feet splashing into sewage.

"Gross," I whimper.

Grabbing my hand, Tristan takes off running, sloshing through the sludge while the blue glow illuminates the round metal sewage tunnel. Despite everything, all I can think about is his hand in mine. It's warm and comforting and somehow I get the feeling that as long as I'm holding onto him, I'll be okay.

I'm jerked from my thoughts when a door on the right

catches my attention. In the pale light, I spy the infinity symbol imprinted on its surface.

"Wait," I say. "I think he went in here."

Tristan surveys the door and then me. "You sure?"

"I don't know how to explain it, but yes. Is that weird?"

"I believe you."

He twists the door handle and kicks against the metal surface, but it doesn't budge. Some letters beneath the grimy surface catch my eye. I swipe at the surface until all the letters are visible. Tristan holds up his glow stick and squints.

"I've no idea what this says." He rakes a hand through his hair. "It's Nazco writing. Languages aren't my specialty."

I lick my lips and with shaking fingers trace the design. "I know these letters and words. Which is kind of freaking me out."

"What does it say?"

"Talia rathum hanada."

The door rumbles, then drops into a slit opening on the floor.

My mouth gapes open. "Did I really open it?"

"Impressive." Tristan steps into the gloom, holding the blue crystal before him. "I think I'll keep you around until we get out of here."

He takes my hand once again. A part of me warns to not hold his hand, but another part begs for his warm security. As soon as I pass through the entrance, the door swishes back up, closing the exit behind us. I jump and step closer to Tristan. We're standing in a small room about the size of Nadia's living room. It's completely empty. A steady plink cuts the silence like a faucet hasn't been completely turned off. The walls seem to be leering at us expectantly.

"Why do I feel like this is a trap?" I whisper.

"Probably because it is one."

The slab of rock under our feet creaks and shakes slightly.

And then it drops.

I scream and throw my arms around Tristan. My stomach slams into my chest as we plummet straight down, riding the rock like a free-fall elevator. Tristan pulls me tight against his chest. I clamp my eyes shut and press my cheek against his hard body, begging for this nightmare to end.

Abruptly, the ground jerks to a stop. We tumble off the slab and roll across a stone floor. I land on top of Tristan, my body sprawled over him. My cheeks flush, and Dion's face comes to my mind. For some reason, guilt threads through me. Quickly, I scamper off Tristan and stand on wobbly legs.

After the groaning of the moving slab and my screaming, the silence is deafening.

Tristan stands warily. "I see that antiqual really opened your lungs."

"I'm never eating ice cream again," I snap back, trying to not think about how my throat is starting to swell again. My head is also starting to throb. "Where are we?"

But really I'm wondering if we're trapped here forever in the darkness.

"Let's find out." Tristan drops another blue crystal and steps on it. It snaps with a crack. Blue light floods the room, revealing every crevice. Every detail.

"Wow," I gasp. "Those glowy things are becoming quite handy."

"If we make it out of here alive, remind me to thank our Light Master for that device."

We're standing in the center of a massive cave. Stalactites hang like teeth above and the walls are carved with inscriptions and paintings. The text is the same kind as the one on the door, which means I must have learned the language in my previous life. I shiver at that thought. It confirms what Tristan has been telling me all along.

Across the cavern sits a mammoth ten-foot carved rock in the shape of a roach. The antennae and bugged eyes almost look alive.

Maybe they are.

My knees go weak as I take in this dreadful place. "I should have never followed you down here," I whisper.

"This is my fault." Tristan pulls out his sword and spins around. "I should've protected you better. Taken you through the Water Channels right away."

"I don't know what you're talking about, but I wouldn't have gone."

Cackling erupts through the cavern, and then a singsong voice calls out in the distance, "Weeelcome! Weeelcome."

"He's straight through there." Tristan plucks another crystal glow stick from his pouch and points to the mouth of the roach statue.

"Are you crazy?" I grab his shirt and tug him back toward me. "This is a *very* bad idea."

"How's your throat?"

Swelling. Not to mention that it feels like someone is poking my stomach with hot tongs. I groan. "You win."

He smiles deviously. "I like winning." And he takes off.

"You have no idea how glad I am to hear that," I say, and scamper after him, trying to keep up with his long strides as we enter the mouth. Even though shooting pain cuts at my insides, there's no way I'm letting him out of my sight.

The mouth is actually a tunnel, roughly hewn rock illuminated by Tristan's light. A skirmish of clacking sounds echo through the rock. Tiny black bugs—cockroaches, I realize—flee from the light as we wind in a downward motion toward what I'm figuring is my death.

The tunnel spits us out into another cavern, this one larger than the last. Taking up most of the cave stands a massive metal throne set up on a dais. It's too hard to really make out the throne's actual shape because it's covered with those awful bugs. They make the throne seem like it's moving.

Two glass pillars, bubbling with brackish liquid, rise up to the ceiling on either side.

"So good of you to come," Roach says, gleefully greeting us from his throne. "I do love a delicious guest list. You are the first Sabian to come to my lair, you know."

I convulse as sharper spasms of pain stab my stomach, and I grab Tristan's arm so I don't fall. The last thing I want is to give this bug guy the satisfaction he's hurting me, but the pain feels like someone is coming out of my insides.

"Hand it over," Tristan growls.

"How rude." Roach snarls. He rolls his head and transforms into his true form. His beady eyes grow larger than a human's. His back arches in a steeper curve, and antennae dangle from the sides of his mouth.

"A shapeshifter," Tristan mutters under his breath,

clenching his sword so his knuckles whiten. "Get out your dagger."

My hands shake as I pull it out. Though the hilt is dull, it's still cool against my sweaty palms. Just holding it is comforting.

"Shalik!" Roach cries out.

"What did he say?" Tristan asks.

The word the Wraiths screamed in my dreams. "Death," I whisper.

"Brilliant," Tristan drones.

The horde at Roach's feet redirects its swarm around the throne to head straight for us. Their skittering feet vibrate through the room.

I search for a place to run, but the only entrance I see is where we just came from. Tristan crouches, holding out his sword. His eyes narrow at the oncoming enemy. He clenches his jaw in that same fierceness he had fighting the Wraiths.

"Please tell me you have a plan," I say, holding my blade before me.

"Plans are overrated."

"Right." Another spasm of pain stabs at my stomach and I double over, nearly dropping my weapon. "So basically we're doomed."

Tristan cuts the air with his blade. With a guttural cry, he shoots out a bolt of fire from his sword. I shield my eyes from its brightness and intense heat. The fire blazes across the air and then lands on the oncoming bugs, incinerating them in seconds. The reek of burned flesh fills the still room.

A mixture of pride and pure fear fills me. Tristan isn't exactly your boy-next-door type. He's a warrior. A killer. And apparently, the enemy of the nation I'm from.

The effort put into creating that large amount of fire must have taken a toll on Tristan though because his breathing comes in and out heavily as if he just lifted a hundred pounds. Sweat drips down his face and his shoulders sag a little.

"Bravo! Bravo!" Roach stands and claps, grinning. "I do love a good show."

"I don't get it," I whisper to Tristan. "Is he delusional?"

"This guy is too happy for my taste," Tristan grumbles.

"But a good show must have a dramatic ending." Roach claps his hands twice.

A rumble pulsates throughout the cavern as multitudes of roaches swarm out of every crevice in the walls.

"Looks like he just called for reinforcements," Tristan says.

"Okay, so I'm thinking dying by a few bites might have been better than being eaten alive."

15
MY SWEET LITTLE ROACHES
ESTRELLA

Florida

"There's something I need to tell you." Tristan rolls his shoulders. "I didn't want to before because I might be wrong. Also, I'm not sure how your mind will react."

"You want to tell me you can transport us out of here?"

"That's not possible for an immortal. Our powers are tied to the elements."

The walls seem to move, interrupting us, as the oncoming roaches rush along the stone and across the floor toward us like hungry beasts. It only takes seconds before the room fills up with roaches.

"Please tell me your fire can stop them," I say.

"For now," he replies. "But I don't have an infinite amount of energy."

He lifts his sword again and sends a bolt of fire across the ground, etching the floor in roaring flame so it encompasses us in a fiery ring like a wall. Though they can't pass Tristan's raging circle, they crawl everywhere.

"My littles!" Roach screams from his throne. "How dare you hurt them."

His words spark a frenzy among the bugs, and they attack with renewed energy. Over and over they come at us. Tristan continues to send forth flames but as time passes, his shoulders sag.

Something hard drops onto my shoulder, and I scream. Tristan flicks off the roach that fell on me.

"They're coming at us from the ceiling now," I choke.

"Tricky little buggers."

The pain in my stomach becomes so unbearable, I drop to the floor and double over, crying out. My insides are being stabbed by sharp-edged glass. I gasp for air, but my lungs can't get enough.

"We're running out of time," Tristan says.

He kneels down at my side as flames surround us, hot and hungry, their tongues licking out like serpents feeding on their prey. Tears stream down my face, but they dry up quickly from the heat. I stare into Tristan's eyes, dark with worry.

"Thank you for trying to save me," I say, choking out the words.

I lean against his firm chest, hot as the flames bursting from his sword.

"I've been letting you touch me," he says. "And every time you did, I believe you've been taking a little of my power out each time."

"What?"

"Which is why my power isn't as strong right now."

"I...I don't understand."

"I think you're a Channeler." He flicks another cockroach off me that had fallen from the ceiling and crushes it under his boot.

I freeze. The memory from my file tumbles back to me.

Ability: *Channeler, high powers*

"My sister was a Channeler, too," Tristan continues. "She once told me a secret. That a Channeler can not only take another's power but give them back."

"How is that possible?" I ask.

"If we make it out of here alive, I can explain everything."

"It would've been helpful if you shared this at the beach."

The room blurs. It's hard to think properly. My stomach heaves, and a piercing pain sears against my mind. I cry out, clutching at Tristan's tattered shirt.

"I was hesitant because we suspected the Nazco put a trigger in your mind to reject certain pieces of information when you hear them. Listen, I need your help if we're going to get out of here alive."

I whimper from the pain. "How can I help when I can barely stand?"

"I need you to push back the power you took from me earlier."

"What? How?"

"I don't know. My sister just did it. She touched me and gave it back. Can you try?"

His words circle around in my head, but they make no

sense. How can I push power into him? That's like something from one of those sci-fi movies the girls watched on Nadia's TV.

The firewall protecting us sputters as more roaches pile up on top of the flames, trying to blanket it and snuff it out. We have seconds before they converge on us. Seconds before my throat squeezes so tight I won't be able to suck in another lungful of air.

Seconds before we both die.

16
ALL HARM, ALL FOUL
TRISTAN

Florida

I cradle Estrella in my arms as her lips part, gasping for air. Sweat drips down her face, and her blonde hair plasters against her cheeks. My heart rips in two. I had sworn I'd protect her. And I had meant it with every bone in my body.

"This isn't the way this mission was supposed to end," I whisper. "I've always said that if I were to be killed, I'd want it to be in battle. I just hadn't thought it would be so soon."

Her eyes flutter, and her breathing wheezes in and out. I push the strands off her face and smile fondly. I haven't told her, but I've been bitten numerous times already. It's only a matter of time before I, too, am lying incapacitated on the ground in agony.

"Next time we skip the ice cream," I say, trying to infuse lightness into my voice. "How about cake with cream?"

The last trickles of my power are being sucked away. The flames guarding us sizzle out, allowing tiny openings for the roaches. Pain from the bugs' poison rages through me, but I will keep her as safe as I can until my last breath. I lift her off the ground, holding her up as the roaches skitter over their comrades' dead bodies and through the newly made paths.

Her eyes close, her head lulling against my chest. She's dying in my arms. There's a slim chance she hasn't lost her immortality and she could still be revived after her last breath. Except there's no way Roach will let us out of here without being beheaded.

After all, it's the only way to make sure an immortal stays dead.

The way he's screaming at us right now from his throne tells me he's eager to rip us apart limb to limb.

Roaches skitter across my boots, looking for skin to bite.

I spin in a circle, searching for the closest exit to run to. If I can hold Estrella up for as long as possible, I— Estrella's hand slips beneath my shirt and presses against my chest.

That's when I feel it.

Power, my visik, seeping from her palm into my skin. Renewed, it races through my veins, reigniting me. Gently, I set her on the floor.

I don't know if Estrella's body can handle the flames, but if she's anything like my sister, she'll be able to channel the power through her body. I pray she'll be okay. It's the only chance we have of survival.

Oddly, the moment I let her go, something snaps within me. It's almost as if there had been a connection between the two of us, bonding us. And now that it's gone, it's like it's left behind a gaping hole I'm desperate to fill. I shake away those unsettling thoughts and push my power to my skin and sword until I become a glowing burst of light. With a cry, my whole body bursts into flames, scorching the roaches swarming me.

I'm death and brilliant light.

My clothes, made to be fire resistant, barely handle the raging inferno I've become. I glance down at Estrella, hoping she's okay since I tried to keep the flames from touching her. Her body lays limp on the floor. Her burns seem minimal, but her clothes are ragged and singed.

It's time to enact my revenge.

Holding out my sword, I blaze a wall of fire around Estrella and then create another path before me. Pain stabs at all the places the roaches bit me, but I shove aside the agony. Running at full speed, I storm at Roach, swinging my sword in sweeping arcs. Flames toss and crash against the roach-infested floor in roaring waves.

More bugs rain from the ceiling like hail, but the moment they touch my skin, they burst into ashes.

"You think you're so smart." Roach cackles. "I already notified the others that you're here. Even if you kill me, you won't get far."

His talons swipe at me like knives, but his words cut even deeper. The fact that he called for reinforcements does not bode well for us. Undaunted, I thrust my sword into the belly of the Roach-man. He screams in agony as blood gushes from his gut.

In a final act of fury, I slice my sword through the air, beheading Roach. His body crumbles at the foot of his throne while his head bounces off the platform to the ground.

"That's to make sure you never bother us again," I mutter.

The roaches that once swarmed the cavern skitter away, leaving behind only silence. Their will must have been tied to his. I slip my sword into its sheath and pull out my last glow rod to illuminate the darkness. Frantically, I scour the throne area for the antidote.

Fear crawls up my throat. Did we come all the way here and fight this battle only for it to be a waste of time? My eyes land on a black case tucked into the stone wall. I throw open the lid. There, lined up in neat rows, lie thin vials of blue liquid.

The antidote.

At least I hope it is. There's a high probability this could be the poison extracted from his creatures, but I snatch up two vials. As I rush back to Estrella, I pop one open with my teeth and then guzzle down the liquid. I need to make sure this is actually the antidote and not something more sinister.

The liquid slides down my throat. Instantly, its effect takes hold. My throat opens up, and the pain from the bites lessons. Encouraged, I pop open the second vial and kneel beside Estrella. I lift up her head and carefully pour the liquid into her mouth. Her body is deathly, terrifyingly still. But then she starts choking on the liquid.

I try to position her head so the antidote continues to slide down. She needs to drink all of it. Her eyes flutter, and her body jerks to life. It's working! She sputters on the liquid, but seeing her skin bloom pink encourages me.

"It's okay," I say, trying to soothe her. "This is the antidote. You have to drink all of it."

Once the vial is empty, I toss it aside and help her to a
sitting position. She rubs her chest and then her stomach,
grimacing.

"How do you feel?" I ask.

"I—I think I'm okay."

"Enough to walk?"

She tries to stand, but her knees buckle. I swoop her into
my arms to keep her from falling into the cockroach ashes
circling us.

"You don't have to carry me," she says. "I just need to
take it slow."

"We don't have time for that." I grimace, thinking about
Roach's final words. "I believe we're going to have company
very soon. Since you gave me all of your power, you're func-
tioning on bare minimum energy. Here, you hold our light
up so I can see in this bug-infested rubbish hole."

I take off running through the roach tunnel, back the
way we came. Every step takes a massive amount of energy
for me, and the muscles in my arms shake a little from the
effort of holding Estrella. Even with the antidote, my body is
still weak between the battle and the roaches' poison. The
thought that I can barely run or carry Estrella is bad. But
should we come across any assassin in our escape, I won't
be able to fight them off. We enter the stone elevator room.

"There must be some way to make the stone platform
rise back up," I say.

Estrella points to an imprint of a roach head on the wall.
"I think that might be our elevator button."

"Good eye." I punch it and instantly the sound of

grinding gears fills the large shaft. The platform begins to rise. I leap onto it, clenching Estrella tight against me. Slowly, we lift into the air.

"I can't wait to get out of this horrible place." She shivers. "You said I gave you my powers. I remember wishing to be able to help you and being absolutely terrified, but that's it."

"I don't really know how a Channeler's power operates. But whatever you did worked."

The platform groans to a stop, and I leap off it. I rush down the corridor, retracing my steps back to the manhole we entered through. The air grows a little fresher. Up ahead, a shaft of pale light pools into the gloom of the sewer.

When I reach the ladder, I pause, staring up into the blue sky. Slowly, I lower Estrella to her feet. She wobbles and clutches onto the metal bars for support.

"Are you able to climb?" I ask, knowing full well she probably can't.

She stares skeptically at the distance. Frustration hits me like a sledgehammer. If we had more time, it would be different. But every moment we take gives more seconds to those who are hunting us.

"You go first," I say. "I'll support you from behind."

"Just don't look at or touch my butt." She quips a weak smile.

"Even if you start to fall?"

"Fine. Only then."

She steps onto the first rung and inches her way up the rusty ladder. I support her as she goes. Her foot slips a few times, but I catch it and place her firmly back on the ladder. I hate the thought of her emerging from the hole above unprotected, but there's nothing to be done about it. We don't have time to wait until our bodies heal.

Finally, her head pops out of the hole, but she freezes in place.

"What's wrong?" I ask.

She doesn't answer. Her body is hauled out of the hole in one swift motion. Panic seizes me. We didn't get out of here in time.

The assassins were waiting for us above.

17
THE IMMORTAL POWER CHALLENGE
ESTRELLA

Florida

Arms yank me the rest of the way out of the sewer. My legs, weak and rubbery, buckle. I crumble onto the hot pavement, scraping my arms. The sludge of the sewers clings to me, and my hair hangs plastered against my face and over my eyes. I struggle against the grip of whoever is holding me, but I'm so tired. Weak.

"Got her!" my captor's voice exclaims in triumph. "Do I get the ransom money?"

"You're such a loser," another says, taking my other arm. "You'd never have found her without us."

I twist and fight against my captors. As I do, my fingers swipe across the top of one of their palms. A trickle of something rushes to my hands. Like an invigorating breath of cold air.

A temptation.

Could that be what Tristan was talking about in the cave? Could this guy have powers? And if so, can I take them from him?

I lift my head and study my captors. It's Chandra and that other white-haired guy I saw in the parking lot. He's pacing off to the side while she leans against the front of a car parked in the middle of the road.

"Chandra," I say. "I should've known you'd be involved with these people."

"Is that why you trembled like a scared kitten every time you saw me?"

"Who are you really?" I ask. "What do you want from me?"

"We're old friends." She smirks. "But you've become far more difficult than I had hoped."

"Should I behead her?" the guy on my left asks, lifting up an ax.

"What?" I gape at the weapon and try to pull free. "Let me go!"

Except I'm not really trying to get away. I'm trying to see if Tristan is right and I can take their power from them. And become stronger.

With a war cry, Tristan leaps out of the sewer. The moment his boots touch the pavement, he pulls out his sword. It smolders in flames. But after seeing his fire against the Wraiths and roaches, his flames now are weak in comparison. He needs time to rejuvenate.

He swipes his sword through the air and stabs the guy

on the left holding me. The man screams in agony, doubling over and releasing me.

I use the opportunity to yank with all my might against the ax guy. I manage to break free. Quickly, I rush to Tristan's side, and he holds one arm in front of me and the sword in the other.

"Well." White Hair chuckles. "She's siding with the Sabian. How unsurprising."

"Can you blame her?" Tristan backs up. "If I had a Euro for every time you made an attempt on her life, I'd be rich."

"Are these people Nazco?" I ask, inching closer to Tristan.

"We can't let the Sabian take her with him," Chandra says. "I vote we chop both of their heads off."

"Only the girl," White Hair says. "We can use him as a bargaining chip with the Sabian king."

A car screeches to a halt behind Chandra's. The door flies open and Dion bounds out of the car, racing over to us. My heart flips at seeing him. Here. What does it mean? How did he know I was here? I don't understand.

This is the face I caressed.

The lips I kissed.

The one who walked with me in my dreams.

His clothes are sopping wet, and there's a hint of scruff on his face like he didn't have time to shave. A part of me yearns to race over and throw my arms around him, but something in the pit of my stomach holds me back. If he's here it means he's immortal.

Whose side is he on?

"Stop!" Dion yells. "Don't hurt her."

"Look who's here to save the day." Chandra rolls her eyes.

Dion halts at Chandra's side. His eyes take in Tristan and how his arm is protecting me. How I step closer to him.

"What's going on?" Dion asks, warily. "Estrella, why are you...why are you with... *him?*"

Chandra grins. "This should be interesting."

"I concur," White Hair says. "Now do you believe me, Dion? She was always destined to betray us."

My head spins. They all know Dion. They're talking to him like he's their friend. He's standing beside them as if he is one of them! The realization splits my heart in half, tearing and ripping it from my core. A whimper escapes my lips at the treachery.

"You're one of them, aren't you?" I accuse him, my voice choking in pain. Dion flinches. "All this time, I thought you were just a guy I connected with. But that was a lie, wasn't it?"

"It's not like that." He takes a step toward me. I take another step back, my heart shattering with every beat.

"But it is," I snap. "They've been trying to kill me. Still are. Which means you must be, too."

Tristan's body tenses. He crouches as if ready for an attack.

"Please," Dion begs. "If you'll just listen to what I have to say, you'll know I never meant to hurt you."

"If Tristan hadn't been here," I continue, "I would've been killed, so that's a lie. Everything you've been telling me has been a lie, hasn't it?"

He closes his eyes, pain etching across his features, and

then he hangs his head. His actions spear me, and the realization nearly sends me to my knees.

"This is so stupid," Chandra drones. "Kill her already."

Tears slip down my face. "I thought..." I thought I loved you, I think, unable to say the words out loud. They cut me like a dagger. "I trusted you."

"I'm sorry. So sorry." Dion sucks in a shuddered breath as if my words had a bite to them. "I never wanted to hurt you. I only wanted to protect you."

"I want to believe your words, but how many lies have you spun?" All this time, I've been trapped in his net and haven't even realized it until now. "This has all been a game, hasn't it? I just can't figure out why."

"That makes two of us," Chandra mutters.

"Trust me," Dion says. "This has not been a game."

"She knows too much," White Hair finally says. "She's become a liability."

"She is *not* a liability, Quadril." Dion's face twists in anger, his hands clenched at his sides. Sparks flutter from his fingertips, which is very, very weird. He has powers, too? "She made one simple mistake. Should she be killed for that? Or is the Empress is too afraid of who she may become?"

White Hair, who apparently is Quadril, glowers. "Step aside."

"No," Dion growls.

18
HOW DARE YOU SAY NO?
ESTRELLA

Florida

Confusion swirls around me. Why is Dion saying no to this Quadril guy? And what does it mean? Chandra jerks to attention, advancing suddenly to Quadril's side. Her hands stretch out. Fear crawls up my spine as I realize she's about to use her powers on us.

"If she can lift a car into the air," I whisper to Tristan, "what can she do to us?"

"No kidding. When I attack, run."

"How dare you say no to me!" Quadril tells Dion. "Estrella's mortalization process has failed."

"You will have to go through me first," Dion says and steps in front of Tristan and me.

I gasp in confusion. What does this mean?

Tristan glances back at me with raised eyebrows. "This is going to be fun."

"You really don't understand what fun means," I say.

"You know this is treason," Quadril warns Dion. "Think carefully about your next actions."

"Trust me," Dion says. "I know exactly what I'm doing."

The guy Tristan stabbed grunts but climbs back to his feet. Blood cakes his hands, and his shirt is wet. He's about to stumble away, but Quadril snaps his fingers and points to his side. The man complies all the while eyeing Dion warily. Ax Guy and Chandra move into line facing Dion and Tristan.

"You really think you can stand against me?" Quadril asks. He pulls out some sort of recorder and puts it to his lips.

Dion swears under his breath and bursts into action, lifting up his hands. Bolts of electricity shudder from his palms, aiming straight for Chandra and Quadril.

I scream.

Chandra swivels to the right, dodging the lightning bolt by mere inches. But the sparks fizzle before they reach Quadril.

The white-haired man doesn't blink, but continues to play a calming, lilting tune.

"Great, a Nullifier," Tristan mutters, rolling his neck.

"What's a Nullifier?" I ask.

"His music carries on the wind and weakens an immortal's powers," Tristan explains.

"Dion has powers as well." I stare at the sparks skittering across his skin. "I never knew."

As if to confirm, Dion flings his hands out on either side. Bolts shudder through the air toward Ax Guy and the one bleeding. The bleeding guy whimpers and covers his head, but the bolts dissipate mid-air.

Ax Guy chuckles. "Think you picked the wrong side, buddy," he tells Dion.

"I'm not your buddy," Dion says calmly. "And I definitely picked the right side." Then he glances over at me. "You are right. I can create and manipulate electricity. I'm sorry you had to find out this way. That was never my intention."

Before I can respond, a gust of wind swoops over us. Tristan and Dion hunker down, fighting to stay standing, but the intensity of it seems to be targeted at me. I'm knocked off my feet and slam to the ground, my head smacking hard against the pavement. Stars swirl in my vision, and I groan in pain. Chandra sneers at me from Quadril's side.

"You will pay for that," Dion says.

"Really?" Chandra snickers. "Are you sure?"

"That wind in the mall and in the school parking lot," I say. "It was you all along."

"Wow." She rolls her eyes. "You're more clueless than I thought."

Tristan kneels at my side and grabs my hand, yanking me back to my feet. His eyes are intense. "You've got to run. Find somewhere to hide."

I nod, but that flicker of his fire power tingles across my skin as if begging to take it as my own. But what good is taking it if I can't use it? Did my old self know how to use my powers? Pain hits my head once again just from the thought, and I blink back tears.

"Okay," I finally say. "Just don't die."

Tristan shoots me a wicked grin and lets go of my hand before moving to stand at Dion's side.

The two look at each other, nodding curtly, as if coming to some sort of agreement. And that's when I realize they're going to fight to their death. For me. I know I'm not worth that. The thought of them sacrificing their lives for me makes me sick. Besides, if I were to run, these assassins would find me anyway.

Fire bursts out of Tristan's sword, and he charges with a battle cry at Quadril.

Dion crosses his arms and then flings more bolts of electricity at our enemies. Silvery zigzag lines spark through the air. They crackle and spark, but it's like an invisible barrier stretches around the four and the electricity dies on its surface.

Tristan's sword smashes into the barrier, fire rushing out in an inferno. It races along an unseen wall as if desperately seeking an opening.

Our enemy goes untouched. I should be running away right now, finding a place to hide. But I can't leave them. Undeterred, Dion shoots out another series of bolts. They rush out in a web of brilliant light. But still, the enemy remains untouched as the music fills the air, drenching us in its haunting tune.

Chandra starts spinning in a circle, holding up her arms. A dark windstorm funnels out of her hands and rises into the air. In moments, we'll all be carried away.

Ax Guy rushes at Tristan in attack.

Tristan turns and meets his weapon with his sword. The clash of steel rings the air. The two twist and spin as they battle it out, ducking up and down. I stand still, torn between staying and leaving. There must be something I can do to help.

The injured guy picks up a chunk of wood on the ground and races toward Dion. As he runs, the wood transforms into what looks like a spear, but Dion is too busy fighting the others to notice.

Frantically, I pull out the knife Tristan gave me and rush at the wooden spear guy. Seconds before he stabs Dion in the back, I leap through the air, landing on Spear Guy's back. We tumble to the ground, rolling across the pavement. There's a shift of energy about us. Did Quadril's barrier get interrupted?

My hands brush across Spear Guy's arm. Instantly, energy within him pulses beneath his veins. I don't really know what I'm doing so I just act on instinct. I grab his wrist and pull as much of his power to me. Instantly, a force rushes into my veins. It bursts through me like I've sucked in too much air or stared at the sun too long.

My body screams in pain. I feel like I might explode.

Dizzy, I jerk away from him.

"What have you done?" he yells at me.

He takes my knife and raises it to stab me.

But he doesn't have a chance because a bolt of electricity zaps him on the neck. His whole body shudders and collapses. I look up to see Dion staring at me.

His whole body glitters. He's beauty and death all mixed into one. A stabbing memory pierces my mind. Another time when the two of us fought together.

In a living room?

Men trying to kill us.

"Run!" he yells, pulling me back to this moment. "Get as far from here as possible."

But something in my gut tells me to do the opposite. My whole body feels like I just drank a case of coffee. There's power running through my veins that hadn't been there before.

And I'm desperate to use it.

What if...

The wind picks up and it swoops Tristan off his feet, slamming him into the car beside us. The ax guy follows him and hefts the weapon into the air, crashing it down. Tristan ducks out of the way just as the ax slams into the hood.

The wind is so powerful now I can't stand. My hair flies around, my clothes fluttering in Chandra's storm. I grit my teeth and crawl over to Dion, who is completely focused on sending bolts of electricity at Chandra. I'm guessing he's hoping to either break through Quadril's barrier or wear him down.

I grab hold of Dion's back, using his body to pull myself up.

He glances over his shoulder, frowning. "I told you to run."

"Trust me?" I ask.

"Of course," he says gruffly, pain searing his features.

I slap my hand on his, sending a bolt of power to him. He lifts his eyebrows in shock.

"You have your powers?" he asks. "You should keep that to save yourself."

"I don't know what I have, but you need this."

He starts to pull away, but I shove more energy from

Spear Guy into him. His body jolts like he's been hit hard. His eyes widen and become almost platinum in appearance.

"Thank you," he whispers.

"Save us," I say and then run to Tristan where he's battling Ax Guy.

Tristan's limping. His clothes are bloodied and torn.

Ax Guy crouches before Tristan, and the two glare at each other as they circle one another. Another whirlwind comes rushing down at us again. It barrels toward Tristan, slamming him to the ground. Ax Guy lifts his weapon to finish Tristan off. That's when I pull out the blue dagger from Nadia's secret room and stab him in the back. He roars in anger, spinning round on me. He's too slow. I've already grabbed hold of his wrist.

"Do not let her touch you!" Chandra screams over the storm.

"Too late." I smirk.

The second my skin touches his, I suck out as much of his power as I can.

His eyes open in shock, and he crumbles to the ground as if I've ripped out the oxygen from his lungs. "You said she was mortal!" he yells.

Once again, the intensity of the power slams into me. I stagger from its impact. My heart races, and the pain in my head blinds me momentarily. I blink, trying to focus. When I do, the ax swings right at me.

I scream. Seconds before it hits me in the face, a flaming sword slices the guy's head off in one fell swoop. The ax clatters to the ground along with the body. I'm left staring face-to-face with Tristan, his blond hair hanging over his eyes. Blood splatters across his skin. His face is dark with fierce intensity.

The wind howls around us, bringing with it debris. Tristan pulls me into his arms for shelter. I bury my head in his chest and shove all of the Ax Guy's power into him. Suddenly, Tristan's whole body is hot as fire.

An inferno.

I lift my head up in time to see Tristan hold out his palm and send an explosive burst of fire at the car behind Quadril and Chandra. The impact sends the two staggering. It's enough that Quadril's lips leave his lute for a brief moment. Instantly, Dion pushes out another bolt of electricity. Windows shatter and alarms burst through the air.

Chandra shudders and falls to her knees. Meanwhile, two black cars skid onto the scene.

"We need to get out of here now," Dion announces. "Do you have a car? Mine—"

He glances over at his car, now lying sideways against the wire fence, steam drifting out of it.

"This way." I point to Tristan's car.

"He's not coming with us," Tristan says. "How do we know this isn't some sort of trap?"

"He's coming with us. End of discussion," I say and rush to Tristan's car, flinging open the door. "Get in the car. We can discuss this later."

19
A GHOSTLY GIFT
DION

Florida

I leap into the backseat just as Tristan cranks the car's engine and squeals out of the parking lot. We're flying down the road at 120 miles per hour.

I grip the edges of the seat. "If you kill her thanks to your incompetent driving skills," I growl at Tristan, "I'm going to kill you."

"If you wanted to kill me," Tristan shoots back, "you should've done it back there."

"Don't worry," I say. "The option is still on the table. After I make sure Estrella is safe."

"Dude." Tristan spins around a corner, making the tires on the left side of the car lift off the ground. "If anyone is going to die, it's you."

"Stop it," Estrella snaps. "Both of you. Enough of the dying. Where are you taking us, Tristan?"

"To the Water Channels," he says.

Palms and oaks rise up along the sides of the road. The car's GPS indicates for us to make a turn onto a dirt road. Tristan takes the turn so hard, I'm thrown across the backseat of the car. Then again, that might have been on purpose.

"You're the worst driver!" I yell at Tristan. "Listen, Estrella. You can't trust this guy. You think he's good, but he definitely isn't. He's a Sabian and one of the worst of his kind."

"And I should trust you more?" She gives a dry laugh. "You're obviously friends with all those people who tried to kill me. I'm such an idiot to have fallen for you."

My heart dies. The car slams to an abrupt stop. Through the trees, I can make out a pond. My heart kicks up in fear.

No. No, no, no.

Meanwhile, Estrella practically leaps out of the car, and I scramble out after her.

"Estrella," I say. "I can't let you go with him. He's dangerous."

Tristan snorts and pops open the trunk of his car, grabbing a bag from the back. "Don't you think it's time you let Estrella make her own decisions? She's not some little girl you can coddle. You saw her back there. She's a force to be reckoned with."

She storms up to me, pointing at my chest. "I know the truth about you now. You're an immortal with powers and you never told me. If I didn't know better, you were helping Nadia to make sure I would never get my memories back."

Her words freeze me cold. Because she's not wrong.

"It wasn't like that," I try to explain. "I was protecting you. If you got your memories back, I knew they would kill

122

you. And I was right, wasn't I? They nearly did kill you. If I had come a minute later, you'd be dead."

"That's because I didn't know the truth," she says. "I walked right into danger. And that's on you. So you failed. Epically."

Her words gut me. "You're right."

Tears stream down her face. I reach for her, but she pushes me away. "No. You don't get to act like you care about me. You should've told me the truth. You should've let me make the choice."

Her words slam into me like a sledgehammer. "Yes. I see that now. I was just so desperate to keep you safe that I was willing to do anything to keep you from being killed."

"We don't have time for chitchat." Tristan starts marching down the path toward the pond. "A whole slew of Nazco will be here in moments. I can't have them following us."

Estrella hesitates, staring at me, tears still streaming down her cheeks. "I remembered you. I thought they were hallucinations or dreams, but they were memories. And maybe I once loved you, but I don't remember those feelings. I do appreciate you risking your life to save me, but whatever we had before is over."

She takes off after Tristan, and I nearly crumble from her words. My heart is splintering.

But I can't leave her. I can't—live without her.

"I have a plan," I call out, following them. "I found a place where no one will find us and we can disappear. It will be just the two of us. We'll leave all this madness behind. I don't care if you're mortal or immortal. All I care about is you."

Tristan stops at the water's edge, his eyes darting between Estrella and me. As much as I despise the guy, I appreciate him letting us have this moment.

"But I don't want to disappear," she says. "I want my powers and freedom. My friends are in captivity, living under Nadia's horrible rules as they slowly lose their minds. I can't stand by and let that happen. Especially when there's a chance I can save them. For their sake, I can't give up."

I drink in the sight of her with her long blond hair blowing in the wind. Her ocean blue eyes that I could swim in for eternity. My heart lies shattered at my feet. I don't know what to say.

But I do know what I must do.

I reach into my pocket and pull out the Ghost locket. Its surface shifts like a phantom in the night as I hold it out to her.

"What's that?" Tristan suddenly jerks to life and marches over to us.

"It's a Ghost locket," I explain, glaring at him. "It's infused with a Ghost's powers before he died. A family heirloom. Please, take it. It will keep you hidden from any Tracker. You will be like a Ghost when you wear it. When it burns red, it's warning you that you're in danger."

"Is that a thing?" Estrella asks Tristan, looking to him for guidance. The action cuts me deep.

"Yes." Tristan eyes it skeptically. "Appears like it's infused with power like that dagger of yours."

"I was planning on giving it to you so we could—" My words break. "Escape."

She takes it and slips it over her head. The moment she does, the gem in the center brightens into a fierce crimson.

"Does this mean I'm in danger from you?" She points to the red glow. Then she faces Tristan. "Or from you?"

"Probably both of us," Tristan mutters.

Dion nods. "He may be right. Your path is still undecided."

She presses her lips together, and for a moment, I sense her hesitancy. But then she takes a breath and lifts her chin. "I should go."

I brush my knuckle along her jaw. "Be careful, and never let your guard down. The Sabians can't be trusted."

I give a pointed, dark look at Tristan.

He shrugs. "Touché."

Suddenly, the roar of engines fills the silence of the forest.

"They found us," Tristan says tightly. "We need to leave. Now."

"You should come with us," she says. "They'll kill you otherwise."

"I have a few cards up my sleeve." I shrug. "Besides, one foot in Sabian land and they'll kill me on sight."

"Can't blame them," Tristan says.

He has a point.

"Come on," Tristan says and wades into the pond.

"Why are you going into the pond?" she asks. "This makes no sense."

"Heads up. Estrella doesn't like traveling through the pools," I tell Tristan.

They both glance at me, startled at my words.

"It's the ancient way of the immortals," Tristan explains. "And it's a little intense."

Two trucks barrel next to Tristan's car, spewing dust in their wake.

Estrella runs into the pond and takes the hand Tristan is holding out to her. As her fingers slip into his, I turn and walk away, unable to watch.

I leave my heart behind on the banks of the pond.

Sparks flicker along my palms as I stride toward the assassins jumping out of their trucks, determined to protect my love one last time.

20
WHO CAN COMPLAIN WHEN PRINCE CHARMING IS YOUR BODYGUARD?
ESTRELLA

Slovakia

"I don't understand," I tell Tristan, my sneakers sinking into the mucky pond. "Why is going in water the Immortal Way?"

Tristan glances over his shoulder, his eyes widening. "We need to hurry."

I follow his gaze to discover trucks barreling into the lot while Dion is striding out to meet them. Is he greeting them as a friend or enemy? Once I thought I knew the type of person he was. But now I have no idea. It makes me sick to think that Chandra was right about not trusting him all along.

Tristan takes my hands, jerking me back to this horrifying situation we're in. Bubbles are forming in the water around us.

"I suppose this will be like the first time going through the Water Channels for you," he says.

"Water Channels?" I lift my eyebrows and look down at the water's surface. It's starting to churn around us. Fear crawls up my spine. "I don't think this is something I want to do."

"I need you to hold on tight to me and not let go, no matter what. Got it?"

I move to pull away from him, but the tree branches hanging over the pond's surface suddenly start growing, stretching out like vines. And they're moving straight for us as if eager to strangle our necks.

"We have to go now." Tristan wraps me into his arms, shoving me hard against him in a vice grip. "They have an immortal who can manipulate trees."

And then it's like the ground has opened up.

We freefall into a tunnel. Our bodies shoot through the empty space as water churns around us. I scream, unable to hold in the fear as we sloosh and twist through what looks like a tunnel of water illuminated by a glowing light. Sparkling. Iridescent. Magical.

My mind reels to make sense of this along with everything that happened today. It's too much. I grip Tristan's firm body tighter, clinging to him for life. Water spits over my body, and even though we're not actually swimming in the water, I'm getting wet.

"These are magical channels," Tristan yells over the churning water. "You must think about your destination, and it will take you there."

I clench onto him as our bodies twist and turn because I know that if I let go, I could easily get lost. Or worse, fall through the water and drown. Soon, I lose all sense of time as we travel—up and down, left and right.

It's dizzying and terrifying.

Until finally, we are shooting straight up like a rocket. I scream, looking above to find a glow above. Then with a whoosh, the surface opens and our heads burst through the surface of the water. Fresh air fills my lungs. The tunnel hole in the water vanishes, and I find myself swimming in a lake. Without the power of the Water Channel, my body instantly begins to sink. Water gets in my mouth, causing me to choke. My feet and arms scramble to start swimming.

"This way." Tristan holds me up and directs me toward the shoreline.

Thankfully, the channel spits us out toward the edge of the lake, so it doesn't take long for us to get to the shoreline. My knees buckle beneath me as I stagger out of the water, choking and gasping for air.

"Do not move another inch," a voice says.

A sharp steel tip touches my neck. I freeze and slowly lift my eyes to find a man, wearing a leather vest over a forest-green shirt. Weapons hang from his leather belt. He has thick brown hair, a beard, and dark blue eyes that are narrowed on me like he's seriously thinking about killing me. I'm getting really tired of people trying to kill me.

"Štefan," Tristan says. "It's okay. She's with me by orders of the King."

Štefan's eyes flick to Tristan's, and he warily pulls his sword back. I take in a shuddered, relieved breath. But as I glance around, I realize that this Štefan guy is one of ten men eying us, weapons ready to take us out. No, they aren't just men. They're guards.

"Prince Tristan," Štefan says. "Please accept my apologies. I hadn't received notification you were returning today."

"Emergency," Tristan says gruffly. "It's been a rough day. Call in the reserve guards in case we've been followed."

"Prince Tristan?" I turn to face him. His blond hair hangs over his eyes and his clothes are shredded, revealing corded muscles beneath. He looks wild and dangerous, and nothing like the princes I read about in fairy tales. "You're a *prince*? Why didn't you tell me that?"

He grimaces, dragging his hair out of his eyes. "I was going to tell you, except a lot was going on. You know between the Wraiths and Nazco trying to kill you."

"You encountered a Wraith?" Štefan's eyes widen. The other guards begin murmuring in shock.

"Like I said." Tristan leads me by my elbow and marches us through the wide-eyed guards toward a wood-beamed building up ahead. "It's been a rough day. We're heading to the castle," he calls over his shoulder. "Tell my father to be ready."

I take in my surroundings as I scramble to keep up with Tristan's long legs, my soggy sneakers squishing on the soft grass. The lake we emerged from is settled in a small valley, surrounded by jagged mountain peaks. Thick evergreens rim the valley and then slope up the hillsides like a soft blanket. But what stops me in my tracks, capturing my attention, is the castle tucked between snow-capped mountains.

Tall spires reaching for the pink and purple beams of the

setting sun. Swooping stairways curving up to towers skimming the clouds. Turrets jutting out from the imposing walls, and flags fluttering in the wind.

"That is the most beautiful thing I've ever seen," I say, gaping at the castle, luminescent in the fading light.

"That's home," Tristan says. "It's not so bad. Most of the time. Come on. I want to get you inside the castle walls before dark. The world is not safe for you right now. You know too much, have too much power for one who's been excommunicated, and yet not enough power to defend yourself."

A part deep in my core screams at me to run into the forest—far from that castle, these guards, and this prince. It warns me that these are not my people and they can't be trusted. But where else would I go? I'm exhausted, hungry, and soaking wet with nothing to my name other than a dagger. I wouldn't even reach the forest before they captured me.

No, it's smarter if I play along for now, get as much information and resources as I can, and then sneak away.

Tristan opens the door and I'm met with a strong earthy scent. Swaying lanterns, illuminated not by fire but by some other glow, hang from the thick wood-beamed ceiling. Stalls line either side of the building where horses peek out, staring at us.

"Have you ever ridden before?" Tristan asks. "These are going to be our mode of transportation."

"These are horses, aren't they?" I say, unable to hide my excitement. I know I must sound like a child, but I don't care. "I've only read about them."

Tristan side-eyes me with raised eyebrows before

heading to a shelf and hauling out a saddle. "You've never seen a horse before? I suppose that makes sense considering where you are from."

I frown at his words, hating how he probably knows more about my home than I do. Tentatively, I edge up to one of the stalls, staring at a beautiful brown horse, its coat shiny in the lantern glow. "Can I pet it or will it bite me?"

"That's my sister's horse. His name is Tricks because he is a tricky beast. No one has been able to ride him since she…" He goes silent and pauses mid-stride to stare at the horse. From the pained expression on his face, I know he's thinking about his sister's death. "Since the last place she rode him was here, here the beast remains. I wouldn't get near him. He'll bite your finger off."

An assistant runs into the barn and bows to Tristan. "Your Highness," he says and goes to take the saddle from Tristan's hands. "Allow me."

The two head further down the barn and open a stall at the far end while I turn back to Tricks, eyeing him.

"I get it," I whisper to the horse, and think about my necklace where the pictures of my parents are hidden inside. I'd placed it in my backpack, but since I left that behind at school, I doubt I'll ever see it again. "I also lost loved ones. It's like losing a part of your soul."

The horse eyes me intently. It's weird. It looks like it actually understands me.

Cries and the sound of a horn vibrate through the air, dragging me from my musings. I dart back to the doorway to find two people emerging from the waters. The moment my eyes land on them, fear spikes my heart.

21
RUN LIKE WILDFIRE
TRISTAN

Slovakia

"Tristan!" Estrella calls out from the barn door. "We need to go. The assassins found us."

"That was fast." I'm about to saddle my horse, Wildfire, but abandon the idea. "You'll have to ride with me. We won't have time to saddle a horse and teach you how to ride."

I swing onto Wildfire and hold out my hand for her. She races to me, fear clouding her Arctic-blue eyes. Her hand slips into mine while the assistant helps her up behind me.

"I don't know how to ride," she says, her voice quivering. "Or what to do."

"Hold on tight," I say. "This is going to be a fast ride."

I spin the horse around to face the back entrance of the

barn, and the moment the assistant opens the doors, I yell, "Ha!"

Wildfire responds with eager anticipation, leaping into a gallop. Estrella clenches me in a vice grip, her soft body pressed against mine. We burst out of the barn and fly like Wildfire's namesake across the valley. I breathe in the sweet mountain air drenched in evergreen, already feeling my powers being revived now that I'm back in my homeland.

Estrella was right. At the lake, the guards are battling against three Nazco warriors, one of which is that Chandra girl from Estrella's school. Her wind power is strong. She will be a problem. I can't worry about that right now. The important thing is getting Estrella to the safety of the castle. The Empress would have to bring a full-out war to break down our gates.

And without a Conduit, there's no way she'd risk it.

Wildfire hits the wooded trail with power, sensing my urgency. We begin to climb up the mountain's side, a long path of twists and turns. Soon the cries of the battle below fade, replaced by singing birds and the sighing of wind through the trees. I allow the horse to slow and rest.

"Why are we slowing down?" Estrella asks, her voice full of worry. "Shouldn't we be worried about the assassins?"

"It's a long ride up the mountain and I want to make it tonight even if we have to ride in the dark."

"I don't get why don't you take a car?" she asks. "That would be so much faster and easier."

"We avoid modern technology as much as possible," he explains. "It dilutes our powers. Most of us Sabians are what we immortals call traditionalists. Those who cling to the old ways and the deeper powers."

Her grip loosens on my back, and she adjusts herself. I try not to think about how her presence fills me with desire. It's only because she's a Channeler and once was a Conduit, I remind myself. It's a part of their power, the ability to have people crave to be near them so they can seep the power to themselves. She probably has no idea what she's doing. Most immortals have no idea how a Conduit's power actually works, but my sister and I used to tell each other nearly everything because we always felt that we were the only ones we could truly trust in this world.

"I guess that makes sense," she says. "It's hard to process everything right now. It's been a lot."

"Once we get to my home, you'll have time to rest and get food. Then we can figure out what needs to be done to get your memories and powers back."

"But I used my powers back at that parking lot, right?"

"You did, but you were not at your full potential. To be honest, I don't know if you ever will be."

"You're risking a lot to help me," she says. "If I decide I don't want to continue helping you, are you going to kill me?"

I grit my teeth, knowing what my father's answer will be. "I promise I will not kill you. But you should be wary. There are many Sabians who hold a deep hatred for the Nazco. You need to be careful who you trust."

A rushing wind pulls at the trees, and the birds perched on the branches above us take flight with screeching cries. My eyes narrow on the path.

"Something isn't right," I murmur.

"Look. It's coming through the trees," she whispers and points to an opening in the tree's canopy where a spiraling funnel of wind lowers through the opening. Then her hands fist my shirt and she gasps. "It's Chandra!"

Sure enough, Chandra floats inside the wind funnel, her dark hair flowing around her, hard onyx eyes narrowed on us as she slowly lowers toward the path, blocking our way. Anger surges up inside of me.

"I should've taken care of this girl at your high school when I had the chance," I mutter.

"Can you get around her?" Estrella asks.

The moment Chandra's feet hit the path, she calls out, "Hand Estrella over to me, and I'll go away peacefully and never bother you again."

"Considering our kingdoms have been at war for a thousand years," I say, "I have a hard time believing you."

She smirks and then whips her body, spinning around. Instantly, wind picks up speed, gathering strength as she rotates. Leaves and branches start falling. The trees around us groan.

"We've got to get out of here!" Estrella says. "Can we go back?"

Wildfire rears up, fighting against the intensity. Tree branches snap off, revealing how close we are to the sharp cliff on our right, which plunges into the valley below. I bend lower to Wildfire's body to keep on top of him.

"Hold on tight!" I scream to Estrella over the wind. Then I urge Wildfire to take us off the path and into the thicket of forest. It's a risk because we might hit a dead end, but there's no way I'm going back down the mountain to face more assassins.

Trees begin to topple and crash around us. Bushes rip

from the ground, flying toward us like bullets. Wildfire neighs and rears up, but I press a steady hand to him.

"There's another trail deeper in the mountains," I tell Estrella as I direct the horse. "If I can find it, we might have a chance."

"Might?" Estrella asks.

It's almost like a dance. Wildfire runs to the left, only to halt as a tree trunk slaps down, blocking our way. I direct him right and then left again, sometimes leaping over fallen logs or ducking under them as we weave through the forest in a desperate escape.

And then I spot the path. It's a little overgrown—unlike the main one, which is well-kept—but it will work.

"Found it!" I cry out in relief. "Run, Wildfire, run like you were born to run."

I press my hand against his mane, letting my fire power sink deep into his core. Sparks shiver across his body. Instantly his speed intensifies as he takes on his namesake.

"We're on fire!" Estrella screams.

"It's okay!" I yell over my shoulder. "You're a Conduit. You should be fine. You survived my fire in Roach's cave."

She mutters something, but my whole focus right now is infusing my last trickles of power into Wildfire.

The horse hits the trail at full force, thundering into the woods, dirt and fire spewing in our wake. Trees stream past us in a blur of green. Wildfire's hooves thrum against the forest floor as we climb higher and higher up the mountain.

We are fire and power. Death to all who dare cross our path.

Soon the land changes from thick evergreens and a dirt

path to ice-crusted ground and chilled snow. A gust of wind rushes up from behind us.

"Chandra has found us again," Estrella warns. "That girl just won't give up."

"We're close," I say. "The gates are not far."

Straight ahead, the castle shimmers in a silvery glow under the rising moon. Cries call out from the ramparts. They must have finally spotted us galloping along the final stretch to the castle's entrance. Flames stream out of Wildfire, but his speed is waning. It was too fast and hard of a climb. Normally, it would take hours, and yet here we are doing it in less than an hour.

"Three people are pursuing us now," Estrella tells me. "I'm going to try to push my power into Wildfire."

Her left hand leaves my side and presses onto the horse. Wildfire shudders, and at first, I feel him hesitate upon sensing Estrella's touch. But then with a half-growl, he dips his head and suddenly takes off even faster, power renewing his body so we are crimson in a world of white.

Wildfire's hooves are torches. Snow melts upon impact as we stream in a blaze of fire across the final stretch of land.

From the ramparts, a volley of arrows fly over our heads, aimed at our pursuers. The gates lift before us, allowing us to burst through the entrance. And then with a tremble, they close, encasing us in the castle's protective walls.

22
ENEMY SWAP: NOT RECOMMENDED
ESTRELLA

Castle of Stará, Slovakia

My insides tumble in fear as I take in the guards that surround Tristan and me, swords and spears pointed up at us from where we sit on the horse. I clutch Tristan tighter as if making myself as close to him as possible will keep me alive. They wouldn't kill their prince, would they?

Unless everything Tristan has told me is a lie.

The wind wails against the air, snow flitting around, and the guards murmur as if they're worried. My eyes cast to the gate we just came through, now firmly shut. Something thuds hard against the doors and they shudder. Is Chandra trying to get through? Who else is with her? What about

Dion? Did Chandra kill him like she seems so desperate to do with me or did he somehow survive?

The guards on top of the wall shout. A zinging sound fills the air. Then sudden silence. It's so quiet I can hear the snowflakes flutter through the lantern-lit courtyard and Wildfire's hooves clack against the stone impatiently.

"All clear!" a guard from the top of the wall calls out.

Tristan's body relaxes, but as I take in the steel-tips aimed at me and the harsh gazes, I'm feeling anything but relief.

"I think we just exchanged one evil for another," I whisper into Tristan's ear.

"Don't worry," he tosses over his shoulder. "These are my people. Just follow my lead." Then he calls out to the group, saying, "You can put your weapons down. She's with me."

A large, older man pushes his way through the armed guards, his body covered in leathers with a thick silver cloak lined with fur and imprinted with a dragon symbol and steel-tipped boots. Gray hair crowns his head, and his face is pulled tight into a thin line as if his mouth has forgotten how to smile or frown.

"Idiots!" he calls. "Put your weapons down. That's your prince."

Quickly, the guards lower their weapons, but my head spins as the reality of who this guy I met at my school settles in. Tristan swings off the horse and helps me slide off next. My legs feel like mush as I try to stand. I wobble a little, but he offers me support and I gratefully lean against his warm body. The mountain air shivers around me, and my teeth clatter from the cold.

"General Sage," Tristan says, holding out a hand. "It is good to see you."

The two grab elbows and shake. I wrap my arms around myself to try to stay warm. And that's when I realize the amulet Dion gave me is glowing red on my chest. What did he say? When it glows red, I'm in danger.

How long had it been glowing? I'd been too panic ridden earlier to check. Worry creeps up my spine as I think about Dion's warning about Tristan.

"I see you accomplished your mission," General Sage says, nodding to me. "You brought Nazco to our doors. I hope she was worth it. How capable is she or were your efforts a waste of time?"

Tristan's smile wanes. "I'd say it was successful since we're both here alive. I'm going to speak to my father now."

His hand touches my elbow as if to lead me away, but the general stops him, placing a palm on Tristan's chest.

"You know I trust you explicitly," General Sage says. "But she will need to be questioned before she can be taken into the King's presence. She must wear resistant bracelets before she steps another foot in this place."

My muscles tighten in panic. I'm not sure what these bracelets are, but one thing I do know is right now I feel more like a prisoner than one who's been rescued. I look to Tristan for support. "What is he talking about? I'm not putting on any bracelets or whatever those are until you tell me what's going on."

Tristan doesn't glance my way. Instead, his gaze glowers on the general and heat drifts off him like he's holding his anger in check.

"She's harmless," Tristan practically growls.

"That is unfortunate," General Sage says, his voice tinged with superiority and some hidden meaning that I'm not aware of. "Because if that is the case, then she's not worth keeping, is she?"

"Fine." Tristan turns to me. "Are you okay wearing the bracelets? They're like handcuffs, but they won't hurt you."

"Handcuffs?" I lift my eyebrows, glancing around as worry creeps up my spine. "Like I am a prisoner?"

A guard steps up to me with silver cuffs. I back away, only to be met by a pointed blade in my back. I bite back a cry, suddenly feeling trapped. The guard moves closer to slap them on me, but I grab his arm first. Instantly, I can feel a thread of his power under his skin.

"Don't let her touch you!" General Sage cries.

Before I can react, another guard steps forward, grabbing the cuffs and slapping them around my wrists.

"What are you doing?" Tristan yells and shoves one of the guards back, tossing him to the ground. "I was giving her a chance to choose."

"Apologies, your Highness," the guard mutters and scrambles away.

"You sure have a way of building trust," I snap at the general. The cuffs sting my skin. I'm not sure if it's from the pain or from the feelings of betrayal. I push back the tears. I won't let them see me as weak, especially not how betrayed I feel. "You act like I'm here to hurt someone."

"Sure looks like she is dangerous," one of the guards says and points to my wrists.

The cuffs glow faintly in the lantern light. I lift my wrists to study the strange shimmering bands.

"Well," General Sage says. "Appears as if she isn't

completely worthless and we were right to put the bracelets on her. She has a weapon, too. Disarm her."

The guard goes to take it, but Tristan holds him back. He pulls my dagger from its sheath on my waist.

"I'll keep it for you." He slips it into his own weapons belt.

"I trusted you," I say, anger pulsing through me. "You tricked me into coming here only to make me a prisoner?"

He flinches as if I physically slapped him. His jaw ticks, but he doesn't say anything. Instead, his hand presses against my elbow and pushes me forward.

"Move!" he orders the guards before us. They scatter, creating a path.

We cut through the courtyard, partly created from bricks and partly from the stone of the mountain. Tristan leads us down a cobblestone street lined with a mixture of stone and wooden houses illuminated by glowing wrought-iron lanterns, sparkling with what looks like glitter-infused light. The intricately fluted roof houses are designed with arched wooden doors and white-trimmed windows that belong to fairytales and magical lands.

What have I gotten into? What sort of place is this?

"I can't believe this is happening," I say, my stomach twisting in fear. "Where are we going?"

"To the Grand Hall to speak to King Julian."

"You mean your father." I wince as the cuffs on my wrists sting as I stumble on the cobblestone street. A wave of dizziness washes over me. I grit my teeth, determined not to pass out.

Tristan reaches out to steady me, but I stiffen against him.

"You're tired," he says. "After we talk to my father, you'll have time to rest."

I try to keep my hands steady. "Why didn't you tell me your father was the king? I should never have trusted you. I feel like an idiot, falling into your trap."

"I wasn't trying to trick you." He sighs. "I wasn't sure how much you could handle. Plus, I wasn't sure how you'd react knowing who I was."

"How much I could handle? I literally helped you fight off roaches and all those people who were trying to hurt both of us. If that doesn't prove anything, I don't know what will."

His lips press together. "You're right. I should've been honest with you. But I'm going to make sure you're safe while you're here."

"Something tells me I'm hardly safe." I point at my necklace burning red.

He flinches as if the sight of the necklace pains him.

The road leads us to a set of wide steps that trails up into a stone building that's the most prominent part of the castle. Its rectangular shape rises up multiple floors with four rounded corner towers spearing up around it like the tips of a crown. Square stained windows arching to pointed tops are set into the stone along with arched designs.

It's stunning, and I hate how beautiful it is.

"This is my home," Tristan says as if he's admitting something terrible. "And where my father's throne room is."

Dread fills my chest. "Why does that sound ominous?"

Tristan doesn't look at me but indicates for us to head up the steps. Just before we reach the top, he pauses, eying the two guards manning the massive carved wooden door.

"While you're here," he whispers into my ear, "don't tell anyone how you were able to channel my powers during the fight."

"Why?"

He looks away and then his eyes find mine. "Because very few immortals in this world understand how a Conduit's power works. And if they truly did, they would be terrified."

"I don't have a reason right now to believe anything you say." I swallow hard, trying to make sense of this new world that I've stepped into.

The guards open the doors wide, and we enter. What will this king do to me, and why did I ever think I could trust Tristan?

23

DON'T DEAL WITH THE DEVIL

DION

The Midnight Kingdom, Antarctica

Blistering stars, my head hurts. I grunt and roll over. I'm on a hard stone floor in a dark room, the cold seeping into my bones. My vision swims, but I force my eyes to focus.

Three stone walls crusted with ice and blue quartz bars create my prison. My wrists are bound by resistant bracelets. So, this isn't ideal. I must be in the Reckoning Hall in the Midnight Kingdom.

Which is bad, but an improvement from beheading.

Which leads to the question, why? Why am I still alive? Why haven't they chopped my head off and burned my body to a crisp?

They must want something from me.

Slowly, I sit up and lean against the frosty wall. The last

thing I remember was facing off the group of angry immortals. Six of them, actually. Even with my powers being nearly depleted from the fight earlier, I'd been able to take care of them all. They'd been lying like incapacitated zombies. I should've gone and chopped off each of their heads one by one.

But I had been the fool. Again.

When faced with Chandra, I couldn't do it. Couldn't kill her like I should've. She recovered faster than I expected and slammed me onto a rock by the pond, knocking me out.

So now? Now, I'm here lying in prison with a wicked headache while Chandra is likely chasing after Estrella.

Or worse, has found and killed her.

"Estrella," I whisper to the walls. "It was supposed to be me that was killed. You never deserved any of this."

A heaviness folds over me and my heart tears, remembering her last words.

You should've told me the truth. You should've let me make the choice.

Bitter winds, she's right. I should've told her. Should've trusted her. In the end, I listened to the Empress's lies and my own fear of losing her. Maybe it's because I thought I finally found her and I couldn't stand the thought of losing her again. But if there's anything I should know, it is that fear always loses.

As much as it killed me to watch her leave with Tristan, deep down I knew that was the safest place for her to be. I can only pray she made it to safety. And if she still is alive, I'm going to do everything in my power to show her the truth of my love. She's my everything. My world.

A click yanks me out of my dark thoughts. A guard

swings open the gate, and the flickering sapphire bars that keep an immortal's powers in check return to solid metal.

"The Empress is ready to see you," he says.

The Empress? Interesting. I'd expected Quadril. Or perhaps to be brought to the Overlords for an official trial and execution. There are a few Overlords who would love to serve my father my head on a platter.

"Tell her I'm too busy napping," I mutter, wishing I could stop the pounding in my head.

A guard lunges inside the cell and zaps my side with one of his wands. Pain snaps through me. My body buckles, and I bite my lip to keep from crying out.

"Fine," I growl. "Since you asked so nicely."

I climb to my feet and sway. Blazes, I really could use a healer right now. Each movement makes me want to throw up. As I step out of my prison cell, I reach up to touch the back of my head where the pain radiates from and find a thick bandage. *Stars and skies.* I must have been bleeding badly. Usually, my body can heal itself fast enough that I don't need bandages, so I must be in bad shape.

"Follow us," another guard waiting by the door says.

My legs resist movement, but somehow I force one foot in front of the other and shuffle after my captors. Carved metal torches shimmer blue light across the icy walls, making it almost feel like I'm walking through a glacier. When we head up a spiral staircase, dizziness washes over me, especially when we step outside of the Reckoning Hall and head to the Ice Palace's bridge.

I stumble a few times and stop to throw up in a snowbank. A group of women chatting on an ice bench shoot me worried glances.

"This is what happens to those who disobey the Empress," one of the guards tells them.

Their eyes widen and they scurry away.

I glare at the guard. "Be careful who you insult," I warn. "Give my body time to heal and our situations could change quickly."

The guard pales and swallows hard. The other guard nudges me with his security wand that I plan on snapping in half if I ever get out of these cuffs. "Move along. The Empress doesn't like waiting."

The wind howls and the flicks of icy snow nip my skin as we cross the ice bridge and enter through her arched gate. I grit my teeth. This is my penance for allowing fear to dictate my decisions. For hesitating when I should've killed Chandra. For not finding a way to save Estrella when I had the chance.

The throne room is as glitzy and spectacular as ever, glittering with diamonds and sapphires. Her snowflake emblem shimmers in the blue light and the ice throne looms before me, terrifying as usual. My heart clenches in fury.

If it weren't for her, Estella would never have suffered like she has.

"Your Highness, I present to you Dion Cabral," the guard says with an annoyingly elaborate bow that makes the Empress smirk. She waves her hand lazily, and my two guards scurry away.

"Welcome back, Dion." The Empress taps her razor-sharp nails on the curved armrests, their ends carved wolves. "It feels like only yesterday that I assigned you to watch over our little ex-Conduit."

"Feels like an eternity to me," I mutter.

The last time I was here, I knew she loved to play games, but now I see how greatly I underestimated her. The fact I'm still alive is a reminder the Empress's games are still very much in play.

And I'm just another pawn.

"Took you long enough to get here. Thought you may have died along the way."

"I didn't want to disappoint you."

She tilts her head and the spikes on her crown flash like knives. "And yet you fought alongside Estrella and the Sabian prince against our own Nazco."

Well, I see we're getting straight to the point.

"You tasked me to protect Estrella. I was merely keeping her trust. She thinks your assassins were trying to kill her. I don't know what gave her that idea."

It's too hard to keep the sarcasm from escaping my lips.

"Those were not *my* assassins," she snaps and rises out of her throne with her jerk. Her sequined white dress gleams like fresh snow as she steps down to where I'm standing. "Quadril made that order, not me."

My eyebrows lift, and my façade fails me for a moment. It's hard to keep the shock from my face. Is this another of her tricks or is she being honest?

"Why would Quadril not follow your orders?" I ask.

"He's following the Nazco code, which we all follow. Of course." Her ice-blue eyes study me warily.

"Of course," I grit out.

"But between the two of us." Her voice lowers into a winter's whisper. "I do not wish her dead."

I take the bait. "What do you wish?"

"To have her memory wiped just enough that I can

rebuild it from scratch. Mold her to become an abiding citizen of the Midnight Kingdom, where she will follow our rules."

"It's too late for that now, don't you think?"

"By Nazco law, any immortal who betrays us means instant death." She begins pacing, her long train sweeping across the ice floor. "But let's be honest. We can't afford to lose a Conduit, and there aren't any promising students in the academy. She's the only Nazco who can go through the Ring of Power into the World of Between and bring back our power source. We need her if we're going to defeat the Sabians."

"I couldn't agree more. Except she doesn't remember being a Conduit. Most of her memories are lost, which means she also has lost those powers. Her ability to be our Conduit is not an option."

I decide not to mention that Estrella was able to use her powers with Tristan and me in the battle. True, her powers were a fraction of what they once were, but they weren't completely lost.

She turns to me, her white lips curling into a wicked smile. "That is not entirely true."

My heart kicks a beat. "What do you mean?"

"As long as she has a spark of her power, she has the potential to refuel her visik. We've done it before with those in rehabilitation centers. In fact, Nadia has done it twice now at her Home for Girls. Which is why I had Estrella sent there."

Hope flares inside of me. The mere idea that Estrella could gain all her powers back changes everything. But this time, I curb the Empress's words with caution. Every word this woman says is coated with a sugary layer of half-truths and devious motivations.

"Fighting alongside a Sabian," she says, "aiding a prisoner in escape, and attacking a fellow Nazco is punishable by death."

"When you put it like that, it sounds like I'm a scoundrel."

"Don't get snooty with me. I'm the only thing keeping you alive in this world."

"What do you want from me? Because that's what this is about, isn't it? You want me to do something illegal. Something against the Nazco code."

"I want you to kidnap Estrella and bring her back here. We'll wipe her memory again. She'll never remember that disgusting prince, whom according to my sources she happily trotted off with, leaving you alone. We'll get her powers back and the two of you can have your happily ever after."

"You wouldn't let the two of us stay together," I say, masking my shock with skepticism.

"If all goes to plan, you two can marry and have ten babies as long as she does my bidding."

"And Quadril approves of this plan?"

"Quadril is a hindrance and nuisance. But once Estrella is on our side, we will be too powerful for him to stop us. What do you say, Dion? Are you in?"

"When do I get started?"

Her eyes twinkle like dark stars. "I knew you would see things my way."

24
LET'S BE FRIENDS. AT LEAST FOR TODAY
ESTRELLA

The Castle of Stará, Slovakia

My knees threaten to snap beneath me as Tristan and I stand before the king sitting on the throne. Not just any king, but also Tristan's father. My head hurts at that thought. He's an imposing figure with a large frame like Tristan's, but instead of the blond wild hair, his is sandy brown hair that hangs straight beneath a shining golden crown. He has a thick beard and his thin eyebrows are drawn together as his gaze takes me in. His face remains stoic, giving me no clues to what he's thinking.

The throne room is huge, with a vaulted golden ceiling held up by white stone pillars. Intricate designs are painted on the walls and torches light the room in a golden glow. It's the most beautiful place I've ever seen.

I don't belong here, standing in my jeans and sneakers.

"Father." Tristan bows. "I am pleased to introduce to you Estrella Milton, the Nazco outcast that I rescued. Estrella, this is King Julian."

"Estrella." The King rises from his throne and steps down from the raised platform. "Welcome to the Kingdom of Stará."

"You have an interesting way of welcoming your guests, your Majesty." I hold up my handcuffs as if to emphasize my point.

"General Sage insisted," Tristan says. "Wouldn't listen to reason when I told him she was harmless."

The king frowns. "Uncuff the girl."

A guard darts out of the shadows and slips a thin pin into the side, releasing the resistant bracelets from my wrists. As soon as they're off, I shake my hands to get rid of that weird feeling they gave me.

"And find General Sage!" he adds.

The King eyes me and my dagger warily as if he's ready for me to attack him or something. Which, even if I could, I'm not that stupid, considering he has guards lining the perimeter of the throne room.

"We don't wish you harm," King Julian says. "In fact, it's just the opposite. I sent my son to rescue you from the prison the Nazco put you in."

I glance over at Tristan, who tries to give me a smile, but it's stretched tighter than usual. Right now, I feel so lost. I don't know who I can trust or who is truly on my side. But he is right. I had been in a prison of sorts and I couldn't have escaped those Wraiths without Tristan's help. I'm just hoping I didn't exchange one prison for another. I want to trust Tristan because if I can't, then I'm all alone in this world.

"I do appreciate his help," I say, "but I don't know if I'm the girl you were hoping to find. You all may have wasted a lot of time and men trying to save me."

"I disagree," Tristan says. "She has lost her memories, but her visik isn't completely gone."

I rub my chest, trying to put the pieces together, but honestly, I'm just so tired. Tired of fighting. Tired of running. Tired of worrying about who to trust.

"A report came in from the Traveling Pool that you were followed through the Water Channels," King Julian says. "All the way to the castle gates. Which means the Sabians believe she's still valuable or dangerous."

"Absolutely," Tristan says. "Assassins and Wraiths were sent to kill her. If Conrad and I hadn't shown up when we did, they would've killed Estrella and her friend."

Those words spear at my chest and I shiver because everything he said was true and the memory is too terrifying. My thoughts return to Lexi. Is she okay? Was Conrad able to heal her?

"I have friends at Nadia's house," I say. "Will they be okay? I'm worried that by leaving it might put a target on their backs."

"I do not know," King Julian says, gravely. "But I will send out scouts and we will assess the damage. It is unclear what this all means. Never in my entire reign have the Nazco dared to be so open in their attacks and enter our lands than they have been in recent weeks. It is alarming."

"Tristan told me about your daughter, Ivana," I say. "I'm sorry."

A shadow falls over the King's features and his jaw tightens. "The Nazco are ruthless, but ever since the Empress has taken the throne, they have become more cunning. It is a deadly combination. You will have to be patient with us as we are slow to trust any Nazco. Even you."

"I lived at Nadia's," I say. "I know what it's like to live a lie and be deceived. But even if I still have this visik Tristan's talking about, I don't know how to use it properly. And my knowledge of your world is limited to only what Tristan has told me. I'm afraid you've gone through a lot of effort for no reason."

"That may be so," the King says.

Which isn't great. When they slapped the cuffs on me, all I wanted to do was leave, but where would I go if they released me? And if they realize I'm worthless, what will I do? The Nazco—who are apparently my own people—want me dead, so I can't go to them. I am literally dependent on Tristan and his family and that sucks. Big time.

"We're both very tired," Tristan says quietly as if he can read my thoughts. "We need rest and food."

The King nods, taking in our shredded clothing. "Indeed. We will talk later. Tomorrow, I wish for you to meet the Queen."

I gulp at the thought of meeting a queen. Then, like a dart, pain flashes through my head. I cry out and shut my eyes as an image—a memory? —flashes through my mind.

A woman as white as snow in a glittering gown and ice tips for a crown that claws at the sky.

We saw it with our own eyes, the ice woman is saying. *She will betray us. She must die.*

The vision slips away, leaving me shaken to the bone. My eyes blink open and I find myself on the floor. Warm hands hold my shoulders, keeping me grounded.

"Estrella," Tristan says. He's kneeling beside me, worry in his eyes. "Are you alright?"

"I don't know," I say. "I saw someone. A queen."

Tristan looks at his father. "Your words must have triggered a memory." Then he focuses back on me, asking, "What did this queen look like?"

One part of me wants to tell him everything, but another part holds me back. Especially the part about my betrayal.

"She looked like snow and ice," I admit. "I don't know how else to explain it."

He rubs his forehead, grimacing while the King smiles. "So it appears you do remember some things," the King says. "This is good."

"The woman you saw was the Empress of the Nazco." Tristan helps me to my feet. I hate how I can't stop shaking and am forced to lean on him for support, but he doesn't seem to mind. "My mother, Queen Kelli, is nothing like the Empress. You might even like her."

The thought of being interrogated by yet another immortal royal doesn't settle well in my stomach, but right now I can't worry about that. I just need to focus on standing and remaining strong enough to get through all of this. The King snaps his fingers, and two guards rush in to stand before me along with a woman with long blonde hair woven into a thick braid down her back.

"Take Estrella to her room and make sure she's well

cared for," the King orders them. "She will want for nothing while she is here in our lands."

Want for nothing? I frown skeptically. That feels too good to be true.

Tristan's lips press into a tight line. "I'll escort her," he tells his father.

"Thank you, son," he says and then switches his demeanor. "Sage!"

General Sage storms the throne room with his head bowed. But as he strides past, he glares at me like he would kill me right here. The moment we leave the room, my body begins to break down. The stone hallway wavers a little and my legs feel like wood as we follow the young lady through the castle's passageways. I'm forced to hook my arm through Tristan's as we walk. I'm grateful he doesn't question me.

"That went well," Tristan says in a low enough voice only for me.

"You sound surprised," I say.

"I am. The moment they put resistant bracelets on you, I wasn't sure how my father would respond."

"That was a very generous command of your father's to say I wouldn't want for anything. It seems too good to be true." I nod to the two guards escorting us. "I still very much feel like a prisoner."

"I respect my father greatly, but he hasn't kept his throne because of his generosity or kindness. You need to know that my father's welcome and apparent generosity is only because he believes you can be an asset to him. It has nothing to do with your well-being or him being kind."

A lump forms in my throat. "What are you saying?"

We stop at an arched wooden door, etched with intricate carvings of deer and trees. The girl pulls out a key and unlocks it.

Tristan leans in close and whispers into my ear, "Be careful who you trust, and keep that dagger close." A wave of heat washes over my skin. "Get some rest," he says, this time loud enough for those watching us to hear. "I'll find you in the morning. There's a lot more I need to talk to you about."

He takes off down the hall. A chill replaces his presence, and I shiver. I want to call him back, tell him to stay with me. We've been through what feels like hell together and now that he's gone, I feel even more alone.

"Miss," the young woman says, waving at the open door. "Come. Your room is ready."

I step inside and take in the surroundings. It's a room fit for a princess with a large four-poster canopy bed covered in a velvety green blanket, plush chairs, and carved wooden furniture scattered about the room. It's complete with a painted ceiling, fire crackling in its hearth, tapestries, and even a small bathroom attached to it. The air smells of fire and cedar.

It's all so beautiful, so perfect, and yet nothing feels right. Right now my world is upside down, and I don't know what is right or wrong anymore.

I miss my friends; Lexi, Jamie, Zayla, and even cranky Mara. My thoughts flicker to Dion and a deep yearning to hold him in my arms fills me. I touch the amulet hanging around my neck, but my trust in him is shattered after learning the truth. I push my thoughts of him away because if I think about him, I might fall apart. And right now I can't do that.

I need to be strong, stronger than I ever was before because I need these immortals to help me get my powers fully back. That's the only way I'm going to be able to rescue my friends.

25
WATCH YOUR HEART, IT MIGHT BETRAY YOU
TRISTAN

The Castle of Stará, Slovakia

I don't want to leave Estrella. In part for her safety, but also that vulnerable look on her face haunts me as I consider all she must be dealing with. I storm down the hallway, anger surging through me at how General Sage treated her. Like a prisoner, like an enemy. Now everyone in the Kingdom will be talking about how she can't be trusted. Or worse, they'll take out their revenge for the Nazco killing my sister out on her.

I rap on Katka's door, even though it's after sunset. She might be out at dinner, but knowing her, she's probably eating while working on one of her inventions. The door swings open, revealing Katka in her work overalls, smeared with grease and her hair pinned up in a haphazard bun. She fists her hands onto her hips.

"Bummer," she says. "I was hoping you'd lose an arm or leg after that battle you had with those assassins."

I keep my face hard. A flash of remorse hits me for the friendship we once had. "And that would be helpful because..."

"Then your father might authorize my proposal to work on prosthetics for immortals. I've always wondered if it were possible. Like could your powers transfer—"

"Stop." I breathe in deeply. Katka knows how to get under my skin more than anyone, and I can't have her derail me now. "I need you to get me information."

"Of course you do. The answer is I'm very busy. Good-bye." She goes to shut the door, but my hand presses against it, keeping it from moving.

I try another tactic. "Hello, Katka. How are you? I hope your latest invention of—" I cast my eyes about her lab and spy some sort of water suit. "Your water gear is going well."

Her eyes narrow, and she presses her lips together but releases her hold on the door. She leaves me and walks over to her desk. I duck inside before she changes her mind.

"What do you want?" she asks and sits at her computer desk.

"A status update on Conrad and Lexi. How are they? Was he able to get Lexi to the hospital? Is he safe?"

"He reported in an hour ago. Said they both were alive and she's recovering." Her fingers tap on her keyboard. "Let me see if I can patch him through."

Recovering. This is good. A ring fills the computer monitor and then Conrad's voice comes over the line. "Katka. What can I do for you?"

"I'm here with Tristan," she says.

"Tristan? You're alive!"

"We made it." I lean close to the computer. "A huge thanks to you, Estrella and I both are unharmed. A little beat up and weary, but we'll be fine. But it's you and Lexi I'm most worried about. How is she? Estrella's been worried about her so I came for an update."

"We're at the hospital. I told the nurse it was a hit-and-run, which was the best explanation I could think of due to her injuries and blood loss. Nadia and two other Nazco just arrived, but Lexi was sleeping. They wanted to take her back with them, but the doctors told them she needed to be monitored here for a few days."

"That's good." I let out a long breath. Estrella will be pleased when she finds out. "Does Lexi remember what happened? Does she know not to tell Nadia?"

"She remembers everything but agreed not to tell Nadia what happened, so that's a relief. I might stick around and make sure she recovers without any issues."

"Don't get attached," Katka interrupts. "Your job is to get the situation under control and make sure we don't have any information leaks. As soon as you think you can leave, text me and I'll let General Sage know you're available for your next field assignment."

I roll my eyes. Conrad is totally attached. I saw how he looked at Lexi. In fact, I bet Lexi is totally fine right now and he just can't bear the thought of leaving her.

"Be careful," I say. "Nadia is far smarter than I gave her credit for. And Tiffany might not be the only girl at that home pretending to be one of the victims but is actually a spy. There might be others, so stay on high alert."

"Will do. Lexi is waking up now. I'm going to check in on her and see if she needs any food or whatnot."

"Food?" Katka huffs. "Do not give her food. Do not get attached."

"She's not a dog, Katka." Conrad chuckles. "Glad you're safe, mate. Gotta go."

"Be careful," I tell him. "And get yourself back here soon."

The line goes silent. Katka glares at the computer, drumming her fingers on the table.

"He's falling for a Nazco," she mutters, and then her eyes dart over to me. "You're not being swayed as well by that Estrella girl, are you? You do know that if she gets her memories back, she might not be as nice or sweet to be around. Those Nazco are pure evil."

I cross my arms and grin. "Pure evil, huh? Just because they're our enemy doesn't mean they're all evil. Keep a close tab on Nadia's Home and any unusual activity. And find out everything you can on these memory inhibitors the Nazco use. I need Estrella to get her memories back sooner than later."

"Watch that heart of yours, Tristan," Katka yells to my back as I head to the door. "If you don't, that girl might break it."

I swallow, but my heart stutters just a touch as I hurry away from her words. Because Katka's right. I have been feeling things for Estrella that are beyond the realm of a pure business relationship.

There's no doubt somewhere along the way we entered

the friend zone. Maybe it's because of all that we've been through. You can't help but feel bonded to someone you shared your powers with. It's intimate and dangerous. When she pushed my powers back into me, I felt stronger than ever, like she not only had given them back to me but amplified them. And that's slightly terrifying to think about because I could totally get used to that.

I need to shut down any feelings I have for her because deep down I know her heart still yearns for Dion. And if my heart was broken, I'm not sure I'd ever recover.

26

COFFEE AND CAKE WITH THE QUEEN
ESTRELLA

The Castle of Stará, Slovakia

S unlight trickles over me as I toss off my thick velvet blanket. Instantly, I shiver, not used to the chilled air here in Slovakia. The wooden floor bites my bare feet as I slip out from the massive canopy bed and pad across the room.

The small clock on the table tells me it's past noon. I can't believe I slept so long. I grab the thick robe I left on a chair and shrug my feet into the slippers I found last night in the closet, eager to get warm. Curious about my surroundings, I push open the arched double doors, which open to a stone balcony dusted with snow. As I step outside, my breath leaves me.

Sure, it's cold, but it's the view that has me stunned. My

balcony is perched on the side of one of the castle towers with an overarching view of the grounds below. People are walking around; shopping, talking, and just living their everyday lives. It's a totally different world than my life in Florida.

Snowy mountain peaks rise up around the castle walls, and plunging below the cliffs lies the vibrant green valley where Tristan and I first entered from the Traveling Pool. It's like something from a fairytale and...oddly familiar. Almost as if I've seen this place before in a dream or vision.

I try to remember the details, but pain pierces my head and I cry out. The door to my room bursts open and the woman who escorted me last night comes running over to me.

"Are you alright?" she asks, holding out a hand to steady me.

Sweat drips down the sides of my face as my body shakes from the sudden pain. I lean against her as she directs me back inside. I sag onto the couch.

"I'll be fine in a minute," I say. "Sometimes I get bad headaches."

"I'm sorry," she says, her forehead puckering. "You stay right there. I've got breakfast prepared for you. I kept it warm while you were sleeping."

The room spins, and my stomach is twisting hard like it's trying to squeeze everything out of me. I close my eyes and lean back in the chair, waiting until the pain and dizziness fade. These episodes are more frequent, but at least I feel like I'm able to handle them better. The reality is they're incredibly inconvenient and I could see them becoming a huge problem.

Last night is a great example. I literally fell apart right in front of the King. I can't keep living like this, but I don't know how to make them stop other than Nadia's tea.

"Here you go," the woman's soft voice breaks through my pain. "Cook Barkas's fresh bread and sausages are the best you'll ever have. And I've brewed you a cup of coffee, too."

"Thank you." I try to smile. "What's your name?"

"Sofia," she says and goes over to the large closet, pulling out shirts and pants and laying them on the bed. "Go on now. Eat up. You look half-starved."

The scent of the homemade bread makes my stomach rumble. I slather butter across the brown bread and take a bite. The rich nutty flavor settles my stomach right away.

"This is wonderful," I say, sipping my coffee. "Thank you."

"Once you finish eating, I've been instructed to take you to see the Queen."

My stomach dives. So much for eating. "She wants to see me? Now?"

"After you finish, of course," Sofia says. "You need to build up your strength."

I nod. She's right. How am I supposed to get my powers and my memories back by starving myself? I need to pull myself together. I know the Queen wants to assess and see if I can be useful to the Sabians, but she's not the only one who's looking for answers.

I shove down my fears as Sofia escorts me into the Queen's sitting room. The walls are papered with flowered designs and edged in gold. The crystal chandelier scatters light across the space, making the room almost feel like you're walking into an open field.

"You'll wait right here." Sofia points to a satin chair. "Queen Kelli will be here any moment."

I swallow, my mind whirling, wondering what to expect. I settle into a blue satin chair and wait, listening to the ticktock of the large grandfather clock in the corner. With a bang, the set of double doors is shoved open by two guards. I jump up from my seat, startled by the sudden noise. I reach for my dagger, only to remember that the guard outside of the room requested I leave it behind.

The Queen breezes through the doors. The woman might be Tristan's mother, but she doesn't look a day over forty. She's wearing a purple velvet gown edged with silver ribbon. A golden crown sits on her blonde head of hair, which is braided into an intricate web.

Her blue eyes, so similar to Tristan's, quickly assess me. They land pointedly on my necklace, glowing faintly pink today. I stand there awkwardly, unsure if I should curtsy or nod or do nothing. I decide to bow my head.

"Greetings, Estrella," Queen Kelli says. "Thank you for agreeing to meet with me. I've been looking forward to chatting with you. Please. Sit."

She waves to one of the chairs in the sitting area by the fire. Regally, she seems to almost float to the long couch.

"I spoke to my son this morning," she begins. "It sounds like you had a time of it trying to escape."

I nod. "There was an assassin and Roach along with a few others. If it weren't for Tristan, I would've died."

"That sounds simply dreadful. I've always hated roaches myself. Thankfully, we don't have to deal with those types of creatures here."

A servant bustles into the room holding a tray. He sets a coffee cup before each of us followed by a platter full of beautifully designed sweets.

"Lovely." The Queen nods to the servant, and he bows and darts away. She picks up a plate and sets a cookie on it. "You must try our laskonky cookie. It's a traditional Slovak treat of two meringues filled with buttercream. It's simply scrumptious."

"It does sound delicious." I take a bite of one. It tastes like walnuts and coconut with the inside being a caramel buttercream. "These are really good. I could eat the whole plate."

She laughs and nods in agreement. Her voice is light and warm like a bit of sunshine, I realize, and instantly I find myself relaxing.

"You must know we are very happy to have you here," she says after finishing off her cookie, "and that Tristan was able to rescue you from that horrible place they had you in."

"It wasn't a good place, but there were some good things there. Sure, we all were dealing with our memory loss and being lulled into taking on mortality, but I did love the beach and lighthouse. I made a lot of close friends there, too."

She nods thoughtfully. "Around the same time you were sent to Nadia's Home, a group of Nazco attacked and murdered my daughter while she was visiting friends in Paris. We are still deeply upset and in mourning."

The word murdered echoes in the space between us.

"I'm sorry for your loss," I say. "I had a friend, well, I thought she was a friend. Her name was Tiffany. The Wraiths killed her accidentally when she was trying to stop me from leaving. It's still really upsetting thinking about it even though she wasn't close. I can't imagine how hard it must be for you."

Queen Kelli studies me and then sets down her coffee cup. "My daughter was our Kingdom's Conduit. Do you know what that means?"

I grimace. "Not really, but Tristan told me a little."

"Some immortals born with the Channeler ability are so powerful that they can rise up to be a Kingdom's Conduit. They are able to enter the World of Between and gather up a power source there and bring it back to our world. That power source fuels and renews our bodies and our powers, our *visik*. Without that renewed source, our powers weaken over time."

"Tristan told me about Ivana, his sister."

"For the Nazco to kill her, it was more than just offending the King and myself. It kept us from renewing our powers. We believe the Empress did this because the Nazco recently lost their Conduit. And that Conduit, we believe, is you."

"Me?" I say in confusion.

Once again that pain spears into my brain like a knife hurtling through my skull, cutting deep. I scream, dropping my cup as I reach to press my temples as if to hold back the pain. The porcelain shatters at my feet.

Servants flood into the room and the Queen's guard is at her side in a second, the tip of his sword at my neck.

"Put your sword away," Queen Kelli says with annoyance. "There is no need. She's merely suffering a massive amount of pain."

The servants clean up the mess, and by the time I'm able to see clearly again, everything is righted just as before. A new cup, fresh coffee, and an assortment of pastries this time.

"I'm sorry about that," I finally manage, kneading my forehead. "It happens every once in a while."

"Do not be sorry for a terrible act that others did to you. I want to help you, Estrella. I know you don't trust me, but I want to prove to you that you can. I will assist you in getting your powers back, and then I'll train you in the ways of a Channeler just like I did for my daughter."

Excitement crowds away the pain. "You will? But why?"

"I, too, am a Channeler, but my channeling skills weren't strong enough to be a Conduit like my daughter. We don't know much about the Nazco's ways, but we believe they put some sort of inhibitor in your brain. If we can get rid of it, you may gain some of your memories and powers back. You'll be able to live your life without pain and grow into a powerful immortal. If I help you with this, I only ask that you consider joining us and becoming a Sabian. Will you consider this?"

My mouth dries up as I consider my options. Agree to her terms and get a chance to get my powers back or say no…and then what? Roam the planet, always being on the run, never having a life? And who would help my friends?

Seriously, there is only one path to freedom and retrieving my powers. It's with the Sabians.

"Yes, I will," I finally say. "I don't know what my memories will show me or if I'm able to get them back. But I do know that my own people kicked me out and took my memories. The moment I tried to get them back, they attempted to kill me. They're not exactly on my friend list."

A smile bursts across her features, and it's as if the room brightens. "I'm so pleased to hear you are willing to work with us."

"This may seem weird, but you've actually given me hope for the first time since I came out of that hospital. I've been feeling so lost and confused. So to hear you say you might actually get to help me makes me happy."

"I'm glad. You deserve a little happiness after what you've been through and what you've lost. We will begin right away then. Today I'm going to have you start working with our family's tutor on the history and customs of the immortals. I trusted him with my children, so I think I can trust him with you. There are many here who wish for your death, so we must be cautious. Tomorrow, you and I will begin channeling sessions to help you tap into your powers."

"I was able to use my powers with Tristan."

"That is a start. And if you show promise, we can also consider a visit to Zmeya, the Dragon Seer."

"Did you just say dragon?" I ask, eyes wide.

"She is both a dragon and a woman. It is a risk though to take you to her for if she feels you are unworthy of her presence, too mortal, or a threat to our nation, she will kill you with her dragon fire. But if she feels you are worth her time, she will tell you your destiny."

"So stand before a dragon to see if I'm too mortal, when all I've done the past month is become more of just that? It doesn't sound promising."

Except the idea of hearing my destiny is more tempting than I'm willing to admit.

Queen Kelli sighs and looks away, her face pinched tight. "It is not ideal. And we should only consider it if your powers are great enough. First, train and we will see what you are capable of. If we believe you have the abilities, we will take you there. But I will not sugarcoat it. Zmeya is dangerous, but she is also powerful. She will reveal to you secrets only she can find."

Secrets.

My body trembles at that word. Somehow deep down I know that I, too, have a secret. A powerful one hidden within me.

"Okay," I say, determination rising inside of me. "Let's get started."

27
LESSONS IN THE LIBRARY
ESTRELLA

The Castle of Stará, Slovakia

"My lady," Sofia says with a bow. "If you'll come this way with me."

I stiffen but nod and trail after the servant. Just yesterday, these people were holding swords to my throat and now I'm being treated as if I'm royalty. It's enough to make my head spin.

There are many here who wish for your death, so we must be cautious, the Queen had said. A shiver of fear shudders through me. I don't know who to trust. The fact that the Queen isn't one hundred percent certain who she can trust either doesn't help my peace of mind.

"The Queen must really like you," Sofia says as she leads me to two double doors adorned by the coat of arms of a lion wearing a crown. "Only a select few are allowed into the royal family's library."

"I don't know if *like* is really the right word," I say. "Maybe useful?"

Sofia flashes me a sympathetic smile as she ushers me inside. "There are many who are useful and yet don't have access to this place."

The scent of aged wood, leather-bound books, and candle wax fills my lungs. Shelves packed with books tower high on three of the walls, many with spines worn and weathered as if they've been read a thousand times. Tall wooden ladders are mounted on rails along the top of the shelves to make it easier to access the books on the top.

Sunlight filters through stained glass windows, pooling patterns on the polished wooden floors. Dust motes dance in the light. It's almost like this place is infused with magic.

"You can wait here." Sofia points to an oak table set in the center of the room. "Professor Henrich will be here any moment. Can I get you some coffee while you wait?"

"No, I'm fine. Thank you." These Sabians are really trying to make me happy. They must be eager to get another Conduit.

The door shuts, leaving me alone. Instead of sitting down to wait, I begin strolling along the shelves. The air is quiet like the place is holding its breath. As I read the spines, I notice the books are in all different languages: Slovak, English, German, Latin, Greek.

I jerk to a stop.

I can read these titles. Which means I know these languages. Frantically, I open a book written in Latin. I scan down the page, having no trouble reading it.

"How is this possible?"

"What is possible?" a man's voice says from above.

I peer up to find a tiny balcony hanging over the doorway I came in from. It appears to lead into a study. The man standing atop it has a thick gray beard that hangs down his chest and bushy eyebrows. He starts down a narrow spiral staircase tucked in the corner of the room. He's wearing a simple brown tunic and black pants.

"You're old," I blurt out before I can stop myself.

He chuckles. "What gave it away? The gray beard? Or the wrinkles around my face."

"I'm sorry. That was rude. It's a little startling after seeing everyone else here look so young and well, you..."

"Don't?" He snorts as he crosses the floor to place a thick volume on the table. "Never worry. I am not offended. I get plenty of side glances from people who do not know me. Let us just say people who look like me are not running around these halls."

I tuck the Latin book away and move to him, holding out my hand. "I'm Estrella."

He eyes my hand warily. "Rule number one. Never shake hands with a Channeler. And definitely do not let a Conduit touch you. Not unless you want to be completely drained."

"Oh. I'm assuming being drained is bad." I tuck my hand behind my back. "So you're a Channeler?"

He chuckles again and settles at the table, waving to the seat across from him for me to sit.

"No, but what I have heard from the Queen is that you are. Which means shaking hands with you would be a very bad thing for me to do. Especially since I have also heard you lost your memory, so you probably do not know what you are doing. A Conduit can drain any immortal of all their powers."

"That makes sense." I grimace. "I never thought about it like that."

"Immortals do not shake hands. It is too dangerous." He flips open the book. "That is a mortal custom that you have taken on. You were living with the mortals, correct?"

"Yes. At Nadia's Home for Girls."

"I have no inkling who Nadia is, but that most assuredly was not a home. That was a facility to which the Nazco sent those who were allowed to finish off their life as a mortal."

I swallow and nod. "Yeah, Tristan said something along those lines."

"My name is Henrich, the King's scholar. I taught both Tristan and his sister, Ivana. And I also taught King Julian and his two brothers. And their parents and grandparents. You might say I have been around a while."

"Is that why you look so old?"

"No." His bushy eyebrows dip. "I was tricked into drinking something I should not have and aged into a seventy-year-old man. Trust me, I was not happy. It is also why I avoid all parties and most individuals. You could say I am not social."

"I'm sorry."

"Normally, I would never come within one hundred feet of a Nazco Conduit, but I admit that when the Queen told me about your situation, I was desperately curious. So I agreed to teach you a thing or two."

"I'm very grateful for that. Most of the time I feel like a normal high schooler, but then other times I don't feel normal at all." My eyes drift to the bookshelf. "For instance,

I was looking at those books and realized I could read Latin and Greek and German. How do I know all those languages? I saw my report card. I'm a straight C student. Not the kind who is fluent in numerous languages."

He eyes me carefully as if trying to sift through my words and find the truth in them.

"All immortals are taught at a young age to read and speak multiple languages. English is universally spoken, but within each immortal group, we have our own language. But to know so many languages, you may have attended the Nazco's prestigious Midnight Academy."

"Midnight Academy? That sounds familiar." The words spark a sharp pain in the back of my head. I rub it. "It seems like I get these painful episodes whenever my mind finds a memory tied to it. Like it's fighting against a barrier."

"Highly likely. Sounds like a very Nazcoian thing to do to someone."

"You all really don't like the Nazco, do you?"

"What gave it away?" he grumbles. Then he pushes the book to me. It's opened to a page penned in ink in a delicate script. "See if you can read this."

I study the page. One side shows a picture of three beautiful women in shimmering white gowns and crowns of flowers on their heads. Four other women in torn clothing and bruised bodies are bowing before them.

The letters float around as if they don't want to stay in place. It reminds me of how the words looked at first when I was trying to read the writing in Roach's cave with Tristan.

I blink a few times and focus hard on the letters. The words finally solidify. I start reading out loud.

"In the First Age of the world, four women who had

been beaten and misused sought out the Three Fates who live beneath the Tree of Life," I begin. I look up at Henrich. "Do you want me to keep reading?"

He rubs his chin, studying me again with those sharp eyes. "Please." He waves his hand. "By all means."

"The four women begged for the Fates to help them be strong enough to stop those who were cruel and misused and abused them. The Fates took pity on these four and decided to give each a scroll of alchemy. One of water, one of earth, one of fire, and one of air. Should they create the formula in their scroll and drink it, they would become more powerful than any human has ever been and nearly impossible to kill."

I pause and look up at the professor. "What is this? An old myth?"

"Not an old myth." Henrich rises from his seat and begins pacing before the table. Light from the stained glass window behind him scatters color over his body. "It is the origin of the four immortal races. The origins of you and me. One that every immortal child is told by their mother at a young age. Please, continue."

Curious and intrigued, I focus on the words and read out loud.

"Never share your gift with another immortal," one fate warned. "Lest they should gain the power of your gift and overcome you."

"Never share your gift with a mortal," the second fate warned. "Lest they should gain the power of your gift and overcome you."

"Never abuse your gift," the third fate warned. "Lest we should reclaim your power and overcome you."

"The four mortal women agreed," I continue reading. "And wisely took the warnings to heart. They created their formulas and drank the elixir. Fire burned through their bodies, killing off their mortality. They died that day but were reborn anew as immortal. Then—"

Henrich pauses mid-stride and turns to face me, waiting as if he's holding his breath so he doesn't miss my next words. "Then?" he presses.

"There is more," I say. He waves his hand eagerly, so I carry on. "Because they knew how powerful their alchemy scrolls were, they searched the world for a secret place to hide and protect their formulas. They chose the most sacred ground and crafted a tunnel deep beneath the earth where they laid their treasured scrolls, entombing them forever so no mortal or immortal could steal their power."

"That's it?" Henrich asks.

"That's the end of this section. The next section is the Battle of Northrong." I lean back in my chair. "That was fascinating. I feel like I understand this world of the immortals better. Thank you for letting me read that."

"No, thank you," he says. "I haven't ever read the actual legend before. The full legend."

"I don't understand. It's all right here."

"I suspected it was there because of the picture. But since I don't read Nazcoian, I had no idea. And all records of our origins were destroyed in the Great War. I suspected that tome held one of the last records of our origins, but I didn't know for sure until now."

"Wait. You've never read this?" I gasp, both shocked and angry that he used me to get information that only I could retrieve. "You tricked me."

"Perhaps a little. Think of it more like a test. First, to see how much of your head knowledge was lost—and now I suspect not as much as I first thought since you read Nazcoian fluently. But also, how cunning and deceptive you are, which again, not as much as I suspected. You should be more wary of who you trust."

I glower at him. "Well, you just showed me I can't trust you."

"Hardly. I just handed over to you the most coveted pieces of information in the entire immortal world. Think of it as a partnership. I owned the tome, you owned the knowledge of the language."

I roll my eyes. "I suppose you might have a point. But you said that every immortal is told this story."

"Very few immortals know the *full* story. The part explaining how the four women hid the scrolls has been lost in our oral tradition. There are some, your Empress to be one, who would kill for that piece of information."

"But it doesn't say where these scrolls were actually hidden. Only in a tunnel under sacred ground."

"I would choose wisely who you tell that information to. If anyone at all."

"And you? Who will you tell it to?"

"No one," he says darkly and swoops over and closes the book, snatching it off the table. "That information is dangerous. Too dangerous for any immortal, if you ask me. If someone sought after the Fates' scroll, it could change our world. It is best if we both forget we even read it and never speak of it again."

I eye him warily as he sets the book aside and pulls out a

new stack. Is he actually telling the truth or am I being naive and too accepting once again?

We move into safer subjects such as immortal etiquette and customs, but I know I'll never be able to forget what I read. Because a niggling sensation in the corner of my brain tells me that there's another piece to the hidden scrolls' puzzle.

And I think I used to know what it was.

28

HOW TO BE A BEST FRIEND
TO AN ESCAPED CONVICT

DION

The Midnight Kingdom, Antarctica

I t's amazing the difference a simple conversation can have in one's life. Less than an hour ago, I was imprisoned, shackled, and counting down the hours until my head was severed from my body.

Now I'm the prize of the Empress. Her hope to find a Conduit who can give her exclusive power.

It took only a snap of her cold fingers for the servants to scurry over and escort me to a Healer. And now I'm set up in a comfortable room in her ice palace with a stunning view of the entire kingdom outside of my floor-to-ceiling paned windows.

Once I've bathed and changed into a fitted black shirt and pants, I almost feel like myself again. My powers are still weakened and it will take more time for them to restore fully, but I plan on avoiding Quadril and his god-forsaken Wraiths and assassins for as long as possible. In theory, I'm under the Empress's protection. That said, an 'accident' could very easily happen.

I finish buttoning my shirt as I stare out the window, debating my next steps. The snow falls gently outside, but all I can think about is where Estrella is right now and if she's safe.

A knock on the door interrupts my worries. I ignore it, but then there are two raps, a pause, and then two more.

I hurry and fling the door open to find my best friend, BJ, leaning against the doorframe as if he hasn't a care in the world. His dark curls are as wild as ever. He looks like he might be headed for a hiking trail with khaki pants and a tight blue shirt that he likes to wear to show off his muscular frame.

"Barden Jasper," I greet him with his formal name, grinning. "What a surprise."

"A room in the palace?" He lifts his eyebrows and reluctantly pushes himself off the wall. "Quite fancy for an escaped convict."

Chuckling, I widen the door and let him inside. "I decided I wanted to keep my head in place for a few more years."

"Heard you're under the Empress's protection," he says and drops into the long chaise in front of the fire. "Not going to lie, it was a bit of a shock. But you know me, I don't care which devil you make a deal with as long as you're still alive. Besides, it saves me the work of having to spring you from that hellhole they call a prison."

"Thankfully, I was in too much pain to fully appreciate my previous accommodations." I grin and pour him his favorite drink and then make one for myself.

"I could get used to this life." He leans against the soft cushions, sipping his drink. "What was the agreement?"

"Nothing gets past you, does it?" I take a long sip of the orange juice mixed with pomegranate berries and then rummage through the cabinets for food until I scour up a tray of cheese and bread.

"I may not have gotten flashy powers like you, but my ability to get information and resources does come in handy."

"She wants me to kidnap Estrella and bring her back here."

"What?" BJ sputters, spitting out the juice he just drank.

"Once she's here, her memories will be wiped again so she won't remember what happened in Florida. Then the Empress will then work to get Estrella's powers back."

BJ's eyes narrow. "Is that possible?"

I shrug. "Apparently."

"She promised the two of you could be together after Estrella gets her memories back, didn't she?"

I nod. "Which is why I told her I'd do it."

"Man, I know that sounds great, but do you really trust the Empress?" He switches to a whisper, glancing around as if the walls have ears. "That witch is evil incarnate. Knowing her, she'll just kill you once you've got Estrella back into her clutches. You will be worthless to her."

"Oh, she'll definitely get rid of me. There's no doubt." I chuckle and load up cheese on a slice of bread. "I'll be a liability. Which is why I'm creating a plan of my own. Want to join?"

BJ's eyes narrow, and he sits up. "What kind of plan?"

"I want to overthrow the Empress."

"Have you lost your mind?" He leaps to his feet. "Did they mess up that brain of yours in prison? Man, you know I'm your best friend, but it's one thing to be buds when you're an escaped convict, but a whole other thing to be friends with a rebel eager to commit treason."

"Think about it. If we could get Estrella on our side and she could get her powers back, it would shift the power from the Empress and give us the upper hand. There are a lot of immortals who would be willing to join our side. They're just too scared right now."

BJ paces the room, his relaxed attitude forgotten. "This is intense. But what Nazco would dare cross paths with the Empress? Those who have tried aren't around to talk about it."

"I was thinking of not limiting ourselves."

"I'm not following."

"I'm thinking of joining with the Eien, Caladrians, and even the Sabians."

"The Sabians?" His eyes squint at me suspiciously. "What happened to you while you were in Florida?"

"Let's just say I made some non-traditional allies."

"Sounds risky. Not to mention the logistics. Like how are you going to get to her? And even if you could, how will you convince her to join you?"

I stare out the window, wondering how she's doing. Is she safe? Are they holding her hostage or taking care of her?

I have so many questions, and they're all demanding answers.

"First, I've got to find out where she is," I finally say.

"That's easy."

I spin around, my heart stilling. "Easy? What do you mean?"

"I saw Chandra's report. Estrella made it to King Julian's castle. Chandra tracked her all the way to the gate."

I close my eyes, relief flooding me. "That's good. She's safe."

"Good?" BJ gapes at me. "Estrella's in enemy territory. No Nazco has ever infiltrated their walls."

"That's where you come in, my best friend in the whole world." I slap my hand on his shoulder, earning me a wary glower. "I need you to find a way for me to get into that Sabian castle undetected."

"Sure." BJ laughs manically. "Because that is possible."

"I thought you liked challenges."

"This may be true." He sighs dramatically. "But let's just say I find a way through those impenetrable Sabian walls, how are you going to convince her to trust you?"

I rub my chin and turn back to the window. My eyes land on the library, where snow piles up on its rounded roof. "I don't know yet, but I think I know the place that might give me some clues."

My feet can't take me fast enough out of the Ice Palace while BJ hurries alongside me.

"What does the library have to do with convincing

Estrella to come with you?" BJ asks as we step into the library's grand rotunda entrance.

"Her two best friends were excommunicated after an incident during a field trip at a museum in New York," I explain. "She was distraught over the whole thing. Can't blame her. They were like her family, especially after what happened to her parents."

"Can't imagine," BJs says softly.

Our boots echo against the marble floors as we enter the main room. Bookshelves stretch to the beams on the ceiling and wooden tables are packed with Midnight Academy students preparing for their exams. We wind our way through the narrow shelves.

"Estrella spent every spare hour here," I continue. "She was determined to find some way to get her friends' powers back."

I come up to a square table by a set of arched windows overlooking the Ice Garden. My fingers scrape across the wood. This is where she sat. Day after day. I close my eyes, remembering her long golden hair falling over her shoulders as she scoured book after book in search for answers.

"This was her favorite place to sit." I nod to the snow-laden trees and ice sculptures glistening. "She loved that garden."

"What does all of this have to do with getting Estrella back?"

"The night of her Conduit ceremony, she told me she found a secret." I tap the table and scan the shelves nearby. "She was going to tell me what it was afterward, but never got the chance."

"You think she found a way to get her friends' powers back?"

"Maybe." The air smells of leather and ancient tomes. I get why she loved this place so much. "But if I can find her secret, I think I can use that as leverage to get her to come with me."

"Except if she's lost her memory, how will she know you're telling the truth?"

"One problem at a time," I say. "Right now, I just need to figure out which books she was reading."

"That's easy. We just ask the circulation desk for a record of every book she checked out."

"They'll give us that information?"

"No, but you are under orders by the Empress to get her back, right?"

"This is why I keep you around." I point at him, wagging my finger and grinning, and hurry off to the circulation desk.

"I thought it was because I was fun to hang out with," BJ calls after me.

29
ATTACK IN THE NIGHT
ESTRELLA

The Castle of Stará, Slovakia

A thump out on my balcony drags my attention from my study of immortal histories. Frowning, I close the book and sit up in bed, staring at the drapes hanging over the windowed doors. Is someone out there? Could the Nazco have found a way into the castle?

Or worse, it could be a Sabian eager to enact revenge. The side-eyes and wary looks haven't escaped my notice since I've been here. There are many who don't seem to care that it wasn't me who killed their Conduit. They just want someone to pay. And I'm the closest Nazco.

A creak spears the silence. The curtains billow ever so slightly, and the candle burning on my night stand wobbles as if a hint of a breeze has snuck inside the room.

Fear slams into me. Someone has opened my balcony door.

My dagger sits on the table beside the candle. I close my palm around its handle, and I draw it to me. Tidebreaker's power may have been sucked out of it, but it still can serve as a weapon.

My breath is caged inside me. Slowly, I rise from my chair. My gaze never leaves the curtain. Inch by inch, I creep toward the door.

But I'm not fast enough.

In a blink, the curtain wavers. A woman slips through its folds. She has long braids the color of the sun and bright, orange eyes. Her red lips curl into a snarl when she sees me. She holds up her hands—crimson red like the burners of a stove.

"You will pay, you Nazco filth," she growls.

Terror clutches my chest in an iron hold. I back up, holding my dagger between the two of us.

"You think you can kill me with that little thing?" She chuckles.

I swallow. "I don't want to kill anyone."

"Is that what your people said when they killed my best friend?"

Crap. Crap, crap, crap. She's here for vengeance. There's no way she's going to let me out of here alive.

"I'm going to make you burn." She inches closer. "Burn for so long you feel the amount of pain that I felt when I heard they killed her."

"I know the feeling of losing someone you care about." My body trembles. I edge closer to the door. "But you have to know that my people also tried to hurt me, too."

"Really?" She advances. "Is that why you're still alive? Is that why you've managed to enter our stronghold when no other Nazco has? Why our Prince is protecting you? Maybe even falling under your spell?"

"No. It's not like that."

"Oh, but I think it is."

She springs. Pounces on me like a lion. Her hands wrap around my neck. They are iron-hot. I'm on fire. Raging pain roars through my body, and the dagger clatters from my hand. I scream.

The world is red.

"I know why you're really here," she yells. "You're a spy. Admit it!"

"I'm not!"

I take her wrists, desperate to rip her off me. The pain from the burn makes it impossible to think. The door flies open. Someone barrels inside. The burning woman is flung off me, and I collapse to the floor. The world spins. My skin sears. A man bends down, his form swimming before my vision.

Tristan.

He hovers over me, eyes full of worry.

"Estrella!" he says. "Estrella, can you hear me?"

I reach for him. Needing him.

My vision darkens, and the voices and pain vanish.

Two days in the infirmary. I don't remember the first day at all. Only fragments of pain and fire. The Healers worked diligently to restore my neck. They said that in time my skin should completely heal. It depends on how tapped into my powers I was.

Today, I'm finally able to move around without too much pain. The attack has only made me even more eager to find a way to get my powers back. I was lucky that Tristan showed up, but I can't keep relying on him. There's going to be a time when I'm going to get attacked and he won't be able to save me.

The ward I'm in is nearly empty. People don't stay for long—another reminder of how quickly these immortals heal. There are ten cots lined up along the wall with large windows casting golden light across the large room, but only two are full: me and a soldier who apparently lost his arm fighting against Chandra's group when she attacked.

I'm eager to see how bad my burn marks are, but thick bandages ring my neck. So I'm restricted to lying on my cot, haunted by all the immortals trying to kill me. I clench my fists. I need to get my powers back. How can I defend myself against my attackers otherwise?

Voices at the end of the hall echo through the room. It's Tristan, arguing with one of the nurses. He darts around her, storming toward me like a hurricane. My heart races seeing him. His wild hair. Broad chest. The man who saved me over and over. I owe him my life.

I owe him everything.

Is that why my heart is pattering like a bird ready to fly? Or is this more than that?

He sits on the edge of my cot. His spicy scent replaces the cold antiseptic smells of the ward, making me want to lean closer to him.

"Estrella," he says, and his eyes darken with worry as he

takes in my bandages. "How are you? I came to check on you yesterday, but they said you were not well."

"I've been better." I lightly touch my neck. "Thank you for saving me. I don't know what I'd have done if you hadn't arrived in time."

He takes my hand and squeezes it. His fingers are rough but comforting. That heady warmth of him fills me just like it always does when I touch him. The memory of him holding me in his arms, my cheek pressed against his chest, ricochets through my core, and a need to be that close to him again fills me.

"It was lucky that I was in that section of the castle when you were attacked," he says, yanking me from my thoughts. "And that you have a loud scream."

This last part comes with a smile as if he's trying to joke this off, but there's pain in his eyes. I pull my hand away. What am I doing? I can't let myself get attached to him? He's a Sabian prince and I'm an outcast Nazco who is wanted by no one because everyone I come close to gets hurt.

"You shouldn't hold my hand. The woman who attacked me said I was trying to bewitch you." I glance over at the Healers hovering by the medical carts. "I'm sure she isn't the only one who thinks that."

"I don't care what they think," he says. "We've been through the storm and survived. They can't understand what we've gone through."

I look into his eyes and reach out, skimming my hand across his cheek. "I don't know who I am or even what kind of person I was. What if I regain my memories and suddenly I'm not the girl you think I should be? That scares me. Honestly, everything scares me right now. Especially me."

"I know." He takes a deep breath. "And that's okay. I wish I could do more to protect you."

"The woman who attacked me said I had to pay for what happened to her sister."

"That was Nina. She was Ivana's best friend. We're all dealing with my sister's passing in different ways. But there's no excuse for what she did."

"It made me realize more than ever that I need to get my powers back. I need to learn how to defend myself. And sitting here in this infirmary isn't helping. How can I continue to work on my training if I'm just lying in bed?"

"You're right. We need to train you and get your powers back. But right now you need to rest."

"Can you get me the books that Henrich wanted me to read?" I ask. "I feel like I don't understand this world I'm living in, and reading about it has helped."

"Consider it done." He fidgets with the blanket. "Another thing. It's not safe for you to be sleeping alone in your room."

"Don't tell me you're going to start sleeping in my room," I joke. When he doesn't smile, I give him a look. "Your life can't revolve around me. Nor are you responsible for me. I'll be fine. I'm still alive, aren't I?"

"Only because I've been there for you," he says.

I cringe and look away because he's right. I hate that I can't protect myself. I don't know how I'm even going to sleep at night anymore.

"Don't worry," he says. "I'm not going to sleep in your room. Yet. But I think it's best if I set up a guard on your balcony and outside of your door. That will be a deterrent.

I've also got my men working on adding an alarm button that you can ring if you ever need me."

"I thought you said you avoided modern technology."

"Avoid is the keyword. We use it when needed."

"See if you can get me out of here sooner." I grab his hand. "I want to start training with your mom as soon as I can."

"I'll do what I can." His lips quirk. "That said, something tells me they aren't too happy with me right now. But I did want to give you some good news."

"Good news? I didn't know such a thing existed."

"I talked to Conrad."

I sit straighter. "Conrad? The guy who's been watching over Lexi? How is she?"

"She's recovered and back at Nadia's Home. As far as Conrad can tell, she's doing fine. She even went back to school today."

"This is great news." Tears spring to my eyes. "Knowing she's back at school is the best news you could've given me."

"Conrad is secretly meeting up with her. He's trying to convince her to come here with you, but she doesn't trust him."

"Can you blame her? But I don't think she would leave the other girls. She has been protecting them even before I arrived." I grip the edge of my blanket. "If I had my powers back, I think I could help them all get out of that place."

"Right now you need to focus on getting yourself healed up." He rises from the cot, but his movements are slow as if it's taking all his effort to leave me. "Now get some rest."

He lifts my hand to his mouth and kisses it, his lips lingering on my skin. Heat flutters through me, and my heart does another flip. Then he strides away, leaving me cold and wanting. I stare after him, waiting for him to turn around and come back. But he doesn't. And he shouldn't. I told him to stay away.

I throw the blanket over me, my head spinning in confusion. Not only do I not know who I am or what my powers are, but I also have no idea what my heart wants.

And maybe that's the worst part of all of this.

30
TRAINING 101 SURE ISN'T FUN
ESTRELLA

The Castle of Stará, Slovakia

Sunlight pours through the paned windows, scattering golden light across the stone walls. But its warmth isn't what is causing the sweat to bead on my forehead. I've been training for an hour with the Queen, but I don't feel I've come any closer to accessing my powers.

"You must concentrate," Queen Kelli says from behind me. "Focus on your visik deep in the heart of your soul. That's where all immortals' power stems from."

"I'm trying," I say in frustration. "I just don't really get how to reach for it."

I've attempted to both close and open my eyes to help concentrate, but I've no idea how to focus on this visik. Every time I try to think about my core area, my stomach decides to rumble from hunger instead of power. But since

I've gotten out of the infirmary, I'm more motivated than ever to get my powers back.

Now it's the Queen's turn to sigh. I turn to face her. She's wearing an evergreen velvet dress with golden embroidery that glimmers in the light. A frown puckers her forehead and she paces, her gown skimming across the floor.

"When you battled against Roach and the other Nazco," she says, "how did you access your visik then?"

I consider her question. "I suppose it was pure panic. It's like something inside of me rose up when I needed it. Does that make sense?"

"It does." She taps a finger to her lips. "I want you to close your eyes and remember that battle."

I suck in a deep breath and comply. But the memory that tumbles back to me is a different one. I'm standing in the parking lot. Quadril, Chandra, and two other assassins are desperately trying to kill Tristan, Dion, and me.

The feelings of shock, betrayal, and fear rush back to me like terror racing at the speed of light. But there was also the realization that if I didn't do something, I'd lose both Tristan and Dion. That in itself was motivation.

"Now I want you to search the memory for the place where your power came from."

I remember Tristan standing at my side, fighting with his flaming sword. Dion is battling on my other side, his lightning streaking through the air. My heart twists as I remember Dion's expression when I left him on the shore of the pond. Did those other Nazco attack him when we left? But it doesn't matter. He lied to me. He didn't tell me the truth about my past or my abilities.

How could I trust him again after that? I shake my head of those thoughts and focus back on the battle.

"There was this one assassin," I say. "My hand brushed against his. I felt his energy pulsing beneath his veins."

"Very good," the Queen says. "Did you take his power from him?"

I frown because the concept is so strange but at the same time, her words make sense.

"Yes. I grabbed his wrist and pulled that energy to me. It felt like something slammed into me and raced through my whole body. Thinking back, it was really painful. I almost felt like I would explode if I didn't do something with it."

"Your body wasn't ready for that much power. You had been deprived of power for so long that when it finally was back in your body, you weren't able to handle it."

"So that horrible feeling isn't normal?"

"Come, sit down." She waves for me to join her on a settee by the fire. "Your visik is like a muscle. If you don't use it, it gets weaker and smaller. Everyone's muscles are different sizes and grow in different ways. The same is true about your visik."

"When I think about the memory," I rub my chest, "the need for that power came from here, but the thought of doing something like that again scares me."

"What you did, taking that assassin's power, was very dangerous. Your body wasn't ready for it. In fact, you're lucky his powers didn't burn your insides out."

"Are you serious? Can that happen?"

"Not often. Channelers are trained at a young age to be careful how much power they take from another immortal. Then they slowly learn to grow and expand their ability to take on more. But since you have no memory of that, you wouldn't have known to be careful. Also, knowing your body stores its visik in your chest gives you a good idea where to start. In time, it's my hope you will relearn everything you lost."

She rises and goes over to her bookshelf, pulling out a large book from it. She sets it on the table and I read the title, *Rules and Responsibilities of a Channeler.*

"This book was Ivana's." She runs her palm across the engraved designs.

"This was your daughter's?" I whisper.

"She was so powerful. Had so much potential. The Nazco came one night and..." She shakes her head as if to dispel those evil memories and pats the cover. "But I want you to have this book now. Study it and learn from it. Your body must know a little about how to be a Channeler, which is why your instincts kicked in. I'm assuming you were once far more powerful than you are now. Your visik muscles, if you will, have shrunk and are weak. You must practice and learn how to take powers and then use them, but not take too much that you burn yourself out."

"Thank you." I flip open the book, studying the layout. "I do have a question. Can you tell me more about Conduits?"

"Conduits are very, very rare. Sometimes there isn't one born in a thousand years. They are extremely powerful Channelers who can take on enough power for an entire kingdom. Their main role is to travel into the World of Between and retrieve our power source. Then they bring it back to our world and set it on our kingdom's pedestal. That power streams to every Sabian—or in your case, every Nazco—and replenishes their power."

"That sounds like something from a fantasy novel. How do the Conduits go to this other place? And what is that place exactly?"

"Don't worry about being a Conduit yet. We suspect you may have been a Conduit at one point because of information we stole. Even if you were, you may not be able to get that level of power and ability back. What we do know is that you do have Channeler abilities. So you must focus on that first. The rest will come later."

"Okay, I can do that. But how can I practice channeling? I don't want to steal anyone's power. Not to mention, no one seems too eager for me to even touch them."

"Tomorrow you will work with Tristan in the training room. There is a power source we set up that Ivana once used. It's not as effective as using a real immortal to pull from, but it's enough for what you need. Now that you know where your visik is located, the next step is to learn how to take and give back powers."

"And what if I can't control it?" I ask.

"You must learn. Or you will die."

31
THE SECRETS OF THE FATES
DION

The Midnight Kingdom, Antarctica

"Are you sure this is the full list?" I ask the librarian in frustration.

I scan the piece of paper he handed me. It's a long list of titles that Estrella checked out, but none of them give me a clue as to what she was after. Most seemed to be books she needed for her lessons.

He stares at me wide-eyed from behind the circulation desk and nods, but there's something about his tight-lipped expression that tells me there's more. So I wait, lifting an eyebrow.

It pays off because finally he clears his throat and says, "She did go into the Restricted Section on, let me see, March 2nd. Escorted by Librarian Norts."

"You have a Restricted Section here?" BJ says eagerly beside me. "Now that is something we need to see."

"Indeed. It's in the back by the statues of the Fates, but it's restricted." The librarian clears his throat. "As the name says."

Now it's my turn to give a tight-lipped smile. "Of course. But since we are here on orders of the Empress, I'm sure you'll be eager to give us access."

"You'll need an official letter with a stamp of authorization. You also need a Head Librarian to escort you inside. No one is allowed to enter alone."

Sparks flutter beneath my skin as my anger rises. I'm getting impatient with this man. But the last thing I need is to lose my cool. It would bring the Empress's attention to what I'm doing and where I'm investigating. I need her to stay in the dark as much as possible.

"Thank you for your assistance." I spin on my heels and march back through the library.

"That's it?" BJ asks, hurrying after me. "You're just going to back down to that guy?"

"I must," I say as I take the stone stairway in the back of the library. "If I seemed too desperate, word could get back to the Empress. We need to keep this lead to ourselves."

"So what's your plan?" BJ asks. "We've already scoured this entire library for whatever Estrella was looking for. It closes in an hour."

"I don't know." I sigh. "The more I think about it, the more I'm wondering if this is an impossible task."

The four statues of the Fates rise up along the back wall of the library, imposing and rather ominous. They're wearing chitons while crowns rest over long, flowing hair. An arched wooden doorway is set in the middle. Engravings of the infinity symbol with vines intertwining around them are carved on each side. Two large oval door knobs are set in its center.

"This must be it," BJ says. "I tried opening this earlier, but it can't hurt to try again."

"We need the key," I grumble, staring morbidly at the Fates' faces.

BJ attempts the door once more, but it's firmly locked. "A minor setback. We'll just find an unsuspecting student who has power over wooden objects. I'll hold them down and you threaten to electrocute them."

I rub my chin, staring at the door as something tickles the back of my mind. A memory.

"What?" BJ asks, studying me. "You have that look. Like you know something."

"There's something she said about the Fates," I murmur.

"She, as in Estrella?"

I nod and hurry back to Estrella's work area. The alcove remains empty when I step inside, probably because it's in the far back corner of the library and no one even is aware that it exists. Outside the large window, a couple strolls hand in hand in the Ice Garden. I move to the room's large desk in the center and study it, hoping it will conjure back the memory.

"One time when I found her here," I tap the desk lightly, "she had a stack of books."

BJ wanders to the bookshelves lining the one side of the alcove. "Do you remember their titles or what they were about?"

"They were about the Fates." I trace the top edge of the

chair. "It feels like only yesterday she was here, sitting in this very chair."

The memory beckons, calling me back to a better time...

I bent down and whispered into Estrella's ear, "Could I entice you to a study break?"

She looked up, eyes glacier blue, and her lips tilted with mischief. "What are you offering, Dion?"

My stomach flipped as I studied her face. The curve of her mouth. The fullness of her lips. She had no idea the power she had over me. How I would go to the ends of the world for her with just a whisper.

I caught her hand and pulled her up to me so our bodies almost touched. Her hair cascaded over her cheeks, and I pushed back the strands so I could memorize every inch of her face. My finger traced her beautiful lips.

"I was thinking you picked the perfect study spot," I said, my voice low and rough. "No one will see us when I kiss you."

She laughed and pushed against me playfully.

"You are a distraction," she said.

"I think you need one. You've been working too hard. What are you even studying anyway?" My eyes scanned the books on the table. The Lost Temple, The Fates of the Immortals, Origins of Our Kind. I lifted my eyebrows at her. "Something tells me your religion professor at the academy hasn't assigned these."

She shifted her shoulders back and forth and looked

down at the stack. "It's something I'm working on, but it's a secret."

"A secret even from me?" I couldn't hide the stab of regret that I felt. That she didn't trust me enough to tell me what she was working on. But after everything she'd been through, I supposed it made sense she wouldn't trust anyone.

"It's better this way." Her eyes darted guiltily to the bookshelf and then back to me. "If a Truth Seeker would interview you, then you wouldn't have to worry about getting caught."

My chest tightened. The thought of her delving into things that could get either of us probed by a Truth Seeker didn't settle well with me. I study the bookshelf, frowning. Whatever she was working on was dangerous. Too dangerous.

I traced a finger along her jawline. "Be careful. I wouldn't want anything to happen to you. I don't know what I'd do without you."

"You'll probably find some other pretty girl." Her face darkened. "Just as long as it's not Chandra. What did you ever see in her anyway to date that girl?"

That sent a laugh roaring through me, and I shook my head. "I was an idiot until I met you. Dating her was my moment of stupidity. But now you're mine and I'm yours, and we are both all the wiser for it."

She rolled her eyes, but a smile caught her lips. She ran her hands along my chest, sending shivers through my body. "Promise that if anything happens to me you won't get involved. I've already lost everyone I love. I can't lose you, too."

"Now you're scaring me." I glanced down at the books. "What are you researching? And why?"

"It's nothing. Really." She wrapped her arms around me, pulling me so close her chest pressed against mine. "Now kiss me."

All my worries faded. My lips found hers, soft as rose petals. My hands threaded through her hair, and I lost myself in her taste and touch. She was sunshine and honeysuckle. The stars sparkled and the sun filled the sky because she existed.

And nothing in this world would ever keep us apart.

"Dion?" BJ's voice yanks me back to the present. Away from her. "You alright?"

I shudder. No. I'm not. Every moment I'm separated from Estrella, it's like another part of my heart is breaking. Soon, I'll be nothing but an empty shell. Except, maybe I do know a piece to her secret's puzzle.

Maybe she told me, after all.

"I used to believe Estrella chose this alcove to study because of the view." I wander to the bookshelf. "But I think it was much more than that."

32

PLAYING WITH FIRE

ESTRELLA

The Castle of Stará, Slovakia

My nerves are tangled knots in my stomach as I step into the training room. Today is my training day with Tristan. Not only will I have to face him after whatever it was that happened between us the other day, but I'm also finally going to be putting my powers to the test.

The room is oval shaped with tall intricately paned windows at the end, casting morning light across the walls lined with weapons, most of which I have no idea what they are. Mats are set up on one side while on the other is a pedestal with a flickering red flame encased in a wrought-iron lantern frame.

But my focus is on Tristan standing and looking out the windows. I study his broad, muscular back, remembering how his strong arms felt around me as he carried me to safety. How I almost reached over and brushed my lips across his when he came to visit me in the infirmary.

Does he remember that moment the same way I do? Did he feel that connection like I did? Or am I just emotionally connected to him because he saved my life like a million times?

I shake my head. I can't think about this sort of thing. I need to focus on getting my powers back and discovering how far my abilities will take me. My friends at Nadia's need me, and I can't let them suffer by staying there.

"Your mom said that you were going to train me," I say, breaking the silence. Even though he's facing the window, he had to have heard me enter.

He runs his hands through his hair, a habit I'm starting to recognize that he does when he's worried about something. Then, as if wrestling with himself, he turns to face me. He's got an odd expression on his face, almost like it's full of yearning, but then it slips away and he grins back to his usual carefree self, eyes twinkling. Relief slides through me. He's not going to make this awkward.

"You're late," he says. "A warrior is never late to battle."

"So that's the sort of trainer you are going to be?" I grin, crossing my arms. "My lessons with Professor Henrich went long. Today I learned how you and I are mortal enemies and how we can never trust each other."

"Did you?" He comes closer.

I back up a little, feeling flustered and breathless. There's something about him, his presence, that warns me that whatever happened between us the other night has not vanished but has been building inside me. I need to be very careful around him.

"So I guess that will help me when I have to use my powers against you."

He laughs, shaking his head. "This I can't wait to see."

"Where do we start?" I wave at the racks of weapons, but my eyes wander to the pedestal. "What is that?"

"It's Sabian fire, or the formal term, Numinous." He steps up to it and I follow. "It is the power that all our races need to maintain our powers and immortality. One of our Conduits from the 5th century brought it back from the World of Between to harness and strengthen their ability. Every potential Conduit has trained with it since."

I stare at the flickering flame, its crimson fire licking at the air like a dragon's tongue.

"It's bright red," I say, uneasily. "Unusually so. I know this sounds weird, but there's something about that fire that's familiar. Like I've seen it before."

"Doubt that. This is Sabian Numinous, red fire. Nazcos are only able to find and use blue fire."

"You're saying I'm not able to touch that?"

"According to records, no. Then again, I'm not sure it's ever been tested. No one wants to be the first Channeler to be consumed by fire."

"Seriously." I grimace.

"Don't worry, my sister didn't start training with the hardcore stuff at first. She began with this other power source that one of our elementalists created. That's what I thought you could train with. Also, next time you come here, bring your dagger, Tidebreaker. If you touch the blade to this power source, it will rejuvenate the blade's power once again."

"That's good to know."

He draws me through a side door into another room. This one is dark, illuminated only by the light trickling in from the opened door. It's completely empty other than a large metal cabinet. As my eyes adjust, I see that there are no windows and the walls are stone. Tristan opens the cabinet, pulls out a simple metal box, and hands it to me.

"I'll let you open it up," he says. "I'm not a Channeler, so there's no way I'm going to mess with it."

"Now you're scaring me." I stare at the box in my hands. "What's inside?"

"The elementalist took elements of the four immortal categories of powers—fire, water, earth, and air—and made them into spheres for Channelers to train with."

"Is it safe for me to open?"

"Ivana called them her little toys." Tristan smiles softly and his eyes soften as if he's caught in a memory. "I also saw how hard they were for her to use when she was little, so be careful. She did some crazy things with those spheres."

"I know you miss her." I go to touch his arm, but stop myself, remembering Professor Henrich's warning that all immortals are wary of Channelers touching them. "It must be hard for you to do this."

"I think you two would've been good friends if you had met. She would be happy knowing you're here, trying to help us."

Guilt bites me. I do care about these Sabians, but do I really want to help them? How much do I know about who they really are other than what they've told me? Right now,

I've only heard one side of the story. Truth is, the most important thing for me is to help my friends at Nadia's. But if I tell him that, I'm not sure he would be here showing me these secrets.

"So are you going to open it?" Tristan presses.

"I know I've got abilities inside of me and I've been able to use my powers, but I still don't trust myself completely."

"You're overthinking things. Just give it a go."

I pop open the box and gasp in utter amazement. Inside are four small glowing balls of luminescent light, all different colors. Red, blue, green, and yellow. They're about the size of a tennis ball and could easily fit into my palm.

"They're beautiful. It's like nothing I've ever seen before."

"Red is for powers relating to fire, blue for water, green for earth, and yellow for air," Tristan explains. "Let's start with the red one since that's the source of my elemental power and you've been working and using it with me already."

"I just pick it up?"

"That's what Ivana used to do," Tristan says, shrugging, but his face is strained as if he's a little uncertain.

I lock away my fears and set down the box. Tentatively, I touch the top of the red glowing ball. The light flickers across my finger as if it's licking it. Warmth soaks into my skin, and a rush of energy races through me.

"Did that hurt?" Tristan asks.

I look up and find him tense like he's ready to scoop me up and race me to the infirmary.

"No." I grin. "It's awesome."

He lets out a long breath while I scoop up the ball into

my palm. Instantly, that warm sensation slides through my body, skittering over me like fireworks. My skin glows, and I let the rush of power draw through me.

"Good," Tristan says, letting out a long breath. "Okay, once you've gathered up some of its power, set the ball down and then use its power that's now inside of you. See this sconce on the wall? I want you to use your power to light it."

He pulls me over to where thick bars of iron cage an empty disc.

"But there isn't a candle or oil in it," I note.

"A fire elemental doesn't need those things for their light to work."

I stare at the sconce in confusion. "What do I do, just think about lighting it?"

"I'll show you."

He flicks his hand and a stream of golden light sails onto the disc. A flame bursts to life. Then he reaches out and grabs the fire like he's scooping it up. It vanishes inside his palm.

"That is weird and not natural." I laugh nervously.

"You're thinking like a mortal. You need to switch your mentality. Think of yourself like you're one with the fire. Like it's a part of you and it's ready to be shared or tucked away."

"Right. Okay."

I hold out my hand. Remembering how he flicked his palm, I try to mimic his movements, concentrating on sending fire out of my palms to the sconce. A rush of fiery heat races from my chest and along my arm. An explosion of flames bursts out of my hand. Instantly, my clothes are on fire. I cry out in fear.

Tristan deftly defuses the fire, patting my shirt and pants down until all the flames are gone except the single one on the lantern. I stare at my clothes, now shredded and blackened.

"That didn't go so great," I say, grimacing.

"On the contrary," Tristan says. "That was great! It means you have the potential to hold and wield a lot of power. You just need to control it and..." His eyes drift to my shirt, which now resembles more of a belly shirt. His face reddens a little, or maybe it's just from the heat in the air. He clears his throat. "And we need to get you some fireproof clothing like I have."

"Great? I could've incinerated someone."

"Sure, but you did light the sconce, so let's take the win." His eyes soften, and he pushes a sweaty strand of my hair behind my ear. "You okay?"

When his fingers touch my skin, they are warm and enticing. I don't know what it is about him, but it's like his powers call to me. I bite my lip, shoving my thoughts into focus.

"It didn't hurt," I say, trying to ease his worries. "I guess it's just a lot to process."

"How about we try a different method?"

At my nod, he goes back to the cabinet and pulls out what looks like a target, setting it up on the other side of the room. Next, he quickly lights up the other sconces around the perimeter so the room glows warm as honey.

"Stand here." He points at a place on the opposite side of

the room from the target. "You're going to try to hit that target."

"We're doing target practice?" I ask skeptically. "Shouldn't I have a weapon or something?"

"Weapons do make it more accurate and give an added element of power," Tristan says. "That's why I like using my sword. But you're not ready for that yet. Do the same thing you did last time, but aim to hit your fire on that target."

"Okay." Uncertainty builds inside of me. "Here goes nothing."

I flick my wrist like before and aim my palm at the target. A shot of fire bursts out of it, but this one is weaker, thin like a strand of thread. It hits the corner of the room. I crunch up my nose, but Tristan spins to face me, grinning.

"Nicely done!" He holds his hand out in a fist bump, which I return half-heartedly.

"Terrible aim. I didn't even come close to the target. And the fire looked like a limp noodle."

"You'll get it. The important thing is that you can produce fire. Not a small feat, which means you've done this before at some point. My suggestion is to not overthink it. Let your natural instincts take over. Use muscle memory rather than mental energy."

"That actually makes sense."

I plant my feet, and this time, I focus on hitting the target rather than worrying about the fire or how my hand moves. It misses again, but it's closer. Sweat pours down the sides of my face from the effort. Again and again, I work. When I run out of fire, I draw more energy from the sphere in the box. Soon I'm hitting the target edges pretty consistently.

"What do you say we have a contest?" Tristan offers, his eyes mischievous.

"A contest? I'm game. Be careful, I might beat you."

I lose track of time as the two of us battle it out, back and forth, shooting fire at the target. Tristan's flames hit far stronger with more accuracy than mine, but I find myself feeling more invigorated as I play with the element. It's like my body is being awakened.

At one point, I run out of fire but instead of going over to gather new energy from the sphere in the box, I grab Tristan's arm just as he aims for another hit. I pull out the stream of fire he's about to release. His visik races to me eagerly, wild for release. It's far more powerful than that small sphere in the box. I tug out just a little before he releases another blast. When he goes to shoot, nothing comes out. His mouth opens wide in shock, and he spins on me.

I laugh and then aim his flames at the target and shoot off a resounding blast.

"You did not just take my fire," Tristan scolds with a hint of a smile. "Give it back. Right now. That's cheating."

"But is it?" I tease, side-stepping from him as he tries to grab me. "Because I am using my powers."

"It totally was cheating." He grabs my hand, holding it up. "Now give it back."

"But did you see how awesome of a hit I made when I used your powers?"

He doesn't answer right away; instead, he's staring at our hands like he's mesmerized, the flames intertwining between our fingers. There's something about it that's hypnotic and intoxicating, and I don't want him to let go.

My body leans in closer as an ache to wrap my arms around him overwhelms me. I expect him to step away, but he closes the gap between us, allowing the flames to course over our bodies like sparkling threads.

I peer up at his face to find he's leaning toward me. Our lips are a whisper apart.

I need to stop this. Break away. But the temptation inside me screams to just taste his lips. To feel those arms circling protectively around me.

Someone clears their throat. Both Tristan and I stiffen, shocked at how close things had been to nearly going out of control. Tristan backs away as if I've burned him.

"Excuse me, your Highness," a man says. I look over to find it's one of the servants. He looks away, face reddening. "Katka says she has an update from Conrad and Lexi. Said you'd want to know right away."

"Lexi?" I ask, and my heart skips. "Is it good or bad news?"

"She didn't say," the servant replies.

"Thank you," Tristan says. "I'll be right there."

The servant leaves while Tristan widens the gap between us, heading to the door like he's escaping while I'm left standing here, confused and cold and empty.

"Wait!" I hurry after him. "I want to come, too,."

33
JUST A SPLASH OF SCANDALOUS GOSSIP
ESTRELLA

The Castle of Stará, Slovakia

M y pulse pounds against my temples in excitement as Tristan and I step into Katka's workshop. I'm finally going to see Lexi again! I am eager to find out how she's doing and make sure she's okay.

The large room is an odd assortment of modern equipment and random items that look older than this castle. This workshop has more modern technology than I've seen anywhere in this kingdom. My steps falter though when I spy the red-haired woman in the center of it, demanding my full attention. She's wearing a gray apron over a tunic and pants, her hair braided down her back. One glance at her tells me she wants nothing to do with me.

"What is *she* doing in *my* workshop?" the woman asks, green eyes flashing as she assesses me.

"Katka, I'd like to introduce you to Estrella," Tristan says. He pulls me closer, but as I slip to his side, her gaze becomes daggers. It's then I realize what we must look like to her—a couple. "Estrella, this is Katka. You probably remember her when she was giving us directions in the car."

"I do." I smile, but the woman only glares in response. "Thank you for your help."

"You wouldn't have needed my help if his Lordship had just followed directions." She rolls her eyes, then turns her attention back on Tristan. "But seriously. No one is allowed in here except for Tia and me. Well, I suppose you, too, from time to time."

I bite back a snarky comment that tempts my lips. It's easy to make accusations from the comfort of your own workspace safe in a castle. How would she feel if she were kicked out and abandoned by her own people?

"She wants to talk to her friend," Tristan says firmly. "We heard you had both Conrad and Lexi on the line."

"Fine. Whatever." She huffs and waves us over to her computer. "They're waiting to talk to you."

Thank you, I mouth to Tristan.

His eyes soften, and he smiles at me in a way that warms me to my toes.

Later, I'll have to ask him what her problem is. I get why she hates me. I'm Nazco. But everyone else in this land treats Tristan as if he's a gift from the gods while this girl acts like he's her servant. It doesn't matter though. Right now all I care about is talking to Lexi and making sure she's okay.

"I'll pull up the call now." Katka taps on her keyboard, and the computer screen blinks to life.

Hungrily, I search the screen for the girl I consider my best friend. But I only find Conrad, sitting at a desk and wearing a plaid shirt. His short brown hair is combed neatly, and he's rubbing his chin like he's worried about something. At first glance, you'd think he was just some normal guy walking down the street, but after seeing him wield that sword against the Wraith, I know he's just as much of a warrior as Tristan and someone not to be messed with.

"Conrad!" Tristan says, his face brightening. "I see the Nazco haven't detached your head yet."

Conrad harrumphs. "Afraid you can't get rid of your best mate yet."

"Good. I need someone to beat on the sparring mat from time to time."

"You look much better than the last time I saw you. Bet you're happy to be eating Chef Nitra's food again rather than...what was it you ordered at the diner again?"

Tristan groans. "Did you have to remind me of diner food?"

"Ah, mate. I can't deny that I'm jealous."

"We need to get you back here as soon as possible," Tristan says. "Tell me you're headed this way soon. Do you think the plan will work?"

"Well..." Conrad rubs his chin.

Desperate to see Lexi, I squeeze in beside Tristan, not wanting to wait another second. "How's Lexi? Is she there?" I lean forward and press my palms against the table.

"Hello, Estrella." Conrad smiles. "She's coming over right now."

With a flash of long red hair, Lexi squeezes into the chair next to Conrad. She's so close that she's practically curled in his lap. My fears are calmed seeing her skin brighter and her hair a richer red.

"Is that you, Estrella?" Lexi asks. "Oh my gosh. You really are alive. Conrad told me so, but I couldn't believe it until I saw you."

"Lexi!" I can hardly hold the tears back. The memory of her cold, bloody body on the bathroom floor still haunts me. "I'm glad you're okay. I've been so worried. How are you?"

"Hospitals suck but if it weren't for Conrad, I'd be dead." She glances over at him and smiles. I narrow my eyes at how close the two have become. Is something going on between them? She focuses back on me. "But what about you? How did you get away and where are you? Oh my gosh. Are you in a dungeon? Are they torturing you?"

"No." I laugh. "This is someone's work area."

"You could call it a torture room," Tristan mutters darkly while Katka bangs around, swearing under her breath about Nazco.

"Oh, I'm so glad," Lexi says. "The girls totally freaked out when you just up and disappeared. Can we meet up soon? I miss you."

"We can't tell you where we are," Tristan interrupts. "It's a safety thing. And unfortunately, we aren't close enough to meet up."

Lexi frowns, and I can see she's not happy that I'm keeping secrets from her. But Tristan's right. It is for the best. Still, I almost wonder if he still doesn't trust her completely to not tell Nadia.

"I'm so sorry I left you," I say. "We were being chased

and Tristan and I both agreed it was safer for you to go to the hospital. Where are you?"

"Conrad and I meet up here at the local library," she explains. "It's private and the perfect place to pretend I'm studying."

"That's smart. How is everyone? How are Mara and Jamie? Is Zayla hanging in there?

"Everything here sucks just like normal. Mara thinks you're dead, so she's fun to be around. Jamie is plotting revenge and has managed to collect nearly every knife and fork in the house thanks to the help of Zayla. The little thief keeps stealing them and then gives them to Jamie, who's hoarding them like she's preparing for the apocalypse. You can only imagine Nadia's wrath when she realized we only had spoons to eat with at dinner last night."

I smile, imagining Zayla in action. She likely knows that Jamie categorizes the utensils by their deadliness. Zayla must have snuck them into Jamie's room and stolen them. A yearning fills me, and my heart aches. I miss these girls. Sure, we don't know much about each other, but they're still my friends. A thought niggles at the back of my mind. Once Lexi told me that she thought we used to know each other. Not that any of us remember our old lives. Still, I wonder if that's true. Could that be why our bond feels so strong?

"What about Nadia?" I ask. "Does she suspect anything?"

"Oh, definitely." Lexi scrunches her nose. "She found your love notes scratched into the floor and the stolen folders under your mattress. But she hasn't said anything more about you in the last few days. I think she's hoping we'll all just forget your exit."

"You need to be very careful. We're trying to figure out a way to get you out of there."

"I'd leave right now if I could." Her brow bunches up, and she nibbles on her bottom lip. "After those horrible creatures attacked us and then finding out that Tiffany was a back-stabbing traitor, I honestly don't know who to trust anymore or even where to go. I can't sleep just thinking about it. Conrad and I brainstormed some ideas, but every time I think about escaping, I worry I'll make some mistake that will get me killed. Or even murder one of the other girls."

We're all silent as we take in her words.

"I wish I had answers or could be there for you," I whisper. "I feel like an awful friend for leaving."

"Conrad and I are working on a plan," Tristan says. "If all goes well, we're going to try to get them out of there in less than a week."

"Really?" My eyes widen. "Is it safe?"

Conrad nods. "It might be safer than staying. I get the feeling that having the girls stay there is more dangerous to their minds every day."

My head spins. What if she tries to escape and she fails? Will they kill her? Leave her mauled on the floor like they did in the bathroom? The thought squirms its way down into the pit of my stomach. I'm about to tell her to stop all thoughts of escaping when an alarm starts beeping on the wall.

"That's a team reporting in," Katka interrupts. "We need to get off the line so I can check them in."

"We have to go," I tell Lexi, blowing her a kiss. "Please take care and don't do anything stupid."

She blows me a kiss back as the call switches over to another team of three members. Their khaki pants and short-sleeved shirts are still dripping wet, which means they must have traveled through the portal and just arrived.

"Reporting in through the south gate," a man with a beard and long scraggly hair says. "Security code 5489, arriving from Mexico."

"Excellent." Katka presses several buttons on her panel. "Releasing you for entry."

"We have the tablet to return to the Artifacts Room as well," one of the women says.

"Got it." Katka nods and types something. "Access has been granted. Head up to the north tower and I'll let you in."

"Let's pray they found something," Tristan says. "That team has been wandering the earth like a bunch of nomads for years."

My curiosity is peaked, and I study this group on the monitor as they enter through the gate. One woman in particular catches my attention, and I lean closer. She's got long blonde hair like most people here at the castle, but the whole side of her face is scarred from what looks like burns.

"That woman." My mouth dries up. "She's familiar. I think I know her."

And I think I gave her that scar.

34
FORGOTTEN SECRETS
DION

The Midnight Kingdom, Antarctica

I rub my chin as I study the rows of bookshelves, wondering what secret they disclosed to Estrella. The air around BJ and me smells of old books and leather bindings. The wooden floor creaks as I pace before the shelf, trying to think how she might be in this situation.

"Do you really think there's a clue here?" BJ comes alongside me to inspect the rows.

One book catches my eye. The top of its spine looks different—firmer perhaps, and not as worn and bendable as the others. Curious, I pull on the book, except it doesn't come out. Instead, the top pulls toward me while the bottom remains where it is like it's some sort of lever.

A soft rumbling sound reaches my ears. BJ gasps.

"Blazes," I say, stepping back in shock as the bookshelf shifts forward. "I think we've found something."

"You could say that." BJ steps to the corner of the room where the bookshelf has pulled back to reveal an opening.

I hurry to his side, and the two of us push against the portion of the shelf wide enough for us to peer inside. A waft of brittle, chilled air hits my face.

"What in the Fate's name is this place?" BJ whispers.

"Shh." I glance over my shoulder, and seeing that we're still alone in this alcove, I say, "Come. Let's be quick about it."

Darkness sweeps over us as we step inside. Based on the sliver of light pouring into the space from the library, I realize this is a smaller room. More bookshelves line all four walls with no windows. Books and scrolls pack the shelves, and by their haphazard layouts, it appears as if they'd been stuffed into these spaces like they'd been deposited in a hurry.

"I think I heard someone out there." BJ darts back over to the crack in the bookshelf and peeks out. "I'm shutting the door."

"What if we can't—" Before I finish, he yanks the shelf back into place and there's a clicking sound that fills the air. Instantly, we're thrust into blackness. "—reopen it."

"Ah. Hadn't thought of that."

I'm about to pull out my phone for some light when suddenly pale white lines begin illuminating the floors and ceiling. They almost seem to move in a swirling motion.

"What's happening?" BJ asks.

"Whatever it is," I say in a hushed whisper, "it's unlike anything I've seen before."

Like the rise of dawn, the lines brighten so they're distinct enough for me to recognize constellations across the ceiling and floor. It's breathtaking and allows just enough light for us to read the print on the book spines.

I bend down and trace my finger across a design on the floor. The light tickles my skin, and the essence of its power coats my fingers like stardust.

"A Light Wielder must have infused their powers into this place," I say. "Whoever did this must have had significant powers to create so much light."

"I bet it's protecting these books from decay as well. This place is incredible. Do you think anyone else knows it exists?"

"Hard to know. But if so, that is a mystery in itself. Why is it hidden and who hid it?"

"Take a look at this." BJ points to a lever on the wall. "What do you think? Our ticket out of this room?"

Inwardly, I cringe waiting for something else to go wrong but when he pulls down on it, the shelf creaks open once again.

"You're like a kid in a candy shop," I say, shaking my head at him, and he winks back at me before closing the opening once again.

"Can you blame me? I can't think of a time I've found a secret door."

Relieved we found a way out, I take a deep breath and begin studying the rows and rows of books and scrolls.

"The library closes in an hour," I say. "Our main focus is to find the books Estrella was reading as soon as possible. There were three that I vividly remember: *The Lost Temple*, *The Fates of the Immortals*, and *Origins of Our Kind*."

"Based on those names, I think we can take a good guess that she was looking for the Fate's temple." BJ joins me in combing through the shelves. "Except the temple was destroyed in the War of the Ancients. If it was found, it would be nothing but ruins. It doesn't make sense."

"Unless there's something about the temple she needed to know." I remember how tireless she had been to save her friends who had been taken away. Could this have been the answer to what she was seeking?

My heart thunders as I find the large tome with the words *The Lost Temple* scripted on its spine. I pull it out and hold it up.

"This is one of the books she was reading," I say. "I'm sure of it."

"Do you think it tells the location of the temple?" BJ comes to my side. "But more importantly, why?"

"I wish I could find out," I say, gently flipping through the worn pages, "but the text is written in Old Castilian."

"Of course it is." He chuckles. "Wasn't that the language you cheated on? I remember you saying you could get by on your Spanish."

I glare at him. "And how is your Old Castilian?"

"Better than yours."

He holds out his hands, and I reluctantly pass the book to him. While he settles on a small wooden chest in the corner of the room and begins reading, I continue the search for the other titles. But there are hundreds of texts here. It could take days to go through them all. As I scan each shelf, my mind wanders, wondering what Estrella is doing right now. Is she safe? Does she still resent what I did?

That expression of shock and pain on her face when she

realized I had kept her true identity a secret from her haunts me. I don't know if she can ever forgive me.

That thought alone sends a shot of pain through me.

"Okay," BJ interrupts. "So this mainly goes through the story of the building of the temple, its overall design, and the materials used."

"Does it give a specific location?" I rush to his side.

"Not that I can tell, but my Old Castilian isn't perfect. We could take it to a language expert."

"We must be careful who we show this to." I rub my chin, contemplating the implications of this find. "It's far too dangerous and probably why it's hidden away in this secret room."

"You're right. It's huge. Probably why Estrella didn't tell you either."

The thought that she didn't trust me enough to share about this place and her secret worries me. It wasn't until the Wraiths held their knives to her that she even dared to mention it.

For the next hour, BJ continues scouring the text for more information while I search for the other two books. Finally, I find *Origins of Our Kind*.

I'm about to start reading through it, but a glance at my watch warns me we're out of time.

"The library is closing soon," I say. "We need to leave."

"Then we'll need to take these with us. We need more time to study them. Besides, the light is crappy in here."

He has a point. We gather the books into our arms and open the secret entryway. I'm about to step out when I hear voices. Freezing, I turn to BJ and press a finger to my lips.

The last thing I need is for anyone to spot us slipping out of this hidden room.

"I think they came this way," the librarian's voice from the desk floats down the hallway. "They're likely in one of these study rooms."

BJ and I duck out of the secret room and settle at the table in the center of the alcove area, pretending to study when another voice speaks. This one chills my blood.

"Quadril appreciates your service, and it won't go unnoticed." There's no doubt. The voice belongs to Viamire.

"Blistering stars." I whisper-yell to BJ. "Since when does he report to Quadril, the head of the Council?"

"It doesn't make sense. Always thought he was the Empress's little henchman."

Viamire continues speaking, "We'll keep looking for him on the upper floor, but make sure if you see Dion Cabral that he doesn't leave this library without speaking to me first."

Their voices grow closer, but when I hear my name, my eyes bug out. He's specifically looking for me. I jerk my head back toward the hidden room. BJ nods, face turning white. Quickly, the two of us duck back through the secret door and quickly shut it.

The second it snaps closed, I press my ear against the door, wondering how soundproof this place is. I get my answer seconds later when I hear the librarian talking again, clear as day.

"I thought they might work in this alcove area," the librarian says. "This is where his friend, Estrella, used to come and study."

"Is that so?" Viamire says. Boots clomp across the floor like a death toll. "Any idea why she would choose this spot?"

"The view of the ice garden obviously," the librarian says. "I admit, it's one of my favorite spots."

"Hmm..." Viamire mutters something I can't quite hear. "You can leave us. Be sure to watch the exit and make sure he doesn't leave without speaking to us."

"Of course. A good day to you both."

BJ and I stare at each other, holding our breaths. If Viamire looks as closely as I did, he's sure to notice the same book that opened this door. And something tells me if he caught me hiding in this room full of valuable—and perhaps forbidden—texts, even the Empress couldn't save me.

"Cabral is up to something," Viamire tells whoever is with him. "He's just as dirty as his father. Never trusted the guy. It's only a matter of time before I catch him in the act of treason."

Footsteps leave, and BJ and I settle on the floor and wait until the library falls into an uneasy silence.

"Appears we're going to be locked in here all night," BJ mutters, rubbing his stomach. "We should've risked it and just left. Now I'm starving."

"You're always starving." I pace the room, wondering what Viamire and Quadril are up to.

Why are they looking for me? They want something. Maybe suspect something? Whatever it is, I'm sure it won't work in my favor. Meanwhile, BJ starts combing the room, peeking behind every shelf.

"What are you doing?" I ask. "You're making me nervous. Next thing we know, you'll set off some sort of alarm."

"Just seeing if your girlfriend left behind some snacks."

He's rummaging through one of the back shelves, grinning over at me. "You never know."

I roll my eyes when suddenly another bookshelf groans and opens up.

"What did you just do?" I ask.

The two of us dart to the opening to find a spiral stone staircase with no railing. Each step is lit by a single star, illuminating a path down into the recesses of the kingdom. BJ whistles.

"Aren't we full of surprises today," I say, shaking my head in shock.

"Considering we're locked in here for the night," BJ says. "I vote we check it out."

"I like the way you think."

35
YOU'RE LETTING A NAZCO ENTER THE ARTIFACTS ROOM?
TRISTAN

The Castle of Stará, Slovakia

"You know Valeska?" My gaze flickers between Estrella's worried face and Valeska's scarred one on the monitor. "How is that possible? She's been on a mission in Mexico. There's no way you would've crossed paths with her."

"I don't know." Estrella's voice is a haunted whisper. "It doesn't make sense, but I know that face. It's ingrained in my memory. Which is weird because apparently Dion and I were close, but I didn't remember him." She shakes her head as if to get rid of those thoughts, and I wonder how hurt she is from his betrayal. "But this woman. There's something about her that..."

Her words trail off and she looks away, pressing her lips together. I rake my hands through my hair as an uneasy feeling creeps over me. Estrella isn't telling me something. Something important.

"Maybe if you talk to Valeska," I say, "it will trigger your memory."

"Or seeing her might trigger Valeska's memory, too," Katka says with a dark, knowing look. "I'm going to meet the scouting team in the Artifacts Room, which means you both need to leave."

"We're coming with you," I tell her. "I think Estrella's memory of Valeska could be a clue to her past."

"That sounds like a dreadful idea," Katka says.

I turn to Estrella and touch her arm. "What do you want to do?"

She looks up at me, those captivating eyes cloudy blue with worry. I see that trust in them, and more than anything I don't want to disappoint her. My heart aches. She's worried about Lexi, her own memories, and now this. I can't let her down.

"I need to see Valeska," Estrella finally says with conviction. "Maybe she's from my past. Maybe she'll give us a clue as to what happened to me and why I remember her."

"Then we'll go together to meet her and see if we can get some answers," I say. It takes all my self-control not to draw her to me and tell her we're going to figure this out. But the last person who needs to see that is Katka.

"Can I speak to you for a moment?" Katka asks me, then stares pointedly at Estrella. "In private."

A shadow flickers across Estrella's eyes, but she says, "I'll wait outside in the hall."

The moment she walks out, Katka whirls on me, eyes blazing. "What are you thinking?" she demands, crossing her arms. "You're actually going to let a Nazco enter the Artifacts Room? It holds some of our greatest treasures!"

My jaw clenches. In the past, I've always thought Katka's and my bickering has been annoying, if sometimes fun since she's the only one who will ever truly cross me. But her challenging me on this doesn't settle well with our history.

"Estrella can be trusted," I grind out. "I once didn't believe she was important to our nation, but after seeing and experiencing what I've been through in the last few weeks, I believe her future is tied to ours. And if I say she goes, she goes. End of story."

"You're making a mistake, Tristan. She's a Channeler, and if she truly is a Conduit, she has incredible power or the potential for it. You of all people know that Channelers are known to manipulate emotions, making immortals yearn to be near them so the Channeler can suck their powers from them. Your own sister was one!"

"Don't cross that line, Katka," I snap. "Do not talk to me about my sister like she was some leech."

But Katka doesn't cower.

"How do you know she's not manipulating you? Has she made you want to kiss her yet? To give her your powers? It's only a matter of time before she'll demand your hand in marriage and take over the throne."

"You overstep your place. This conversation is over."

"You'll see I'm right, but then it will be too late."

I storm out of Katka's workshop into the hallway to find Estrella pacing outside, rubbing her palms together, brow pinched. My heart tumbles seeing her. I take a deep breath. Could Katka be right? Do I yearn for Estrella? Is that natural or is she playing me?

She haunts my dreams.

I make up excuses to see her.

I'd do anything for her.

If we hadn't been interrupted in the practice room, would I have kissed her?

Blast it all. What if Katka's right and Estrella is manipulating me? It's entirely plausible. It would be the perfect Nazco move. They are the experts at sabotage, deceit, and treachery. My sister fell for it. What if I, too, have fallen into their trap?

"Is everything okay?" Estrella asks, reaching for me. But I sidestep her touch and her face twists as if I'd slapped her.

"The scouting team is waiting for us," I growl, unable to hide my anger. "We must hurry."

I march down the hallway that twists around the castle, my thoughts a whirlwind as I try to separate my emotions from my decisions. There's no doubt I've allowed myself to get too emotionally caught up with Estrella. Still, this is my kingdom and I'd do anything for it, even give up my life. Ivana's blood still calls for revenge from the very people Estrella has been trained with. The question is whether Estrella can become our greatest asset.

Or will she be our downfall?

My long legs carry me up the stairs of the South Tower, and I hear Katka and Estrella's footsteps scampering behind.

When we reach the top, I stride to the large wooden door and jam the key into the lock.

"What's the blue stuff on the door?" Estrella asks, stepping beside me.

Before I can tell her to stop, she lightly taps the surface with her fingers. Instantly, she's thrown backward to the ground.

"Ouch," she mutters, rubbing her backside. "That door has a serious kick to it."

"The wood has been infused with an air immortal's power," Katka explains, chuckling lightly under her breath. "They placed a protective barrier on it so only those with the key or the ruler of the Sabians can open it."

It takes all my effort to keep myself from helping Estrella to her feet and snarling at Katka for laughing at her. What's wrong with me? *So what if Estrella fell on her butt?* I think as I push open the door and step into the circular Artifacts Room. My one job is to help get her powers back so she can become our next Conduit.

That's it. Period.

A gasp escapes Estrella's mouth the moment she enters.

"This place is incredible," she exclaims, her voice echoing across the rafters above. She presses her hands together, and her face shines as she spins in a circle like a kid in a candy shop. "There is so much power here. I can feel it."

Katka scowls and gives me a pointed look. I shift uncomfortably, but Estrella doesn't pay us any attention. She steps up to one of the cases scattered around the place and peers through its glass.

"Are these objects like the dagger I have?" she asks. "Because I think I feel an energy source coming out of them."

"Yes." I step to her side, studying her eager expression

for any sign of betrayal. Either she's a good actor and I'm a fool, or Katka is creating an issue out of it all just to be spiteful. "Each artifact has been infused with an immortal's powers and can be used by those who wield it."

"What does that one do?" She points to a compass.

"These artifacts' powers are classified," Katka says.

"The compass's name is Wayfinder," I explain, ignoring Katka's huff. "It will lead the bearer to a location or person they wish to find."

"That is the coolest ability. I love its name, too." She moves to another case, this one full of some of our most valuable and rarest powered artifacts. "And what about that one?" The artifact holding her interest is an old pocket watch.

Should I be paranoid that she seems to be pointing out some of our most precious artifacts? Or that her hands are shaking and her eyes are scanning the cabinet for a way to open it?

"That is none of your business," Katka says and shoots me a look that says, *See?*

I glare back at her. "That one is called Timebender. It manipulates time for a moment."

"What in the Fate's name is *she* doing here?" a woman's voice yells, dragging my attention to the doorway.

Standing at the door are three people, one of which is Valeska. Her scars are prominent, and her mouth is twisted into a snarl. She advances closer, icy-blue eyes narrowed and body leaning forward. Her long white hair crystallizes into icy strands.

"Why have you brought a Nazco Channeler into the heart of our lands?" she demands.

"Finally, someone with sense!" Katka mumbles while Estrella starts backing away.

"You must pay for what you did," Valeska says and lifts her hands. My heart seizes. She's going to kill Estrella.

Shards of ice fly through the air just as I yell, "Stop!"

I'm too late. Daggers of ice hurl across the room, aimed directly at Estrella's heart. She screams and dives behind the case, ducking low. The glass case shatters as icicles slam into it like bullets.

"Valeska!" I command. "Stop this instant!"

Valeska whips her head to stare at me. She doesn't lower her palms, but she does hold off another barrage. The other two with her step to her side, bodies tense and wary.

"She's dangerous. And a murderer. I promised myself if I ever saw her again, she would die," Valeska says. "Let me have my vengeance!"

"She is under the protection of King Julian and myself," I say. "She is not to be harmed."

Valeska lets out a painful sigh and slowly lowers her hands to her sides. Even still, I can see the war playing out behind her eyes. She's not as bold as Katka, but inside she's questioning my orders.

Estrella rises from where she had been hiding and creeps out, her boots crunching on the glass and ice scattered across the floor.

"You say you know me," Estrella eyes Valeska warily, "and though I've lost my memories, I won't deny your face is familiar. You said I killed someone. Are you sure?"

"You killed my best friend and our teammate," she says, nodding to the two standing beside her. Katka gasps, and my heart sinks. Estrella jerks as if Valeska's words physically hurt her. "We fought and you left me with this," she says, pointing to her scars, "to remind me every day the pain you caused. Tristan, you of all people know how I feel. How could you ever protect a Nazco? It's her kind that killed your sister."

Blast it all.

I hate that Katka might have been right all along. I turn to Estrella, desperate for her to tell me it's all a lie, and yet also needing to know the truth. "Is this true?"

Her face is white as ash.

"She speaks the truth," Estrella says in a choked voice.

I heave in a massive groan and rub my palm over my eyes. I trusted Estrella, but I should've listened to Katka's warnings.

Have I doomed us all?

36

SHE WANTS ME DEAD YESTERDAY

ESTRELLA

The Castle of Stará, Slovakia

My skin crawls with fear as an ice spear forms out of Valeska's palm. An Ice Wielder. My pulse thumps against my temples. The same pain that always surfaces in my brain when I'm close to remembering something. It rages in my head, making it hard to think properly. Snippets of a memory cut through the pain.

Broken glass.

Blood.

Friends lying on the ground.

Me touching her ankle and sucking out the power.

And another woman being speared through the heart and falling off the roof's edge.

Falling because I was the one who killed her.

I shudder in horror. Why would I do that? How could I? What kind of person was I before all of this?

Now, the only one keeping Valeska from killing me is Tristan, but I can feel his support wavering. Strangely, this bothers me the most. It's too close to the hurt I felt when I discovered Dion's betrayal.

"I hate to say it," Katka says, interrupting the silence. "But this just proves I was right about Estrella all along. Now do you believe me, Tristan?"

"There's more to the story though, isn't there?" I press, ignoring Katka because as much as Valeska hates my guts, she's the only person here who knew me before I was cast out. She may have answers. "My memories were taken from me, but every so often, I get glimpses of my past. And there's something about our fight that was important. Why were we fighting?"

"You do not remember?" Valeska's brow creases in skepticism. "Is this another of your Nazco tricks?"

"Her memories were stripped from her and she was cast out from the Nazco, sentenced to mortality," Tristan explains.

"Sounds like a trap," the man beside Valeska says.

"Finally someone with sense around here," Katka mutters, rolling her eyes.

"It was on a rooftop," I begin, feeling the memory of that moment clawing at the edge of my brain. "Something about a shard of pottery."

My words don't help. If anything, it makes things worse. The team's expressions darken, and the guy clutches the bag against his chest tighter.

"When did you encounter Estrella?" Tristans ask Valeska.

"She attacked us after we left the Metropolitan Museum of Art in New York City," Valeska says. "We arrived to retrieve the tablet only to discover the place was swarming with Nazco."

New York City? This is new information.

"I think I was trying to stop you," I say, "but I can't remember why, other than I needed that tablet."

"You know about the broken tablet?" Tristan faces me, eyebrows raised.

"She was there when we took it," Valeska adds.

"I was trying to get it," I whisper as shadows of memories dance across my mind. "There was something important about the tablet."

"We thought so too," Valeska mutters and nods to the man on her right. "But it turns out it was a dead end. The tablet Calinda died for was worthless. We still can't quite decipher the message. Go ahead, Nathan. Return it to its place."

Calinda. That was the name of the woman I killed? I shudder at the thought. The man with Valeska nods and hands Katka the leather pouch, who opens it and starts setting the individual pieces into the case. My heart rate kicks up as the need to touch the pottery consumes me.

I inch to the case, but Tristan holds me back. "What are you doing?" he asks.

"I don't know how to explain it," I say. "But the last time I touched it, I think it—"

I can't even say the word *vision* because they're going to think I'm crazy. I press my lips together and study the plaque in front of the case that reads: Dated 1020 A.D. Found in Mexican temple.

"You think what?" Tristan prompts.

"Why are you asking her?" Valeska demands. "Why is she even here? Since when do we work with scum like her?"

I jerk from the verbal abuse, but considering I probably killed her friend, I hold my biting retort in check.

"I think I saw something when I touched that piece of pottery," I tell them. "I could be mistaken—my memories are so cloudy and confusing—but I think you're wrong. I don't think it's a dead end. That tablet has meaning."

"If you took a closer look at it," Tristan rubs his chin as he eyes me warily, "would that help you?"

"Don't let her near that tablet," Valeska says. "It's a trap."

"How is it a trap?" I shoot back, my frustration finally getting the best of my control. "You just said the tablet is worthless."

She bristles and glares daggers at me, swearing under her breath.

"Take a look at it." Tristan nods, indicating for me to go to the case. "See if there's anything there that might trigger a memory."

Katka has set the last piece of the broken tablet in the case. It almost all fits together like pieces to a puzzle. Only a few pieces are missing. My fingers itch to touch it, but when I dip my hand inside the case, Katka's hand slaps me away. I glower back at her.

"Katka!" Tristan growls. "Stand back."

I glance back at Tristan, feeling the heat ebb off of him. The tips of his fingers spark with fire. I can't decide if he's furious at me or the others in the room. His jaw is clenched tight, his eyes sharp as a hawk. He snaps me a curt nod. He's giving me a chance to justify myself, and for that I'm thankful, but today has tested his patience and belief in me.

The writing is vaguely familiar, but it's a language I don't know.

I swallow and refocus back on the tablet. Tentatively, I trail my fingers over the ancient Mayan writing, but nothing sparks a memory.

"It's not triggering a memory," I say, shaking my head.

A cry fills the room. I spin around just as a massive ice spear hurtles through the air, aimed straight for my neck. Frozen with shock, I can't seem to move. All I can think about is the terror that filled the eyes of Calinda, the other Sabian on the roof, before she fell.

Tristan's flaming sword slices through the spear. The weapon jerks slightly from its trajectory. But not fast enough. The icy tip slams into my shoulder. Its force propels me backward.

I'm falling. Screaming. Icy fire erupts through my body. My back smashes against the glass case. But instead of breaking my fall, the case tips over and I go crashing to the ground on top of it.

Tristan stands before me, sword flaming as it knocks away another spear.

My protector.

And then my head smashes against the hard ground. The world blackens.

~

A cool mist sweeps across my cheeks. I'm lying on the ground in a strange place. Slowly, I sit up. My heart races lightning fast. Confusion courses through me as I take in my surroundings.

Where am I? What is happening?

I'm on a stone floor in a long hallway carved out of rock. Strange, blue-lit torches illuminate the passageway. Maybe I was knocked out from the fall and the Sabians put me down here.

Except I'm not wearing the training clothes that I had on. I'm now dressed in a white gown. My long blonde hair falls across my shoulders, and flowers have been tucked into them like I'm entering some sort of ceremony. Is this some weird sacrificial thing that the Sabians do? Knowing my luck, they have some sort of minotaur in here, which will eat me alive.

"Hello!" I call out, rising to my feet. My voice echoes like a distant memory.

I search for an exit, but the only thing other than the smooth stone walls is the white mist, coursing its way deeper into the passage. Standing here isn't going to get me answers or help me find an escape. For all I know, I've been dropped here for some monster to come eat me.

Except, there's something oddly familiar about this whole situation. As if this has happened to me before.

The stone floor is cool against my bare feet. Slowly, I creep my way down the tunnel, straining my ears for the slightest sound. A trickle of music reaches my ears. Fear clamps a hold of me. Is that music a good thing or a bad thing?

I peek around the corner to find the tunnel opens to a

large cavern that looks like a garden. Stalactites covered with flowers hang from the ceiling and glitter-crusted pillars rise from the ground, each studded with what looks like a thousand diamonds. In the center of the cave is a thickly gnarled tree, its boughs laden with pink flowers. Their petals rain over a woman, wearing an iridescent silver gown, sitting beneath it. She's strumming a harp, its melody enchanting.

She appears harmless enough. Maybe she knows how to get out of this place or why I'm here in the first place. Tentatively, I inch up to her, my bare feet sinking into the soft silvery grass.

"Excuse me," I say, but halt a few feet from her. A sense of dread tickles at my chest, warning me not to get too close. "Can you help me?"

The woman stops playing. Her eyes jerk to find mine. They're startling purple like a sunset over an endless ocean. The harp vanishes from thin air.

As if by magic, the woman stands before me. Her long white hair flutters like it's caught in the mist flowing around us. I gasp and step back in terror because there's something otherworldly and terribly powerful about her.

"Yes, I most certainly can help you," she answers, her voice as beautiful as her music. "But are you worthy?"

"I—I don't know," I gulp, and my words choke in my throat. What have I done to be worthy? Nothing.

"Oh, but you do know, do you not? You are unworthy to even be standing before me, and yet, here you are."

My heart slams against my ribcage like a jackhammer. "What can I do? How can I be worthy?"

"The power of the immortals is failing. Our gifts of

water, earth, fire, and air are fading because of corruption and greed. There is great power in you, but it is lost. And because of that, so are you. Which is why you are not worthy."

"I don't understand. Who are you?" I look around. "Why am I here?"

"I am Future's Fate, and I have spoken."

"No." I step closer to her but freeze when her eyes darken. "There must be something I can do. Tell me and I will do it."

She cocks her head to the side. "Destroy the one who seeks to destroy Us."

"Who is this person? And how do—"

My words are ripped from my mouth. Mist rises around me, swirling around until all I see are her violet eyes staring into my soul.

And then darkness sweeps over me once again.

37
FRACTURED TRUST, FORMIDABLE ENEMIES
ESTRELLA

The Castle of Stará, Slovakia

Pain radiates through my shoulder. Cold, icy, shivering agony. I'm shaking all over.

"Estrella!" Tristan calls to me, yanking me away from misty passageways and the strange, purple-eyed woman who calls herself Future's Fate. "You alright? Can you hear me?"

My vision clears. I'm lying on glass and the shards from the tablet. Blood is everywhere. My blood, I realize in horror. Above, Tristan leans over me, his eyes a storm-ridden blue. My gaze drifts beyond him to find Katka, Valeska, and Nathan standing off to the side, vultures ready to slit my throat.

A shudder wracks my body as I remember Valeska's ice

spear aimed directly at my throat, only missing thanks to Tristan's quick deflection. Frantically, I sit up and scoot backward, keeping my eyes focused on Valeska. Her eyes light up, and her mouth twitches.

Despite failing at beheading me, she's loving this. Seeing me bleeding, powerless, and wallowing on the ground. Anger flares up inside me, and I glare back at her.

I never chose any of this. I don't even remember what I did!

"Leave this instant!" Tristan yells at the others over his shoulder. They reluctantly back up to the door and he adds, "Valeska, your actions will be dealt with later."

The moment Tristan refocuses on me, Valeska's hand makes a slitting motion across her neck and she mouths, *I'll kill you.*

My heart dives straight to the pit of my stomach. She fully intends to carry out her vengeance. If I hadn't felt safe here before, I most definitely don't now. I'm not at home here, and I never will be. My own people cast me out. And now it's happening all over again.

The group leaves, but my heart still pounds in part with terror at seeing the blood dripping down my body, but also with anger. She went for the kill, and there's no doubt that if Tristan hadn't been there blocking the spear's path, she'd have been successful.

I need to get away from these Sabians. I need to escape from this castle, but how and where would I go? I may be safe with Tristan, but he can't be with me every second. There's no doubt that if I were left alone with that group, they'd kill me. Sitting around trying to make friends sure didn't help. I need to take matters into my own hands.

My eyes scan the valuable artifacts now scattered on the floor around me thanks to the attack. A timepiece, a compass, a letter opener, and something that looks like a makeup compact. Could one of these help me escape? Each object's power calls to me, tingling across my skin. My hands shake as the temptation to grab one and put it into my pocket tugs at me. But Tristan's sharp eyes are not letting any movement of mine escape his notice. I decide to leave the artifacts—for now.

Besides, I need his trust more than I need an object.

"We need to get you to a Healer," Tristan says. He rubs his warm hands up and down my arms, flickering heat through me. "Your wound is deep."

He pulls off his shirt, revealing a chest of corded muscles and toned abs. I suck in a shocked breath because wow, the guy is ripped.

"What are you doing?" I ask, and the room sways around me. I tell myself it's not because Tristan has taken off his shirt.

But his face is clouded with worry as he rips the shirt in half, clueless to the impact that bare chest is having on me.

"This will slow the bleeding," he explains as he wraps his shirt around my shoulder and tightens it.

His fire power drifts around my body, warm and inviting. He's inches from me, so close I could touch him and pull some of his visik out to heal myself, but I show restraint. He didn't offer it to me, and it feels wrong to take it from him.

"Let me carry you to the infirmary." His voice is low and strained.

"No." I shake my head. One thing I'm starting to realize is I need to find ways to survive without him. If he were to turn on me, I'd be all alone in this world. "I can get up on my own."

Despite my brave words, Tristan helps me stand. The room spins as my movements cause the icy pain in my shoulder to rear up again with a fury. Crying out, I lean against his chest, his hard muscles offering support. My breath hitches as my cheek touches his hot skin. It soothes the aching cold from the injury.

"You sure you can walk?" he asks.

I lift my eyes to stare into his face. His expression burns with intensity, and the sharp edges of his profile warn me how dangerous he truly is. Especially those lips that tempt me with things I must not think about.

Only an hour ago, I almost reached up and ran my hands through that wild hair. I stepped so close to him that our lips were moments apart. And now, despite my pain, the warmth of his gaze curls through me and every inch of me wants to sink into his arms.

No. Stop thinking like that!

I jerk away. I can't believe I almost kissed him. Again.

"You're right," I say breathlessly. "We should get to the infirmary as soon as possible."

He nods, but his fiery eyes tell me otherwise. That maybe he also feels this tension between the two of us. We begin shuffling out of the room, and I shove my feelings for him into a box and lock them up.

What had I been thinking? Tristan and I can never have a future. He's a Sabian prince, while I'm everything his people hate. Besides, I'm starting to allow these feelings for him to cloud my judgment. I need to be smarter about everything.

By the time we arrive at the infirmary, I'm tired and dizzy from blood loss. The Healers get right to work on my shoulder, unwrapping Tristan's bloody shirt and cleaning the wound. Then one of the Healers presses his palms to the wound. A burning fire rushes into my arm and across my skin. I feel my body stitching back together, inch by inch. Tears well up in my eyes from the pain, but I grit my teeth and let him work.

Once he proclaims he's finished, I sit up and assess my shoulder. The pain has vanished, and I'm able to move my arm with ease. It's shocking how quickly my body healed. I'm escorted to a shower room and given a new set of clothes. Once I've cleaned up and changed, it's like the incident never happened. At least on the outside.

Tristan is waiting for me as I step out into the infirmary's vestibule, head down, pacing the room like he's caught in a rainstorm.

"You're still here," I say.

"But of course." Tristan's usual bright and mischievous smile is gone, replaced with lines running along his forehead and mouth dipped into a frown. I can't decide if he's upset that he has to babysit me or if he's starting to worry that the others might be right about not being able to trust me. "Can't have another incident like that happen again."

We weave our way through the corridors in silence until we reach my room.

"What Valeska did was wrong and completely uncalled for," he says. "She will pay for her actions."

"She wanted justice for her friend." I lick my dry lips. "Maybe I deserved it or maybe there's more to the story. But what really concerns me is that you're putting all this work into helping me get my powers back, but what if it doesn't work? What if you're wrong and I'm not this all-powerful Channeler like you think I am?"

He shrugs. "Then you don't get your powers back."

"I don't know who I am, what I've done, or where I belong. And after that attack, I don't even know if I belong here."

I open my door and go to step inside, but he pulls me back to face him. His sharp jaw tightens and a golden curl falls across his forehead, tempting me to reach up and push it back in place.

"What if instead of trying to find out who you were once before, you figure out who you are now?"

The question startles me, and I frown. "I hadn't thought of it like that before."

He's right though. I've been so busy trying to understand who I was that I haven't thought about the person I've become since I first arrived at Nadia's.

"Maybe you're not the same person you were before, but you're still you. Nothing and no one can change that." He lets me go and steps away as if he realized he had been touching a Channeler. "My mother sent a message asking for both of us to have dinner with her tomorrow night."

"Dinner with the Queen?" I gulp. "I don't know if that's a good idea. Especially after everything that happened today."

"Don't worry, she's not going to kill you while you eat cake." His wicked grin is back, and my traitorous heart skips just seeing it. "So you'll come then?"

"You should've started with cake," I say, trying to stay upbeat. "How could I say no to that?"

He nods once and spins on his heels, hurrying away as if one more minute with me is too tedious.

Back in my room, I sag onto the bed. Even though I'm tired, my thoughts fly in a million directions. But they all end up thinking about Tristan's question, which has me more unsettled than ever.

Who am I now?

I'm pouring over a pile of ancient texts when Sofia bustles into my room with a dress fit for a princess. The sunset-purple gown sways from a hanger as she hooks it on the door of my armoire. Slowly I sit up, feeling ragged between my training sessions and Valeska's attack. My hair hangs in tangles over my face, and my clothes are rumpled.

"Greetings, Miss," Sofia says. "I'm sorry to interrupt, but it's time for you to get ready for your dinner with the Queen."

My stomach twists at the thought. I'm sure she's heard about the incident from yesterday. Will this dinner be an interrogation or a welcome meal? Or maybe it's a test to see where my allegiance aligns and how far my powers have grown. Regardless, I need to go and get some answers from her.

"Thank you, Sofia," I say kindly and cross the room. I let my fingers skim across the soft, shimmering material. It's a generous gift. *Too generous*, I think, frowning. "This is lovely, but perhaps I should wear something simple."

"I was just asked to deliver it and help you dress," she says and then hands me an envelope.

I pop open the red seal encasing it to find a note.

Please accept this gift as an apology on behalf of my subjects.
Tristan

I swallow, trying to push away all thoughts of Tristan and my growing feelings for him. Deep down I know there's no way a prince would trot across the world just to help some nobody outcast girl. He's got an agenda, and his people come first. I must never forget that.

"I guess I am wearing this tonight after all," I announce.

Sofia lets out a breath of relief. She slips the material over my head, and the folds settle on my hips. The gown is stunning. It's the most beautiful thing I've ever worn, surpassing the dress I bought with Dion's money at the mall with my friends.

I bite my lip at the thought of Dion. What is he doing right now? Apparently, we knew each other before I lost my memories. What had our relationship been like? He made it sound like we were serious, but if that was the case, why did he lie to me? Why didn't he help me remember my past?

Sofia zips up the back so the bodice hugs my chest tight and the bottom flares out in glistening layers, skimming the floor like. I give a little twirl and the material swooshes out like peonies in springtime. I can't stop the happiness spreading from my lips all the way to my chest. Next, Sofia settles me on a chair and begins to brush out the snarls in my hair.

As she tames my messy curls, I think about that strange woman from my dream when I fell in the Artifacts Room. She said she was Future's Fate and that the immortals' power is failing. What did that mean?

There is great power in you, but it is lost, she had said. When I pushed her for more information, she said I had to destroy the one who seeks to destroy us. I'm guessing *us* meant the Fates.

"There," Sofia says, smiling at me in the mirror, "you're all set. You look beautiful. I'll escort you to the Royal Dining Room."

A portion of my hair is braided, crowning the top of my head, while the rest falls in long golden curls down my back.

"You are a master," I say. "Thank you."

My eye lands on the amulet Dion gave me. I slip it on for safety. Its glass is a murky pink. I follow Sofia into the hallway, but my mind scrambles for clarity. Had that been a dream about the Fate, a vision, or was it more than that? Tonight, I need to get some answers from the Queen, because if anyone knows about powers lost and those seeking to destroy, it would be her.

And if I'm really lucky, Tristan won't be there to distract me.

38
INTO ANTARCTICA'S ABYSS
DION

The Midnight Kingdom, Antarctica

The stairwell sinks into the depths below Antarctica's cold crusted surface. The further BJ and I descend, the atmosphere grows slightly warmer and mustier as if we're breathing centuries-old air. My boots pound on the dust-caked stone steps with the only light from the ancient marks created by a Light Sculptor long forgotten guiding us. Wariness itches at my mind the deeper we go.

"What do you think this place is?" I ask BJ, squinting into the darkness below.

"And why is it hidden away?" he adds. "Maybe this isn't a good idea. It could be a trap."

"Perhaps," I say as I step off the last stair and take in the base of the shaft we just descended. "But why create hidden doorways and secret lighting systems if it's a trap? This stairwell took a lot of work, effort, and power."

The archway dotted with pinpricks of light to my right is the only exit to the rotunda. Clutching the two books I took from the secret room, I step through the entrance. A short tunnel spits us into a cave where we discover a round pool, glistening Arctic blue. The magic of the water illuminates the ceiling, skittering iridescent light across the roughly hewn stone walls.

BJ whistles. "A Traveling Pool."

"Interesting." I chuckle, shaking my head in wonder. "I bet this place was purposely created by someone who wished to be able to enter and exit the kingdom without anyone else's knowledge. And based on the level of dust, that immortal hasn't used this place in decades or longer."

"Or is most likely dead." BJ steps up to the side and stares into it. "The good news for us is it appears as if we've found an exit."

"There is that, but I want to take these books with us without getting wet."

"There must be some equipment around here."

The two of us begin searching the area, hoping to find traveling gear.

"Every Traveling Pool I've ever encountered always has supplies for traveling through the Water Channels," I say as I scour the cracks and roughhewn walls of the cave.

Finally, I find an old wooden chest, hidden in the shadows of the stairwell. "Found something," I call out to BJ, my voice echoing across the ancient stone.

I yank open the chest to find spare robes and oilskins.

The robes were obviously for whoever traveled here to change into, but the oilskin would work for the books.

"You think we should leave the Midnight Kingdom?" BJ asks. "Won't the Empress be suspicious if you just unexpectedly left without any records of your departure?"

He has a point. Every Nazco who exits or enters the Kingdom through the main Traveling Pool is documented.

"We don't have a choice," I finally say and slip the books into the oilskin. "Viamire will make sure we're dead or follow us if we go through the normal channels. I'll send a note to the Empress that I was being followed and had to travel in disguise. And no one knows you're working with me, so you're in the clear."

"Who said I agreed to work with you?" He rolls his eyes. "You're more work than our friendship deserves."

"Your life would be boring without me," I say, heading back into the cave.

"I hate it when you're always right," he grumbles.

I take in a deep breath, gearing myself up for what I'm about to do. Then I step to the side of the glistening pool. "Ready?"

"Why do you sound so ominous? Please don't tell me we're going to see your father."

"It's time for me to finally become the son he's always wanted."

"Oh, this is not going to go well."

Together we pencil dive into the shockingly cold water. I let its magic pull me into the Water Channels.

~

By the look of my father's guard, he wasn't expecting BJ and me to step out of the Traveling Pool.

"Master Dion," he exclaims. "A most unexpected surprise."

"I couldn't agree more." I slosh out of the pool, running my hands through my wet hair. "Please send a message to my father that I've arrived and have important information to discuss with him."

The guard bows and rings the bell, alerting a servant.

"Does your father know you were planning on disappearing?" BJ asks me as we pick out a set of dry clothes from the Traveler's Wardrobe.

"I'm sure the news got back to him about my little run-in with Quadril and his assassins."

"You're talking about when you helped Estrella escape with that Sabian prince."

I glare at him and step into the changing room, pulling the curtain shut as if to indicate the conversation was over.

Once I've changed into dry clothes, the guard alerts us that my father is waiting for me in the library. I nod my thanks and enter the living quarters of my family's mansion. Honey-colored light from the ornate lanterns hanging from the ceiling cast patterns of stars and zigzags across the stone walls like constellations, mimicking my scattered thoughts.

"The last time I was here," I tell BJ, "I thought I'd be leaving permanently. I'd taken the Ghost pendant and planned to disappear from the world with Estrella thanks to the setup you gave me."

The thought sends a rush of anger through me. All my perfectly laid plans are ruined courtesy of Quadril. Tristan showing up and meddling didn't help matters.

"I still can't believe you were planning on living in Eien territory." BJ shudders as we head up the marble stairwell. "I know you're upset it didn't work out for you, but I'm glad to still have you around to torture."

"You might be changing your mind on that soon. This will be a tricky meeting with my father. He's against the Empress, but he also knows I've been assigned to work for her and I stood against Nazco warriors to save Estrella."

"And allowed Estrella to be kidnapped by the Sabian prince."

I shoot him a glare. "Whatever you do, don't remind him of that."

BJ chuckles. "Trust me. I'll be avoiding that conversation."

"Maybe, *maybe*, I can still find a way to fix this and save Estrella."

"Are you sure this girl is worth all this effort? Your life?"

I halt in the middle of the hallway and turn to face BJ. His wet, dark hair hangs over his forehead, and the borrowed clothes are a little too tight for his large, muscular frame.

"When it comes to Estrella, everything is worth it. Got it?"

He lifts his eyebrows. "Loud and clear."

"Good." I continue walking until we reach the library doors. Two guards are waiting for us. My eyes narrow. This is unusual. They open the door for me but hold BJ back.

"Master Cabral has requested only Dion," the guard says. "You will wait here."

"My father doesn't trust my best friend?" I cross my arms.

"He knows of Barden Jasper's ability to suck information from people," the guard says. "Therefore he is not invited."

"Wow," BJ rubs his scruffy chin, "that just makes me sound like a leechy vampire."

Annoyance at my father pricks my neck. "BJ, I'm sorry. You know your way to the kitchen. See if Chef Maria can whip you up some food."

"Don't mind if I do," BJ says, but then leans in close and whispers, "Those books you have are valuable. Use them as leverage to get what you want."

I flash him a grin, clutching the oilskin tighter. He has an excellent point. He gives me a salute and strides away. *Lucky guy.* My stomach growls thinking about food and comfort. But those will have to wait. I need to focus on my talk with my father and how I'm going to convince him to join me in saving Estrella.

I step inside, greeted by the smell of books and firewood. It whisks me back to when I was in the academy, spending long summer nights studying so I could be the highest ranked in my class. Those were the days when I did everything in my power to try to appease my father so he could see my worth.

A total waste. When I moved to the Midnight Kingdom to be closer to Estrella, instead of training to be the next in line to the Cabral family, nothing I said could convince him I was worthy.

"You chose Estrella over your family," he said. "Until you set your path straight and rejoin me, we will not see things equally."

During my last visit, I played the part, making him think

I was finally joining him. This time, he won't be so trusting of me.

"Dion," my father says from where he stands by the fireplace, "this is quite unexpected. After I discovered you stole one of our family's most treasured artifacts, I thought you were planning on disappearing forever."

My gut twists, but I pull myself ramrod straight and turn the conversation in my favor.

"Since when does my father have guards watching his library doors?" I ask.

"Ah, you don't miss a thing. Perhaps I trained you too well." He chuckles and shakes his head. Then his gaze levels on mine. His eyes harden, and his jaw sets. "Why are you here, Dion? What have you come to steal this time?"

"I have found something." I pat the pouch hanging from my shoulder. "Something that could change everything for us."

"Is that so?" my father asks, but his face tells me he's anything but interested. Instead, he pours himself a drink and settles into his chair to stare at the fire.

"I'm here to make a bargain," I press, and move to sit across from him. I set the oilskin on the table between us.

"There isn't an artifact with enough power to entice me to a bargain with you, Dion. You stole from me. You protected an outcast. You allowed the Sabians to take one of our own who is highly volatile, and you fought against your own people. So you must see why I wish to never see you again."

Except he didn't have to see me. He could've locked the entrance of the Traveling Pool and barred me from entering his estate. Yet, here I am. I choose my next words carefully.

"I want the Empress destroyed just as much as you do. I believe Estrella is the key to that."

"It always comes down to that girl, doesn't it?" Bitterness laces his tone. "She has always kept you from achieving your full potential."

"What if I told you I think I found a way to get Estrella's powers back? If I can get her to work with us as our Conduit, then we'd have enough strength to overthrow the Empress. Would you make a bargain with me then?"

He sets his glass down and leans forward. "I'm listening."

39
DINING WITH THE QUEEN
ESTRELLA

The Castle of Stará, Slovakia

My fears are briefly forgotten when I step into the Royal Dining Room. The painted walls are covered with visuals of people feasting and dancing, the images so lifelike that they almost seem to be moving. I blink. Maybe they are. White stone columns ring the room, and the air smells of roasted chicken, herbs, and freshly baked bread. Instantly, my stomach growls and I press my hand to it.

An ornately designed paneled ceiling arches over a long oak table where golden goblets and blue-tipped candles burn from silver holders. A massive chandelier brightens the room, but it's not made of lightbulbs like I would expect. Teardrop glass illuminates the room with an ethereal glow, making me wonder if they are infused with visik like the artifacts are. Three thick red velvet chairs are set at one end of the table, telling me that I won't be eating dinner with the Queen alone. Tristan may be joining us after all. A flutter stirs in my stomach.

I don't dare sit or move until I'm told to. The last thing I want to do is anger these people even more. What would they think of me if they knew I was secretly planning my escape? That I had an eye on those artifacts and had been so close to taking one?

The double doors on the far side of the room are thrown open, revealing Queen Kelli. She looks resplendent, wearing a green gown that shimmers like the forest after it's rained. Tiny gems are sewn to the edges of the gown's full skirt, and the wide sleeves open at her elbows. Her golden crown gleams in the candlelight as she strides confidently into the room.

An entourage follows after her, quickly hurrying to pull back her chair to sit in, but she stops and assesses me with her sharp blue eyes. My body feels like I jumped into a freezing cold river. Someone behind me clears their throat. I'm reminded that everyone in the room has bowed and is now eyeing me warily. Quickly, I dip into a curtsy, hoping that was the right motion.

"Estrella," she says, "I'm glad you decided to join me this evening. From what I have heard, you've been very busy today."

"Thank you for having me," I say, trying to discern her tone, but she's too well-trained at controlling her emotions.

"Now where is my son?" she asks the attendant at her side. "Does he know he is late?"

"Not to worry, Mother!" a voice calls out from behind

me. My silly heart tumbles around in my ribcage. *Tristan.* "I had to deal with some things, but now I'm at your service all evening."

The Prince strides confidently into the room as if he owns the world and goes to his mother's side, giving her a kiss on the cheek. Her face brightens immediately like she just walked through a ray of sunshine. A red cloak is thrown over his shoulders, embroidered with the image of a golden dragon. He tosses it on one of the long tables against the wall, revealing a crisp white shirt underneath that fits his muscular frame.

He turns to face me with a nod but an expression that I can't read. A silver circlet rings his head. It's the first time I've seen him wearing anything that would show off that he's the prince of this realm. I swallow. It's a bit intimidating.

"How are you feeling?" he asks me. "Are you up for an evening suffering in my company?"

"I am hungry." I try to smile, but honestly, my emotions are all over the place. If I didn't need answers, I would run away from this room as fast as I could. But too much is on the table. The conversation with Lexi yesterday nips at me like a festering wound. She needs my help and yet here I am, still so worthless. That must change.

The Queen settles into the largest of the three chairs that sits at the head of the table with Tristan assisting her. Then he goes to another chair and pulls it out. "Please, sit, Estrella."

I hurry and slip into the chair, sinking into the soft velvet cushion. Tristan sits across from me, but when our eyes meet, his intense gaze sweeps over me with such intensity that I feel my face flushing. Quickly, I avert my eyes and focus on the servants setting a plate of food before me.

Roasted duck, herb potatoes, and steamed vegetables served with crusted bread. Ever since I started training, my appetite has increased.

Queen Kelli lifts her goblet and says, "A toast."

"A toast," Tristan mimics, holding up his glass, and I quickly follow suit.

"To new alliances," she says, "and regained powers."

Our goblets clink against one another. I assume this is just a ceremonial thing and not some binding contract between immortals, but I am very much on board with getting the full expanse of my powers back.

"I'm not going to lie," I say, "this food is incredible."

"All our food has been tended and grown by immortals with the power to manipulate plants and the soil. It's what makes our food so delicious."

"Far superior of a meal to what we had at Nadia's."

"I should hope so." The Queen shakes her head. "Dreadful place."

"It wasn't that bad." I shrug, cutting my meat. "Except for the meals when the girls tried to stab each other."

Thinking back to that one meal where Flora and Jamie tried to fight, I should've realized then that we all had powers. Sure, they'd been suppressed, but they were there, lingering under the surface.

"That must have been very hard for you," the Queen says.

"Do you think they can get their powers back, too?" I

ask. "They are all suffering as much as I am. I want to find a way to help them."

"From what my Healers have told me," Queen Kelli says, "the Nazco have placed an inhibitor inside your mind. Every time your mind tries to make a connection to an event in your past, it sends a pulse of pain to keep you from remembering."

"Which must give her those headaches," Tristan says.

"So you think that if I fight against these headaches and push through the pain, I'll be able to access my powers and memories once again?"

"Possibly, but you must realize that everything we know about the Nazco's processes are mere guesses. We could be wrong."

"What you say makes sense." I push my vegetables around my plate. "Nadia would give us tea to soothe the headaches, and they worked."

"I'm sure the tea was made to relax you so you wouldn't fight against the pain," Tristan says.

"I just don't understand why they didn't just kill us," I say.

"The Empress set up the Removal Facilities when she came into power," the Queen explains. "She says it's her way to show compassion to her people. An act of benevolence."

"Benevolence?" I sputter.

"More like twisted cruelty," Tristan mutters.

"Indeed," the Queen says. "I suspect they are used for a deeper purpose. A way to wipe the mind of a powerful immortal so she can then bring them back to her kingdom with no memory of who they once were and who their old allegiances were."

"Ah, so more of a brainwashing facility." Tristan leans back in his chair, frowning.

My eyes widen in shock. "I hadn't thought of it like that before. But what service could they offer to the Empress once they've lost their powers?"

"From what my spies have ascertained," she says, "those in the facilities either die or they're shipped back to the Midnight Kingdom. It is my guess that those who return to the Nazco do still hold some of their immortal powers, but those are a fraction of what they were before. Which is perfect for the Empress. They're moldable, but not too powerful. They become excellent servants."

"Wow." I stare at my plate, my appetite having vanished. "So you don't think I can get my full powers back and neither can my friends?"

"Your powers must have been great for you to have been a Conduit," she says and then turns to Tristan. "You have worked with Estrella. What is your assessment of her powers?"

His firm lips press together as if he doesn't want to say his next words. He sucks in a deep breath and says, "Her powers are like a young child. They are there, but wild and untamed. It will take time and work to mold them. And I suspect they will never be to the levels they once were."

A spearing ache rushes through me. Until this morning, I hadn't realized how incredible it felt to use those powers. I hadn't realized how much I yearned for those powers to come back until now. It's like I'd been given a taste of something so rich and delicious, but only a bite. To know I'll never be the person I once was is devastating.

"So I can't be your people's next Conduit, can I?" I'm

unable to hide the quiver in my voice. "I am a Channeler though, right?"

Tristan doesn't answer; instead he rubs his chin, his thick brows knitting together. The heat of his power seeps across the room, and I want to pull it around me like a warm blanket, keeping away my fears and disappointments.

Queen Kelli studies her son for a moment and then sighs. "It appears to be so," she finally says.

"Then I want to go see the Dragon Seer," I say. "You said she could give me answers and help me find my way."

"The risk is too great now that we know the limitations of your abilities," she says. "If for one moment, she feels you are unworthy or too human, she will spew dragon fire over you."

"Unless she's able to channel the dragon fire," Tristan offers. "She has no trouble with channeling my fire."

"Estrella." The Queen reaches out and touches my hand. Calmness slides over me. It reminds me of the hot day on the beach with Lexi as we laid on the warm sand and let the sun soak our bodies. "I know you want to get your powers back, and selfishly, I do too. If you could be our Conduit, our people's powers could be renewed and we wouldn't have to worry about attacks from the Nazco. But your life is not worth jeopardizing. We will wait and hope our defenses stay strong until another Conduit is born."

"Or try to make an alliance with the Eien or Caladrians," Tristan offers.

The servants exchange our dinner plates with dessert. It's a chocolate mousse topped with smooth whipped cream. I wish I was hungry, but my stomach twists into a knot at the reality that I'm facing.

"I remember those names from my studies with Henrich," I say. "The Eien are from Asia and the Caladrians from Africa. But from what I've learned, they tend to stay out of the war between the Sabians and Nazco."

"This is true," the Empress says. "Somehow we need to convince them that if the Empress conquers us, she will come after them next."

"Then it's clear what I must do," I say. "The Dragon Seer is my only option."

"We will find another way," the Queen says. "I refuse to let you be sacrificed at the whim of Zmeya. It is my mistake for bringing it up to you before. She's far too temperamental."

"Except my life is constantly in danger," I press. "Valeska would've killed me if Tristan hadn't intervened, not to mention that woman who attacked me in my room. I'm not safe here, and I'm definitely not safe with the Nazco. Without my powers I'm a sitting duck, just waiting to be killed. The Dragon Seer is my best hope."

The two stare at me for a moment, and then Tristan rises, muttering and running his hands through his hair. He knows I speak the truth, and yet he hates it.

The Queen presses her lips together and lifts her finger. A servant rushes to her side and helps pull her chair back, and she rises to stand. The servants waiting in the shadows quickly bow, so I scramble to my feet and do the same. My heart beats in hope that the Queen will allow me to see the Dragon Seer.

She turns and glides to the door. My heart dives. She's leaving without granting my request. But then she stops and faces me.

"I lost one daughter already." Her eyes have shifted to the color of the deepest waters in the ocean. "In this short time, you have become like one of my own. I cannot allow you to walk to your death, so we will find another way."

She sweeps out the door, taking my hope with her.

40
FIRE'S KISS
ESTRELLA

The Castle of Stará, Slovakia

The moment the Queen exits the dining room, my legs buckle beneath me and I sag into my chair. Despair threatens to cloud all my thoughts. The Dragon Seer was my last hope and now that has been ripped from me. I can't give up now. There must be something I can do.

"Have you ever played chess?" Tristan asks from across the room.

I blink and focus on his face. "Chess? It's a game, isn't it?"

"Yes." He strides to my side, offering me his hand. "Come, I'll teach you."

I eye the servants standing around, pretending not to be listening. His offer is such a trivial thing to ask, but there is nothing trivial about Tristan. "Based on what my trainer says, you shouldn't touch a Channeler."

"This trainer of yours sounds like he doesn't trust Channelers." His lips quirk, but he doesn't withdraw his hand. "I trust you."

My heart skips at those words. He trusts me? Ever since I can remember, the trust with every relationship I've had has been a fragile thread, snapping all too often. Dion, Chandra, Tiffany, Nadia... even Mrs. Blaire, my caseworker, wasn't who she said she was.

A smile escapes my lips. I rest my hand in his and rise to my feet. The heat of his power flickers across my palm, chasing up my veins. The room brightens and the world shifts, and all I can focus on is him. Tristan doesn't seem affected as he escorts me through a side door.

We step into a sitting room complete with walls of bookshelves and a fire crackling from a large hearth, casting a warm, inviting glow. Positioned around the fire are a set of chairs and a long couch upholstered in a deep midnight blue with gold edges. Porcelain vases and carvings of mythological creatures are scattered across the shelves and small tables. Snow blusters outside the large bay window, but inside it's cozy and inviting. A pair of servants enter the room and line up on the wall along with a guard.

I can't suppress my grin. "Appears as if you need an entourage to stay safe from me."

"You are quite dangerous." His eyes twinkle. He turns to his staff. "You all can step out of the room. If I need you, I'll call."

They bow and find a place to stand outside the open door.

"But they can't quite let you out of their sight," I say.

"You get used to it, but it's more for show." He waves at a small square table by the bay window where a board with pieces is set up sandwiched between two chairs. "After all, no one followed me into the Nazco lair to find you. Not that I'd want them to, of course."

We sit across from each other. "Henrich says I'm one of the first Nazco to be allowed to stay in this castle in over three hundred years."

"Do you feel special?" he teases.

"I can't decide if I'm too special or not special enough."

He begins to explain what each piece means and how they move. I know I should be concentrating on the game pieces, but all I can think about is how his perfectly combed curls have managed to fall over his forehead once again. The curve of his strong jaw. The patient cadence of his voice.

His words still ring in my mind: *I trust you.*

"The ultimate goal is to checkmate the king," he finishes off and then looks up at me. His pupils widen as if he realized I'd been staring at him instead of the board.

I clear my throat, unable to stop the flush from blooming across my cheeks. *Say something quick!* "Basically this game mimics real life. Everyone is after the king or in the Sabian's case, the Empress. And everyone must be sacrificed to do so."

His eyebrows lift. "I suppose so."

"So these pawns, all they can do is move one space? Not much power."

"Yet they are small. It allows them to be sneaky and unassuming."

I move my pawn forward. "After Valeska's attack, I feel even more helpless than one of these pawns."

"You're upset about my mother's decision."

"Do you believe she's right? That I don't have a chance of surviving the encounter?"

"Maybe." He grimaces and moves a pawn. "Or maybe she's being overly protective and the Seer would see your potential and tell you your destiny. But I couldn't live with myself knowing I recommended you to speak to Zmeya and you died."

"I don't have many options." I take his pawn, which unfortunately allows him to steal my knight. "I can't spend the rest of my life hovering by your side, hoping you'll protect me from the next assassin."

"Would that be so bad?"

My heart skips, and my eyes flick to his. What is he saying? That he would be my protector? Or is he insinuating something more? My heartrate kicks up at that thought.

"It might sound fine now, but after a few years, it would get old and you'd eventually resent me." I shrug as if my words don't mean anything, but my thoughts flash back to Dion. Is that why Dion tried to keep me from remembering who I was? Had I become a burden and by making me mortal, it allowed him freedom from having to protect me? I clench my queen in anger, reminding myself to never think about Dion again. I take Tristan's bishop.

He whistles. "Nice move."

"What do you know about this Dragon Seer?" I ask, needing to get my mind off Dion.

"I've visited her twice. Once for myself and once as an escort for my sister. It's my family's tradition to bring every royal child at twelve years old to face Zmeya and receive their fate."

"That young? That must have been pretty scary for you as a kid. What did she say your fate was?"

"My fate is my fate alone." He glances at the door, and then quickly goes and shuts it. The room blankets in a heavy silence as he turns and stares at me intently.

"What is it?" I press.

"What I'm to tell you next, I can't have anyone over-hearing."

"Okay." A trickle of dread pools into my stomach as I rise and follow him to the fireplace. He presses a hand on the mantle, its ends carved into the shape of two dragons, as he studies the flames.

"Only those with high powers can survive her test," he says. "So very few dare to enter her lair. She appears to some as a dragon and others as a woman with flaming red hair and skin covered in tattoos that will remind you of scales."

"Who did she appear to you as?"

"A dragon. When she looked at me, it was as if she could see my very first breath and the very last I would ever take. She knew my secrets and those that were yet to come. It was terrifying. She blasted me with an inferno of fire."

"But fire doesn't hurt you, right?"

"It only physically hurts those who are unworthy." He runs his hands through his hair, which glows golden in the firelight. "But inside, it felt as if she were raking her sharp claws through my core. That's when she gave me my fate."

I gulp, imagining him as a young boy, standing before this creature and trying to be brave and follow his family legacy.

"I remember lying on the ground, unable to get up," he continues. "Finally, my father came and got me and carried me out. He never looked at me in the same way after that day. It was as if he thought since I couldn't walk out of that cave myself, it proved I wouldn't be strong enough to lead the Kingdom."

"Nothing could be further from the truth." I want to reach across to him and smooth out the creases on his forehead. "I've only known you for a few weeks, but from what I've seen, you're the bravest, truest man I've ever met."

His mouth dips into a frown. "That's generous of you, but you've not met many men and you should not think so highly of me. I only came to rescue you from Nadia's for selfish reasons. My people needed a Conduit, and my father ordered me to get you because you were our best option."

"And I'm grateful you did." I step closer to him.

His expression softens. "So am I."

I want to touch him, run my hands through his hair and then down his back. I want to feel those strong shoulders under my palms and the heat of him racing through my body. The fire crackles and pops. Outside, the winter winds howl.

"And now how do you feel about me?" I whisper, my body aching for his heat. "Now that you know I'm not an option for your people's Conduit?"

His gaze catches fire, and he closes the space between us. Those strong hands cup my face, warm as summer's sun.

"Now I don't know if I could ever let you go." His voice is husky and deep. "I don't ever want to lose you."

Breathlessly, I lift my face, my lips hungry for his. A part of me screams to stop. To remember he's the enemy. That he could turn on me in a heartbeat.

But another part is desperate to kiss him. To feel his lips. For him to be mine.

Our mouths crash together, stars colliding. His lips are scorching hot, and the kiss is everything I've fantasized about. I press my body against his hard frame. My fingers drag across his rippled shoulders, firm and solid from hours of practice and training. Adrenaline shoots to my core as his visik races into my body. I gasp from the thrill of it. I return his fire to him, only for him to catapult it back to me.

Our powers are a song, weaving a magical melody of our own making. Embers and fire, flames and passion rise up inside of me. My world is on fire, and every problem and worry is consumed by our inferno.

When we finally break apart, I'm breathless and dizzy. He groans like I'm torturing him and he steps back, putting space between us. Cold air swoops around me as his heat returns to him.

His eyes are dark and heavy. "You are intoxicating."

A spike of fear hits my chest at those words. Is he only falling for me because I'm a Channeler? I never told Tristan, but while Katka had been talking to him privately yesterday, I eavesdropped. I had to know what she was saying.

A chill slithers up my spine as I remember how she said Channelers manipulate emotions. They made immortals yearn to be near them so the Channeler could suck away their powers. Is that why he finds me intoxicating? Is he interested in me or are my powers making him feel this way?

"Has she made you want to kiss her yet and take your powers?" Katka's words vibrate back to me like a poisonous

dagger. *"It's only a matter of time before she'll demand your hand in marriage and take over the throne."*

"I shouldn't have kissed you," I finally tell Tristan, breaking the awkward silence. I back away. I could never break his trust. Never take from him what wasn't mine.

His face jerks and pain crosses his face. "Was it so bad?"

"It's just..."

"It's just what?" he demands in frustration.

How do I explain these emotions swirling inside of me? That I don't know if what he's feeling is even real or something I've manipulated him into thinking.

"I should go," I whisper.

And with that, I flee from the room. Because if I stay for one more moment, I'm going to throw myself back into his arms and demand he never stop kissing me. And maybe prove Katka right.

41
HOW TO GET TO YES WITHOUT BREAKING A SWEAT
DION

São Paolo, Brazil

I can't remember a time when Father actually showed an interest in what I had to say. But the possibility of overthrowing the Empress is too great for him to ignore. The bargain I'm about to offer him is a risk, but skies above, I have to believe he will hear me out.

"Estrella had been studying these three books." I point to them. Father's face remains stoic, clearly unimpressed. "I believe she had been searching for a way to save her two friends, Lexi and Jamie, who had been excommunicated and sent to a Removal Facility."

"What do her friends have anything to do with us?" Father growls.

"These books made me realize she wasn't just looking to rescue them from the facility. She was trying to get their powers back."

I flip open *Origins of Our Kind* and point to the legend of the Fates. "We all know this tale of how the Fates gave the first four women their gift of immortality. But we always believed that the scrolls holding the formula they used to create the first elixir were lost."

Father's eyes darken. He nods slowly as if sensing where I'm going with this. Next, I pull out another book, *The Lost Temple*, and flip it open to where a modern paper bookmark had been placed inside.

"I believe Estrella bookmarked this page," I continue. "It has a description of the Lost Temple of the Fates, where the founding Mothers created the elixirs."

"A description?" Father's voice is breathless, eager. "But that is impossible. All that knowledge was lost."

"Says it right here." I pick up the book and haltingly begin reading the ancient tongue. "Oh, what a sight it is to behold, full of grandeur and perfect beauty. Carved from sandstone cliffs, the temple blends seamlessly with the natural landscape.

"Murals adorn the walls, depicting scenes of the first immortals and the Fates. Symbols of ancient significance are etched into stone floors, guiding the way to the heart of the temple: the Sanctum. Here in this sacred chamber the obsidian pedestal stands, holding the four sacred elixirs."

"Impossible."

"Beware," I finish off, "for the Sentinel watches over all, endlessly safeguarding these hallowed grounds. Only those found worthy will be admitted to unlock its secrets."

"Where did you get this book?"

How much should I tell my father? Do I fully trust him? Hardly. Nor do I wish to give him this information. Keeping it close gives me the upper hand.

"That's not the important thing." I close the ancient tome. "At the time this was written, the elixirs were still active and available. It means that those who have lost their powers could get them once again."

"And in an undiluted form," Father notes, rubbing his chin. "But does it speak of where this temple is located?"

"No." I shift uncomfortably. "That is the tricky part. But if we could find it, Estrella could regain her powers and potentially be able to help us overthrow the Empress."

"I like how you are thinking, son, but no one has seen or had any memory of the Temple of the Fates in over a thousand years."

"Yet this book is obviously newer than that. Someone knew about the temple and kept a record of it, keeping the information tucked away in a hidden corner of the Midnight Kingdom. It would not surprise me if they made sure they were the only ones with this knowledge."

"You are likely correct." Father rises from his chair and begins pacing the room. "I can have my librarian take a closer look at those texts. See if they can divulge any further clues to this mystery."

"There is also Estrella," I press and move to stand before him. "She told me she had a secret. I think this is what she was talking about, and I think she found the location of the temple."

Could it be written on one of the books or scrolls still located in that secret room?

"That is a far-fetched guess."

"If we could get access to her memories, she may be able to help us."

"She's been touched by the Empress' scepter." Father laughs darkly. His words stab at my gut. "There is nothing that can fully restore her memories or powers. She may be able to access pieces and fragments, but to become the powerful Conduit she once was," his eyes swivel to the stack of books on the table, "she would need the Fate's elixir."

"Exactly!" I can't dispel my hope. I refuse to push it aside. "Those fragments of memories could serve us. This information could be a precious memory that her mind refuses to release. Which is why I propose we make an alliance with the Sabian King. Have him hand over Estrella and we offer to work with him in destroying the Empress."

"Trust that hot-headed Sabian?" Father snorts. "Hardly. I've made attempts at working with King Julian, and every time it's been an utter disaster. After that last delivery he sent me, I refuse to speak another word to him."

I sigh heavily and stride to the window that overlooks the garden. The neatly trimmed hedges surround beds of flowers. Their bright rainbow of colors is a harsh contrast to the dull ache shrouding my heart. I thought I had the edge, a way to save Estrella. But once again, I am met with walls, pride, and grievances from the past. There must be another way.

"What about the Eien?" I ask, spinning around to face my father. He's already settling back at his desk and opening up his laptop as if our discussion has ended. "Would they work with us?"

"In what way?"

"Unlike the Sabians or us, they have a living and active Conduit. She could work with Estrella. Maybe even help her recover specific memories."

"Why would they do such a thing?" Father rolls his eyes. "What is in it for them?"

"The Empress knows our powers are the highest they will be for some time since we recently got a resurge to our visik thanks to Estrella. But without a Conduit to replenish those powers, they will fade. The Empress won't wait around. She will attack the Sabians who don't have a Conduit sooner than later. And once she's conquered them, she will come after the Eien."

"True." Father shrugs. "Or the Eien could ally with the Caladrians and stop her."

"And," I press, refusing to give up, "we could offer them information on the location of the temple."

"We don't have that information."

"Yet. We don't have that information *yet*. But if they help Estrella get her memories back, it would be a huge motivator for them."

Father drums his fingers on his desk and leans back in his chair.

"This could work," he says. "But you are forgetting one thing. Estrella is being held captive in the Sabians' stronghold."

"Leave that part to me. Set up a meeting with the Eien and see if we can strike a deal. If we can come to an agreement, I'll find a way to get Estrella to wherever they wish to train her."

"If I do this," Father eyes me carefully, "I want you to

promise me that you'll stand by my side and lead the resistance against the Empress. Will you do that?"

I swore to myself last year to never work for my father. I wanted to be my own man and carve my own path. But if I did this, it could change everything. For the Nazco, the immortal world, and for Estrella.

Pushing aside the hollowness in my gut, I cross the room to stand before his desk.

"You have a deal." I hold out my hand. He smiles, eyes glittering with victory, and shakes my hand.

"Maybe this Estrella girl is working in my favor, after all," he says.

～

"You what?" BJ exclaims after I joined him at the brightly lit sunroom table just outside the kitchen and recounted the deal with my father. "How are you planning on getting Estrella back?"

"You're going to help me."

"Not that again." He rolls his eyes and grabs another pão de queijo. "I already told you I'd need to be magic itself to get into the Sabian King's castle. There's a reason no Nazco has breached the perimeter. Because it's impossible."

He pops the tiny cheese bread ball into his mouth and takes a swig of espresso.

"Will you try?" I press. "If anyone can get information on how to get inside, it's you."

"Now that is true." He sighs. "I am the best. I'll look into it, but you owe me."

"You know I will do anything for you. What do you want?"

"For you to buy me the best tickets to a Flamengo game and come watch it with me."

"You want me to take you to a soccer game?" I ask incredulously as Maria bustles in and sets an espresso in front of me.

"Master Dion," she exclaims in Portuguese. "So good to have you home. I'm going to cook all your favorite foods, so don't you dare think about leaving until you've eaten a full meal."

"Obrigado," I say, giving her my thanks. "You're the best."

She clicks her tongue but smiles as she leaves through the arched doorway and into the kitchen area.

"You're always so busy." BJ shrugs. "So this way I get to force you to spend time with me."

I grimace and take a sip of the hot coffee. Maybe my goal to get Estrella back has been a bit of an obsession. "You're right. I've been a bad friend. I promise to make it up to you."

"Excellent." He grins and pulls out his phone. "I guess it's time for me to start working my magic then." He presses the phone to his ear and starts talking, "André! It has been too long. I was wondering how busy you were today. Uh-huh. Right. I'd just need five minutes of your time."

He winks at me, and I give him a fist bump. He'll find a way. For the first time since Estrella was excommunicated, hope dares to enter my heart. I'm going to rescue her, and once she gets her memories back, she'll remember what we had together.

And how deeply we were in love.

42
A SILENT NIGHT SEARCHING
FOR A SILENT SECRET

ESTRELLA

The Castle of Stará, Slovakia

My lips still burn from the heat of his kiss. The guards eye me warily as I hurry down the corridor, away from the sitting room, away from Tristan. The bodice of my dress feels too tight, and the flowing skirts keep me from running like my feet demand. It's not until I'm halfway to my room that I realize one of them has followed me. I'm not sure if it's for my protection or to keep me a prisoner.

Maybe both.

I stiffen. Is this how I'm going to live my life? Always being trailed? Always being hunted? I want more than just to survive. My steps slow as a new idea forms in my mind.

Just because the Queen doesn't approve of me seeing the

Dragon Seer, doesn't mean I can't go. Instead of taking a right and heading to the West Tower where my room is located, I continue straight until I come to the library where I've been taking my studies with Henrich. I try the door. It's unlocked, but my new guard has followed me here. I need to nip his suspicions in the bud.

"I'm going to work on the homework Henrich assigned me," I tell him.

Thankfully, he nods and positions himself by the door. Breathing a sigh of relief, I slip inside. The moment I do, the luminesce on my amulet Dion gave me softens so it barely registers any light.

The library lies in darkness except for the pale white glow from the snowstorm outside the windows. The wind rasps against the glass like a Wraith's wail, and cold shivers scuttle down my spine.

I dart to the table where Henrich keeps his candle. A matchbox is set beside it, and I mentally thank Henrich for being so orderly. The candle sparks to life, and I grab the brass column and tiptoe to where I remember the map case is located.

The candle's light casts pale beams across the bookshelves. The statues of mythological creatures scattered around almost seem alive. Mermaids with empty eye sockets, beasts with gaping jaws, and serpents with twisted bodies. I bite my lip, reminding myself I survived Roach and his swarm. A few creepy statutes can't hurt me.

The archival map case rests by the back wall. There are hundreds of maps stored inside. I bite my lip, staring at the stacks. I set my candle on the table beside me.

"This might take all night," I mutter.

Resolutely, I start working through the piles. Soon, I realize there's a system to the maps, which speeds up my search. Finally, I discover the one I'm looking for. My heart skips as I gently withdraw it from its rack. An old map dating back to the 1500s.

"There you are," I whisper, smiling down at the layout of the castle and its surrounding grounds.

A quick glance at the doorway tells me I'm still alone, but my heart is now slamming against my chest like an anvil. If anyone here should find me holding this parchment, they would know I can't be trusted. I'd never be allowed the small freedom I've been given.

Gently, I lay the parchment on the table and smooth down the edges. Considering its age, it's well preserved. My eyes scan the lines and layout. It shows the guard station by the lake in the valley below where Tristan and I entered the Sabian Kingdom through the Water Channels. A village called Malá Franková rests on the other side of the lake. I suppose I'd been too busy trying to run from Chandra to notice it. There are several other smaller villages nestled away in the forest surrounding the castle with narrow paths connecting them together.

But these don't interest me. I'm looking for Zmeya's cave. My fingers trace over each section until I find it. Its entrance gapes open like the jaws of a monster. It's set in the mountainside not far from the castle walls. And then I spy something else.

"A path," I whisper, my pulse beating against my eardrums, "and it runs from the castle straight to the dragon cave's entrance!"

If I could somehow get around the guards, I could make

my way to the dragon's cave on my own, face Zmeya, and finally get the answers I seek. Voices fill the silence, and my amulet sparks red. My eyes jerk to the door. Someone is out there.

I'm about to pick up the map and tuck it away when another set of words on the map catches my attention.

Tichá Túnel

I frown, translating the words from Slovak. *Silent Tunnel.* The cartographer wrote those words at an opening in the castle's garden. A tube-like sketch snakes its way from the castle and through the heart of the mountain until it opens up at the mountain's base in the valley below.

Does this tunnel still exist? If so, this could be a way to escape. Do others know about it or has the knowledge been forgotten? Heart pounding, I slip the map back into its slot and shut the case's door.

A figure shuffles through the doorway and I scamper to a nearby shelf, pretending to put a book away. The last thing I want is to be found near the map case, evidence of what I'm up to. The pale light illuminates Henrich's wrinkled face just as I grab a random book off the shelf.

"What are you doing here at such an hour?" he demands.

"Couldn't sleep, so I thought I'd get some extra studying in." I hold up the book. My nerves zing, but I press on a smile and join him.

His frown deepens as he takes in the book and then me. "Since when are you interested in the composition of tectonic plates?"

Crap. He may look a hundred years old, but his vision is sharp. "I've heard that Earth Shifters can cause all sorts of havoc. I figured it might be good knowledge just in case I run across one." His frown deepens, and his eyes cast around the library. I need to get out of here fast. "But you know, I'm feeling tired now. Guess studying geology is the perfect solution to insomnia. I'll see you tomorrow first thing. Good night!"

I set the book on the table and quickly exit the room before he can call after me. When I step into the hall, I rush to my guard with a shocked expression on my face.

"Sir!" I say breathlessly. "You have to help him. Henrich is unwell. Please, hurry!"

The guard's eyes widen, and he bursts into the library. Grabbing the sides of my dress, I break into a sprint down the corridor, darting around the corner and tumbling down a series of stairs until I burst outside into the cold wintery night. Hugging the stone walls, I work my way through the outer courtyard, keeping myself tucked close to the shadows. Snow bites my cheeks, and the icy wind whips my long hair free from the intricate braids that Sofia worked so hard to weave.

I didn't think this all through, I realize. But then there wasn't time nor the opportunity for me to go back and change or put on a coat.

You're from Antarctica, I remind myself. *You should be fine with the cold.*

Except my body trembles regardless as if it only has memories of the thick, hot air of Florida. After some time, the North Gate rises up just ahead of me. It's smaller than the main entrance that I came through with Tristan and only manned by four guards, two striding in front with two others on top of the lookout above.

The gate's iron plates gleam almost silver. They've been infused with an immortal's visik, I realize. Which means it will take more than just barging through to exit. Based on what I saw from the map, the path to the dragon cave is just on the other side, butting up against the mountainside.

Sure there might be only four guards, but how will I get around them or convince them to open the gate? I crouch behind a cart and study their actions. What might their powers be? Could I find a way for them to help me get through without their knowledge? I bite my lip. If I fail or they catch me, I'll likely be sent to prison, especially if General Sage has any say.

But if I don't do something, is my life really any different other than I'll be living in a different sort of cage?

"You are brave and smart." I give myself a pep talk. "You were once a Nazco Conduit with high powers. You can do this."

I take in a chilling breath and rush up to the guards. "Excuse me!" I say, rubbing my arms and pinching my face into a look of desperation. "I need your help."

"What are you doing running around?" the burly guard, who must be over six feet tall, demands in a booming voice. "A storm is blowing in from the north."

"I seem to have gotten lost." I crouch my shoulders and hang my head. "I can't figure out how to get back home."

The burly guard chuckles darkly and shakes his head. He reverts to pacing in front of the gate. He obviously did not recognize me as the dreadful Nazco ex-Conduit. This is a surprise, but maybe these men weren't at the front gate upon my arrival last week or they just lump all women together. Regardless, I can use this to my advantage. I turn my focus on the thinner guard with a goatee. Currently, the man is frowning with worry as he takes in my dress's thin material and slippers. My pale chest rises and falls as if I'm out of air, which to be honest is not far from the truth.

"Please, kind sir, help me." I reach and take his hand, expecting him to jerk back, but he doesn't. A smile curls across my lips. "I have trouble seeing in the dark. Could you show me the way back to the Queen's Garden? I know my way from there."

I don't have to pretend to be terrified or cold. My body trembles, and my teeth clatter like old bones. But that's not what I'm paying attention to. My whole focus is on pressing my hand against his as I search his body for his visik. Then I feel his power. I'd been hoping it was strength or stealth or some sort of skill to escape, but as my mental grip wraps around his visik's thin cord, I realize his power is to seek and find.

Ugh. I should've focused on the bigger guard because Goatee's power won't help me.

Goatee pulls his hand away to pat my shoulder. "There, there now. It's going to be alright," he says calmly. "I'll be happy to escort you back to the garden. Come along."

How can I control his power that's now racing through my veins? A thousand images start to flash before my eyes, one after the next, all calling out to be found.

Gems, gold, immortals, people screaming, artifacts demanding attention, the Queen's voice...

My vision swims. It's too much. Too much information.

"Miss," the man's hand steadies me, "please do not pass out."

What had Tristan told me while training with the fire?

Think of yourself like you're one with the fire. Like it's a part of you and it's ready to be shared or tucked away. This is the same thing, isn't it?

I clench my fists, forcing my mind into focus. I shove back all the objects demanding to be found and focus only on thoughts of the dragon's cave. A tugging yanks at my chest, begging me to turn back to the gate.

It's working. It's trying to take me to the cave!

Except the guard is practically hauling me forward, down the path and away from the gate. My insides twist as if crying out to go back. I glance over my shoulder, every muscle screaming to stop and turn around.

"The Queen's Garden truly is a lovely spot." The guard is rambling on like we're here strolling around for fun. "It's too cold for the flowers this time of year, but in the summer, I try to make an effort..."

He continues, but my mind flickers through possibilities until a new idea slams into me. Plan B. The map had shown a secret tunnel beneath the castle with its entrance being in the Queen's Garden. I'll use his power to find the secret tunnel. How long will his power last inside of me? The last few times I used Tristan's power right away so I'm not sure how long it will last, but if I don't use it up, it might linger for a few minutes.

"And here we are," the guard announces, smiling down at me. "Will you be able to find your way home from here?"

Hedges are blanketed in snow that look like fluffy pillows with tiny stone paths wandering around them. A few barren trees are scattered around, their branches fingering out and bending in the cold breeze. I tilt my head and squint in the pale light created from the intricate lanterns hanging throughout the area. Inwardly, I gather his visik and focus on the image of the secret passage from the map.

My chest jerks as his power grabs at my soul and tries to physically drag me to its source.

The guard frowns. "You alright, miss?"

I must look like a ragdoll being jerked around. "Yes, this is perfect." I clamp on a smile. "Whew, that wind is blowing me all over the place. Thank you for your help. Goodbye."

The guard nods but hesitates. "Should you need anything else, you know where to find me."

"Excellent, and thank you." I need him to leave ASAP. His power is zinging through me, begging to be used or sloughed off. Who knows how much longer it will last?

He strides away while I scramble down the path in my snow-drenched slippers. My toes are nearly frozen. I'm not sure if I can feel any part of my body, but the tug is hauling me forward. I'm a fish dragged through the water. I clench my fists, shrugging off the cold, and hurry through the garden until I come to a fountain hidden behind a row of thin, tall bushes. I push my body through the branches. A few forgotten coins lie in the fountain's outer ring, but other than that it looks as if it's been forgotten. The sides are crumbling, and bushes have grown around it.

My control over the power scatters once again, and suddenly a thousand things demand for me to find them.

A book.

A screaming child.

A sparkling crown.

The Wayfinder Compass.

I clamp my hands over my ears and close my eyes, imagining the tunnel on the map and only the tunnel. And then my fingers itch with the need to touch something.

My eyes fly open and narrow on the pipe on the side of the fountain.

"Okay, so that's weird," I mutter, "but let's go with it."

I follow through with the sensation and seize hold of the pipe and pull. A section of the ground to the right of the fountain rumbles and shifts to reveal a gaping hole. A blast of stale, warm air hits my face. My heart tumbles around in my chest like it's clapping at my discovery. Crouching down, I peer into the murky darkness. It's hard to see very far, but it's clear that a set of stairs leads down to a narrow passageway below.

"Tichá Túnel," I whisper.

Except once I go down there, how am I going to find my way in the darkness? Then I remember the garden torches. I squeeze my way back through the bushes, glancing around to make sure no one sees me. I quickly unhook the lantern from its post and duck back to the fountain's secret hiding place.

Stealing a breath, I slip down the stairs and into the secret passageway, hoping the guard's power lasts long enough for me to find the dragon's cave.

And my destiny.

43
TRIAL BY FIRE WILL CONSUME YOU
ESTRELLA

The Cave of the Dragon, Slovakia

y torchlight flickers across the stone. The shadows are like spectrals dancing on a moonless night. Chunks of rock litter the ground from what I'm guessing is debris fallen from the ceiling. I gather some in my hand and use them as markers every so often to make sure I can find my way back to the entrance.

If I survive the Dragon Seer.

The tunnel splits, one section continuing in a downward slope, which I'm assuming will eventually lead to the base of the mountain. The other section cuts left. Based on my memory of the map, it should lead me to the dragon's cave. A part of my mind dares to entertain the idea of just continuing down the tunnel, all the way to the valley, and then into the forest where I could run, run, run away.

But then what would I do? I certainly can't go tromping through the forest in this dress. I have no money or warm clothes, and my powers are limited and erratic at best. *No*, I sigh wearily, I need to be smarter about this. I may be stronger and wiser in the ways of the immortals than I was at Nadia's, but it's not enough to survive on my own.

I take a deep breath and turn left. This path has been less used, and parts of the walls have crumbled inward, forcing me sometimes to twist sideways so I can shimmy through the narrow gaps. It quickly takes an incline, rising up until the ceiling is so low that I'm forced to duck my head to continue. Finally, I reach a dead end.

"Are you kidding me?" I exclaim in frustration and kick at a rock. Which only earns me a stab of pain in my foot. "There must be some sort of way out of here. They wouldn't build a tunnel for no reason."

Desperately, I run my stiff fingers over the sharp, dusty rock wall, hoping for some sort of exit. I'm about to turn around in defeat when my eye catches a metal lever on the ground nearly covered up in rubble. I push aside the rocks until the lever is free and then pull back on it, praying it doesn't make the ceiling tumble down on my head.

A portion of the wall opens, and a gust of snow-flecked wind swooshes over me. I'm so happy, I practically dance out onto the snow-caked ground. But my delight is short-lived when my eyes land on the gaping cave entrance carved out of the side of the mountain connected by a narrow path above the rocks below. It looks like the maw of a monster, ready to devour those who dare come too close. Rocks cut down from the roof like teeth, and the wind wails across the entrance like a banshee. It snuffs out my torch.

I take in the snowy, ice-slathered mountainside before me and then the cliff's edge not fifteen feet behind me. This wind seems to have a mind of its own, and I can imagine it picking me up and hurling me off the edge. This has to be the entrance.

My legs tremble, a mix from the cold and fear. I walk along the narrow path and dart through the cave's opening. Warm air hugs my skin, heavy as a wool blanket. My ice-cold body soaks in the heat like it's parched. My eyes adjust to the semi-darkness. The walls are full of stick figures and sketches like they were drawn with a rock, but instead of the lines being white, they're red, glowing as if carved from volcanic fire.

Letting the crimson light guide me, I shove my fear aside and creep deeper into the cave, leaving behind the howl of winter's wind. The ceiling opens up, taking me into a large space that looks like a warren of tunnels spearing out of it like octopus tentacles. The air smells of ash and fire and something else that I can't quite place, but it's unsettling and my steps falter. A scratch, scratch, scritch sound cuts through the silence. It's coming from a woman crouched on the floor, carving the wall with a red-glowing coal.

"Zmeya," I whisper under my breath.

Suddenly, the woman is standing before me as if saying her name summoned her. She's nothing like I expected or how Tristan described her. Her gown is a simple hemp shift tied at the waist with a rope. There are no signs of any tattoos or scales like Tristan mentioned. Her hair is brittle and gray as ash. Could she be Zmeya's assistant?

"Are you Zmeya?" I ask. "If not, could you please show me the way to her?"

Amber eyes glitter in mirth as she lifts a single eyebrow. "Aren't you a fun surprise?" Her voice is deep and old, and my heart thrums like a butterfly warning me to flee. "I don't think I've ever had a Nazco dare enter my home. How intriguing."

So, she is the Dragon Seer.

"The Nazco took away my powers and abandoned me," I say, and this time I'm not able to hide the anger and resentment in my voice. "So I don't have any allegiance to them."

"Can you blame them?" Zmeya clucks her tongue and shuffles toward the center of the cavern where a fountain stands flowing with lava liquid. "You were the one who betrayed them first."

I frown. "What are you talking about?"

"The moment anyone enters my home, their mind whispers their secrets to me." She drops her coal into the fountain, and it melts instantly. "It's why very few dare enter and most beg for a swift death."

I've willingly allowed this woman to snag me into her net, and now I'm her captive. I should be terrified. I should fall to my knees and beg for her mercy. But captivity is not new for me.

"I've been a prisoner for as long as my mind remembers." I walk closer to her even as my legs beg to flee. "I'm tired of waiting around for someone to kill me or use me or manipulate me. That's why I'm here. I've heard you can show my destiny, but I'm hoping you can give me more than that."

"Fascinating." She taps her long black nails against her

lips, assessing me like a cat ready to pounce. *No. Like a dragon ready to devour.* "And what is it that you want, Estrella Cortez?"

I hold back a gasp. *She knows my name.* The pendant on my chest flares to a bright red.

"I want to know how to get my powers back."

"Are you sure?" She begins to circle me, and with every step her hemp shift begins to change. Gems begin to blink on it like stars, and the hemp material transforms to a deep ocean blue. Her snarled mane unravels into long red hair, flowing over her shoulders and down her back like lava. Tattoos appear one by one, glowing like the carved embers on her walls. I suck in a startling breath as the weight of her power shivers over my skin, dangerous and inescapable.

"There was a time when every waking moment you trained to get revenge for the deaths of your parents," she carries on.

Shock strikes my chest. "I don't remember my parents. What happened to them?"

"And then there was a time when every waking hour you searched for a way to save your friends, Lexi and Jamie. Do you remember that hidden room where you combed through ancient texts and scoured secret scrolls?"

My head spins, trying to process her words. Or are they lies?

"Your guilt for letting them take the fall for what you did plagued you."

"You lie." I dig my nails into my palms, anger curling through my stomach at her accusations, hitting me like sharp stones.

"So now you come to me asking for something

completely new. But what is it that you really want, Estrella once Conduit of the Dreadful Nazco?"

A raging headache spears my head. I rub my temples. Has she triggered the implant the Nazco placed inside my head to unbalance me? Or is everything she said true and it triggered the implant? Before I can answer, she presses on.

"Or maybe you want the Sabian Prince. He could be the love of your life, but then we Sabians would never accept a Nazco as their princess." My heart stutters at the thought of Tristan, his kiss still branded on my heart, and the truth of her words. She freezes midstride and whips to face me. "Except there is another...one you thought would be your other half. Perhaps you'd wish to be reunited with your lost love?"

My breath is stolen. Is she speaking about Dion? The memory of him fighting to save me haunts me. "Since you know so much more about me than I do, why don't you tell me?"

"It's all there, on the tip of your mind, waiting for you to accept it. But each of these desires leads you down a different path." She opens her palms, holding them face up before her. Flames erupt from them like torches. "And many lead to the destruction of the Sabians, which makes you an enemy. My enemy."

Terror strikes. Her fire is powerful. It would consume me. Tristan always controlled his power, letting it slip through my veins like honey, moldable and ready to be used. But hers is a fiery whip, ready to seek and kill.

"I'm not here to hurt the Sabians," I desperately explain. "You must believe me. You said not all paths lead to your destruction. How can I choose my path when I don't even understand who I am or what my powers are? How can I save my friends?"

"You were born for greatness," she continues as if I never asked a single question. "Your parents knew this and died so you could live to achieve it."

I gasp. Her words slam into me, stronger than any weapon possibly could. Tears well up in my eyes. My parents died? For me? "That's a lie." Except my heart screams that it's the truth.

"But now your powers are a fraction of what they once were. You are weak, powerless, and useless. Easily disposed of."

Each word is a slap in the face. They're all true. And yet, I refuse to believe them.

"No!" I shout, my voice echoing through the mountain like a battle cry. Lexi, Jamie, Mara, Zayla... their faces flash through my mind, and my visik surges deep within me. "I can't, I won't be useless. My friends are depending on me to help them. I promised, and I will fulfill my promise. So tell me, Dragon Seer, my path to regaining my powers so I might save those that I love."

The flames in her hands rise, and she tosses them at me. My vision is consumed with fire as her visik surges around me, seeking to devour. It's a cord of dragon scales, snaking around me. No, it's a dragon tail that has wrapped around my body, squeezing my core so tight I can't breathe. Her yellow eyes home in on me.

Hot tears stream down my face. My skin sears as the flames lick every inch of me, finding every crack and weakness. I fall to my knees, screaming in agony.

"Let go!" I yell.

"You are my enemy," her voice floats through my mind, "so you will suffer the same fate as your father and mother."

Those nails are now talons, which she rakes down my arm. My shrieks are drowned in an inferno. The pain is too great. I need it to stop. Fingers stretching, I grasp her hand and I feel the power of her visik running beneath her skin. I grab hold of it and yank back, pulling it to me.

It surges through my veins, melding with mine. She jerks, and her grip loosens as if I've taken her by surprise. I use that blink of a second to grasp her wrist and take more of her power for myself.

"You dare to take my powers?" She roars and wrestles to free herself of me.

I'm not strong enough. My power is tapped out. I don't have much time.

"Tell me how to get my powers back!" I scream, unwilling to let go. I use every ounce of her own power to survive a heartbeat longer.

"Find Ami," she finally relents. "Have her take you to the World of Between. There you'll find what you seek."

The answer calms me, and I release her.

"You are a greater enigma than I first thought," she says. "They froze a portion of your mind and soul in the mist of forgetting, but your heart is strong. You did not come for your destiny, but I shall give it nevertheless. Caught between fire and lightning's might, your rule may be fierce, but it will also bring light."

The fire vanishes. I'm lying on the ground, gutted. Cold, so so cold. I'm ash and bones. A husk of a soul.

But I survived.

44

AN ENCHANTED AGREEMENT
OR A DEVIOUS DECEPTION?

DION

Chichén Itzá, Mexico

I t would be a lie to say I'm not nervous. My heart clips
as fast as a motor as I walk down the dusty path beside
my father through the Mayan ruins with BJ and our
two guards. Even though my skin is still damp from traveling through the Water Channels, the hot breeze bites at
my skin, and my sunglasses do little to keep the blazing
Mexican sun from practically blinding me.

"I'm still surprised the Eien agreed to meet us, and in
Nazco territory, no less," I tell BJ.

"Chichén Itzá is sacred ground to all immortals," BJ says.
"I figured it made sense to meet here as they know we'd
never defile the ground where our ancestors were once
worshiped."

"How far we have fallen," I mutter. It still shocks me how we immortals had once been so revered and powerful that mortals worshiped us. "Look at us now. Forced to live in secret, scrabbling for position and power in this world."

"If those books you found are accurate," Father says in a low voice so we're not overheard, "perhaps we may regain the level of our powers once again."

"I can't decide if that's a good thing or not," BJ says, eyeing the stone statues of eagles and jaguars consuming human hearts.

I lift my eyebrow. "You may be right, my friend."

We enter the heart of the city where the stone step pyramid spears into the sea-dipped sky. The iconic structure still strikes awe in me even though I've visited it before. It stands almost one hundred feet high with steps that lead to where the temple sits on top like a proud crown.

The most difficult part was securing the grounds and making sure only those loyal to my father were allowed here during this meeting. We need to keep this a secret from the Empress.

A guard steps up to my father. "The Eien ambassadors have arrived. They are waiting for you in the inner sanctuary."

"Excellent," Father says curtly. "Make sure they are searched for artifacts. I don't need any surprises."

The guard nods and hurries off while we head over to a small thatched-roof hut. I duck into a changing room, complete with a bundle of clothes with my name on it along with a stack of towels. I tug off the wet shirt and dry myself.

My mind whips back to that field trip where I'd been secretly assigned to watch over Estrella. It was supposed to be just a job, but the moment I first laid eyes on her, I knew I was in trouble. The curve of her smile. The knowing look in her eyes. The way her hand tucked into mine as we traveled through the channels until her arms were wrapped around my body. I never wanted her to let go.

I rub my chest, the memory sharp as if it only just happened. *Blistering stars, she tortures me.* How did we go from an innocent field trip to trying to overthrow the Empress? I shake my head and jerk on the black pants and collared black shirt. I shrug on the jacket and slip the envelope that I hope I won't have to share into its pocket. Once I step out of the changing room, BJ slides to my side.

"Do you have a backup plan if this doesn't work?" he whispers, eyes darting to where my father is speaking to one of his advisors.

"It will work," I say because it has to. "Any luck on finding a way into the Sabian stronghold?"

"I have a man on the inside. He's working on some options for us." BJ rubs the side of his face, a hint of a beard forming, and winces.

"The options are that bad, huh? Has your insider even seen Estrella? Is she still there?"

"He has confirmed her presence is at the castle. Apparently, she's not a prisoner but a guest of the king."

I should be pleased by this, but a frown pulls at my lips as I remember her holding Tristan's hand as they were sucked into the Water Channels. "Every day Estrella is with them puts her at greater risk. Also, I want to be the one who finds her."

"That's a huge risk." BJ crosses his arms, clearly unimpressed with my idea. "You're a Cabral. They hate your family. Someone will recognize you right away."

"Then tell your man to get creative," I say with a devious grin just as the guard tells us the area is cleared and ready.

"You may owe me more than just a soccer night," BJ grumbles.

"You're absolutely right about that."

Father joins us, taking a swig of a drink as if this whole business is stressing him out. "This meeting will be with only the two of us." He looks pointedly at BJ.

I resist giving my father a dark look. He could've decided this before BJ journeyed all the way here. Right now, I need him working with me, not against me. "Are you okay waiting here?" I ask BJ.

"This might be a good time for me to make some inquiries," he says. "There's someone I want to meet, and it needs to be in person. That said, I'm not looking forward to entering the Water Channels again, but it's the fastest way."

I rest my hand on his shoulder. "Take care. Meet me back at my house as soon as you can. Be careful."

He nods and takes off, grumbling under his breath about how his feet are going to turn into prunes.

The tunnel leading up to the secret temple inside the pyramid is narrow and steep, but my legs eagerly eat up the distance, ready to tackle this problem head-on. I'm about to step into the inner chamber when Father holds me back.

"Don't promise them anything you can't deliver," he whispers. "And trust only half of what they say."

Do I spy a trickle of doubt and worry in my father? It doesn't fit his profile. He has never worried for me, only demanded of me. I lift my eyebrows but nod. My father has gained influence and wealth over his lifetime, and it's not from his charity. During every meeting, his ruthlessness and cunning methods have always spoken the loudest.

I duck through the stone entrance engraved with symbols into El Castillo. Torches are set around the perimeter, illuminating the splotched and tired stones built a thousand years ago. A red jaguar throne rests in the center of the chamber, but my eyes are focused on the three Eien delegates standing still as stone statues.

One man stands off to the side wearing a black button-down shirt. His long hair is tucked back in a knot at the base of his skull. Tattoos run up the sides of his neck, and his eyes look almost silver as he studies me like he's ready to rip my heart out. He must be their guard.

The other man wears a black jacket with a white shirt beneath it. He has short, wavy black hair and dark eyes. He shifts his body sideways as if he's ready to pounce between me and the pale woman beside him. Which tells me she's the one I should focus on. I bow to her.

"Hello," I greet in English. "Thank you for traveling here to meet with us. I am Dion Cabral, and this is my father, Gabriel Cabral."

Her pink lips press together. Her kohl-lined bright blue eyes that only a Channeler would have narrow as if my words hold poison. Could she be their Conduit as well? Not likely since they wouldn't let their Conduit leave the safety of their borders, right?

"I am Ami, and this is Sensei Haruki. We were intrigued by your proposition, which is what brought us to you."

Unlike the two men who are wearing modern clothes, hers is a mix of modern and traditional Japanese. A tight red dress with a thick crimson sash hugs her waist. The sleeves open wide at her elbows, revealing a tattoo of a bird in flight. The bodice cuts open in a V-shape, revealing an ornately gemmed necklace, glimmering with some sort of power that hangs between full breasts. I swallow hard and rip my eyes back to hers.

Now she smiles at me. I'm a mouse caught in her snare.

"Artifacts are restricted from these hallowed grounds," I snap, nodding to her necklace.

Our guard steps up to Ami, holding out a hand. She waves it away.

"This necklace is a part of me, and I, a part of it." Her voice is like a song. "Either it stays or we leave."

"What power does it hold?" I ask.

Sparks flutter over my palms as my wariness for these people intensifies.

She clicks her tongue. "As if I'd tell you."

"She is a Channeler, and her amulet holds a siren's power," Father says, "which makes her words have a strong influence on others."

"So it is true." Sensei Haruki's eyes widen. "You, Master Gabriel Cabral, not only have the power over stone, but you can also identify the power in others. High powers, indeed."

"Enough," Father snaps. "I don't have all day for chit-chat. Dion, go ahead with your proposition."

I nod, clenching my hands behind my back to hide the sparks eager to escape.

"I'll get right to it," I begin. "We wish to overthrow the Empress from her tyrannical rule. Since our nation does not have a Conduit, now is the perfect opportunity to do so.

Especially since we believe that our ex-Conduit can still regain her powers and be swayed to join us."

Ami's eyes flicker in interest. "What role do you see us playing in this scheme of yours?"

"We wish for you to help the ex-Conduit regain her powers," I say.

Ami and Haruki laugh.

"Why would we ever help you find a way to regain immense power when you've done nothing but cause us pain and suffering?" Haruki asks.

"Because we believe this ex-Conduit once knew the location of the lost Temple of the Fates." Their laughter dies at my words. I press on, "And we think this temple holds the Fates' formula for the immortal's powers."

"Impossible." Ami snorts.

"Our proposition," I say, "is for you to help our ex-Conduit regain her powers and memories and we will share with you the location of the temple."

"Intriguing, indeed," Ami says. "But what proof do you bring us? Surely, you don't believe we'll trust a Nazco's word only?"

I didn't want to share this next piece of information, but if I can help Estrella, I have to try. The envelope practically burns in my palm as I pull it out of my jacket pocket. I hold it out to the Eien. Haruki takes it and cracks open the fold. He pulls out the photos I took of the ancient books I found in the secret room and a few interior pages.

"What's this?" Haruki asks.

"These two ancient books were in the possession of our ex-Conduit before she was excommunicated."

"This proves nothing," Ami says, passing back the envelope.

"If you look carefully, you'll find they mention the Temple of the Fates. It proves that the temple was still standing far more recently than any of us suspected. And if we can find it, we can find the formula."

Ami and Haruki begin whispering in Japanese too quietly for me to catch their words. Haruki seems to be against the idea, but interest sparks in Ami's eyes. She's curious. Finally, the two nod at each other and face us again.

"What have you decided?" I ask.

"We agree to your terms," Ami says. "But we wish for it to be a binding agreement of powers."

My heart sinks. A binding agreement of powers is dangerous. It requires all participants to place a portion of their powers into their signature as they sign the document. If either party breaks their agreement, their portion is given to the other party.

Father swears under his breath, muttering, "I knew they'd ask for that." Then louder, he says, "That is not possible. I do not sign binding agreements."

"Then we are finished here," Ami says, and the three Eien make for the doorway.

Panic washes over me like cold rain. I can't let them go without an agreement. I've come too close to let this slip through my fingers.

"Wait," I call out. "I will sign it."

Ami turns around and studies me like she wants to consume my very soul.

"Don't let her influence you with her powers," Father says.

"I'm not." I clench my fists. "I'm doing this for Estrella."

"Estrella?" Slowly Ami's lips curl into a dark smile. "Is that her name? How sweet."

"I'm assuming you brought a parchment," I half-growl, knowing she must have planned for this to happen before she stepped foot in Mexico.

"But of course." Her scent of jasmine swirls around me, tempting me closer. I stiffen against her pull. She snaps her fingers, and her guard whips out a piece of parchment and a quill and hands it to Haruki. "Write the agreement for us."

Quickly, he scrawls out the terms in English and shows each of us.

"This is correct," I say.

Ami takes the quill and signs her name in traditional Japanese letters. The ink shimmers red, indicating her visik has infused into the document. She passes the quill to me, and I sign my name, the ink spilling out silver, sparking like lightning. Ami's eyes flash hungrily at the document and then crash against mine.

"Looks like we have ourselves a deal," she half-sings. "Bring her to Kyoto. We will begin our work immediately. Oh, one more thing. If you betray us, my dear Dion, I'll kill Estrella myself."

She bustles away with her two escorts, vanishing into the dark tunnel. I should feel elated securing this victory. So why do I feel like I've just entered a trap?

45
YOU'VE GOT COMPANY?
TRISTAN

The Castle of Stará, Slovakia

"What do you mean she's gone?" I demand of the guard who just rushed into the sitting room. "You were supposed to watch over her."

I'm tempted to grab the guy and shake him, but I keep my voice steady and the panic tempered.

"She tricked me." The guard is gasping for air, his eyes wide. "Told me something was wrong with Professor Henrich, but when I went into the library, he was fine and she was gone."

"The library?" I frown.

"Yes, after leaving here, she went to the library to study."

Dread spears at my chest. I'm sure Estrella went to the library to find information on Zmeya because she was planning on seeing her without the Queen's approval. I swear under my breath and brush past the guard, hurrying to my room. I grab my sword and a cloak and rush out into the night. A bitter wind nearly sucks the air out of me, but I'm glad for the cold. It chills the fire of panic building inside of me. My best hope is that she got caught trying to escape the castle walls and the guards have her apprehended.

Worst case, she managed to find the Dragon Seer and didn't survive the test. This thought quickens my steps.

"Hello, there," I call out to the North Gate guards. They quickly tighten their stance and snap into sharp bows. "Have you seen a young lady with long blonde hair and blue eyes come past this way? She may have been wearing a blue gown?"

"Yes, your Royal Highness," the thin one says. "In fact, I personally escorted her to the Queen's Garden. She said she was lost but knew her way back from there."

My heartbeat quickens. I was right to come out here looking for her. I'm about to head toward the garden, but I stop as a new thought strikes me. My gaze narrows on the guard.

"Your powers are to search and find, correct?" I say. "Could you find her?"

"Absolutely, your majesty." He nods and holds up a finger. "Give me a moment and I'll tell you what I can find."

The guard steps back and hangs his head, closing his eyes like he's in prayer. Suddenly, his gaze jerks up to lock onto mine. "She's at the Dragon's Cave."

"Open the gate!" I order the guard manning the wall. Instantly, the portcullis lifts, grinding against the howl of the wind. "Your orders are to tell no one about this."

I take off down the narrow path. It winds around the

edge of the mountain like the tail of a serpent. One heavy gust of wind could sweep a person off the path and hurtle them over the thousand-foot drop. But my feet are sure and determined as I retrace my steps to the cave I've avoided ever since my last visit with my sister.

Withdrawing my sword, I let the flames of my fire burst from the blade, in part to light my way, but more to protect myself. Zmeya may be one of my own people, but she's as ancient as this mountain and her idea of who she serves is as fickle as the wind. The mouth of the cave seems to swallow me as I step inside. Between my flaming sword and Zmeya's fiery hieroglyphics, I'm able to work my way through the cavern until I find a woman crumbled into a heap on the ground. Fear cuts through me.

"Estrella!" I rush to her side.

A quick inspection shows me her skin is half-burned off and her hair is singed. Rage fires through me. I'm ready to kill the Dragon Seer myself.

"She's alive if that's what you're worried about," the woman's voice echoes from the other side of the cavern. I hope it's because she's scared to come too close.

"How could you do this?" I growl. "You tried to kill her, didn't you?"

"She's our enemy. Never forget that."

I want to attack Zmeya. Slice my blade across the wretched woman's neck and end her life. But right now, I need to get Estrella to a Healer. She's in pain, and killing Zemlya serves me no purpose.

"Your destiny might be tied to hers," she continues, "but she will always be a Nazco."

"You think you know everything," I spit out. "You may read destinies and minds, but you can't read hearts."

"Those are always the easiest to read," she says and then disappears in a rush of flames.

My feet can't move fast enough to escape this vile place.

I hurry Estrella back to my quarters, trying to ignore how her body hangs limp in my arms. I'm careful to stay out of sight from any suspicious eyes. The moment I enter my room, I request for my guard to send for Milania, the one Healer I trust explicitly. It's not that I don't trust the other Healers. They've proven themselves already by helping Estrella numerous times during her stay. It's the fact that they'll know she went to Zmeya when they see her body. One look at her will also tell them that Zmeya tried to kill her and failed, proving Estrella is a threat.

Gently, I lay her onto my bed, trying to make her comfortable. My heart rips in half, seeing her skin burned, her body ravaged by another once again. I rake my hands through my hair. I've done everything in my power to keep her safe, but I'm failing. Trouble stalks Estrella like a hungry lion. Milania arrives, and once I explain the details of what happened, she gets right to work.

"This must remain between the two of us," I tell her.

"Of course, your majesty," she says softly. "I'll do what I can."

I leave her to work and step into my sitting room, spending the next hour pacing in front of my fireplace, wondering what went on between the Dragon Seer and

Estrella. Did Zmeya give Estrella her destiny? Did Estrella gain the answers she was seeking?

My thoughts are disturbed by a knock on the door. Worry strikes me that someone has heard or witnessed Estrella's little excursion and already reported it to my father, and his guards are here for her. But when I open the door, I'm met with Katka, arms crossed. I'm surprised she's here, and doubly so when she pushes past me and enters my quarters.

"You shouldn't be here," I say, resisting a glance at my bedroom door.

"Why? Because you've got company?" She chuckles and rolls her eyes as if to tell me she knows I never have anyone in my quarters.

That's the problem with Katka. We know each other too well. Some might have once called us best friends. We were inseparable, causing havoc wherever we went. Like the time we hung sheets that looked like ghosts in the guardhouse and raced out screaming that the place was haunted. It took a dozen guards and over an hour for them to realize it was a prank. Not only that, she was the one I learned how to dance with—stepping on her foot too many times—and my first riding partner.

"How can I help you?" I ask her stiffly as the memories resurface.

"Why do you keep talking to me like that?" She sighs, and for a moment I can see the crack in her surface. The sharp hardness of her features softens, and the storm in her eyes dampers.

"Like what?"

"You promised you'd never treat me like I was one of your subjects. Like we weren't equals."

I don't miss the tremble in her voice. It's the first time she's shown an ounce of vulnerability to me ever since that dreadful night. It's the first time we haven't been snapping at each other since then. A spark of anger flares inside of me that she's opening back up to me now.

"I have always kept my promise." It's my turn to cross my arms. I don't want to have this conversation. Not now. Not when the rest of my world is a firestorm.

"You're still mad at me for ruining our friendship, aren't you?"

I look away. "I can't talk about this right now."

"I know I should regret what I did, but I don't." Her expression changes, and the mask she's been wearing for the last six months falls away. I rub my palm across my face, unsure how I should respond because she won't like my answer any way I put it.

"It's just you said you weren't ready for love," she continues, "and yet I see you with Estrella, hovering over her like she's yours."

"It's not that way between us," I lie. It's a lie to myself, and yet it must be a truth. Because she's not mine. I know this deep down even if I don't want it to be true. "She's here to train and regain her powers. That's it."

Katka reaches out like she's about to touch my face but jerks her hand back as her eyes whip to stare behind me. She gasps. I spin around to find Estrella standing in the doorway, barefoot and wearing a white nightgown. Her skin is already recovering, and Milania must have cut her hair because it's now neatly trimmed, golden strands sweeping along her shoulders. But I don't miss that look of betrayal on Estrella's face, which tells me she heard my last words when I implied there was nothing between us. My chest constricts. I want to tell her it was a lie and that my heart wants to be hers, but the voice of warning claps my mouth shut.

Milania slips past Estrella, holding the charred dress. She nods to me and then ducks out without a word.

"What's going on?" Katka takes everything in with her sharp eyes. "What was she doing here in your room?"

Blast it all. If Katka wanted to enact her revenge, this would be perfect ammunition for her arsenal.

"It's none of your business," I clip. "I need you to promise to not tell anyone about Estrella or the Healer."

Katka's fists clench at her sides, and her face hardens to stone. "I can't promise that."

"Please." Estrella steps forward. "Tristan was merely helping me by getting me a Healer without causing suspicion here at the castle. I went to see the Dragon Seer because I needed answers and to find a way to get my powers back to help my friends." She swallows and adds, "And to help the Sabians."

I don't know if Estrella is telling the truth, but her words seem to be working on Katka.

"Tristan's right. Nothing is going on between us," Estrella continues, lifting her chin. Those words stab me hard in the chest, and suddenly all I can think about is how soft she felt in my arms, how her kiss ignited every fiber within me.

"I'm surprised Zmeya let you live," Katka mutters.

"She said I needed to see Ami," Estrella says. "She is the one who can help me."

"Ami?" Katka frowns. "I don't know anyone by that name here."

"Can you find out who she is?" Estrella asks. "Please?"

Katka's gaze darts between the two of us as if she's deciding what she will do. I watch as her eyes harden to stone. I don't like the idea of what I think she'll do next, so I play the card I swore I'd never play on her.

"Will you do this for me?" I ask, my voice low and strained. I take her hand and squeeze it tight. "Doesn't our friendship mean anything?"

Katka stares at our held hands, swallowing hard. Beside me, Estrella stiffens. Finally, Katka pulls her hand away.

"I will do this for our friendship that once was," she says. "But I want you to remember that I was the one who was here at the beginning and will be at the end."

Then she gives a dark look at Estrella and storms out of the room, slamming the door behind her with a boom.

46
A PAWN IN A GREATER SCHEME

ESTRELLA

The Castle of Stará, Slovakia

My body visibly jerks at the slam of the door. Now that Katka has left, the tension should've as well, but instead, it's as if the air is full of sparks and hot coals. One step and I'll burn myself. I look into Tristan's eyes. They're stormy blue, tortured as if he's lost at sea.

"I don't think she likes me," I finally say, breaking the tension. "And now I see why."

"It's not that she doesn't like you." Tristan rakes a hand through his blond curls. "She's protective."

"She's in love."

Tristan's gaze whips to mine. His face twists in pain. "We are merely friends...or at least once were."

I nod, but I'm hardly convinced. It all makes sense now. Her untrust. The way she treats Tristan. The way he treats her. I walk over to the fireplace and pull a framed photo off the mantel. It's a picture of Conrad, Katka, and Tristan standing in a field with some sort of sticks. It must have been taken a few years back because they're all younger. Conrad's face is lit up with a smile. Katka's leaning against Tristan, her face softer than it is now. And Tristan has a devious sparkle in his eyes like he's about to cause mischief.

"You seem happy here," I say.

"It was a polo tournament." Tristan merely frowns deeper and takes the frame from me, setting it back on the mantel. "Why did you go see Zmeya? You could've died. You almost did."

He's right. The Healer may have mended my skin, but the memory of the pain still haunts my nerves and mind. "I had to do it. Being powerless was killing me."

"I hope it was worth it." Tristan crosses his arms.

"It was." I'm tempted to tell him the destiny the seer gave me, but the memory of his words to Katka keeps me in check: *It's not that way between us. She's here to train and regain her power. That's it.* Is that all I am to him? A pawn in a greater scheme? What had that kiss been?

Apparently, it was nothing. A stab of pain shoots through my chest.

"At least I know what our next step is," he grumbles. "To find who this Ami is."

"Do you think Katka will find her?"

"Depends on her mood."

I shift on my feet, suddenly feeling too close and yet too far away from Tristan. I still can't shake the feeling when I woke up in his bed while he was talking to Katka. When I saw his photos on the walls, the chessboard by the window, the miniature knights lined up on a shelf like he'd been collecting them for years. The scent of him still clings to me.

It terrifies me that I've let him get too close to my heart.

"I need to go." I back away from him.

"You're weak. You should lie back down and rest."

This might be true, but I can't stay here. "I need time to process everything that Zmeya said."

"She told you other things?" Tristan steps closer.

"So many terrible things about my past." I rub my forehead. Like how my parents died to protect me. That I was trying to save Lexi and Jamie before I met them at Nadia's Home. "How could I not remember those things?"

His brow furrows. "Zmeya has a way with words. She may speak the truth but she also twists them for her own means."

A wave of dizziness sweeps over me. "I need to go."

"I'll walk you back to your room," he says.

"Making sure I don't run away again?"

"I want you to find your powers and the answers you seek," he says softly. "Believe me or not, but it's true. And keeping you safe is the only way to do that."

We walk back to my room in silence. As the guard opens the door, I pause saying, "Thank you for coming and saving me. I'm deeply grateful."

"You are worth saving, Estrella, with or without ever regaining your powers." He lifts his hand and skims his fingers lightly along my cheek, sending a trickle of heat across my skin. "Sleep well and rest."

A shuddered breath escapes me. I'm desperate to let him

envelop me in the safety of his arms, but right now I can't trust my emotions. Quickly, I duck into my room and shut the door, leaning against it for support.

The next few days, I give myself time to heal, but I still try to practice my channeling. The use of my powers wears me out, and I find myself eating and sleeping more than usual to stave off the headaches. I'm haunted by the destiny the Seer gave me along with information I still have trouble processing, but it pushes me to work harder on using my visik.

She said she wanted to kill me like my parents died. She said before I lost my memories, I'd been trying to seek revenge for their deaths. Did that mean I'd been trying to find their murderer? Was I actively trying to kill Sabians?

And who exactly were my parents?

I have kept up my lessons with Henrich in the library as well, but maybe I'm just avoiding Tristan. The Queen ordered me to have a training session with Tristan using a fake Sabian Numinous fire, but it got so weird and awkward between us that we ended early.

He hasn't sought me out so perhaps he's avoiding me, too. It's better this way. The more I learn about myself, the more I realize my world and his are universes apart.

A week after my incident with the Dragon Seer, a seam-stress arrives and fits me for a gown and mask for a masquerade ball. Once she leaves, I pull in my maid, Sofia, and ask her if I really need to attend. The last thing I want to do is dance around with hundreds of people who want me dead.

She laughs. "But of course, you should. The King just announced that the ball will be in honor of you surviving the Dragon Seer."

"So he knows what I did." I sag onto my settee.

"This is a good thing." She settles beside me. "It means he's finally accepted you. By him hosting this ball in your honor, it means you are one of us."

"I'll never be fully accepted by the Sabians." She tries to disagree with me, but I say, "That's what the Dragon Seer told me."

"Oh." She swallows. "But this is a good step, is it not?"

"And the ball will be a great night for all of my enemies to show up to kill me."

"The Queen knew that might be the case, which is why she made a decree that it would be a masquerade ball."

"Is it strange that I trust and admire your queen far more than any of the leaders of the Nazco?"

"Well, they are Nazco, so it does make sense."

She pops up from her seat as a servant arrives with my breakfast. But her words sink heavily in my heart. Are all Nazco inherently evil? If I regain my memories, will I become like them?

I stand in front of the mirror hardly recognizing myself. The dress is the color of moonlight dusted with sugar, cascading in a waterfall of tulle to the floor. The tight bodice is pressed with intricate roses and pearls. Sofia pinned silver flowers into my hair and then allowed the rest of my long blonde curls to tumble down my back. I pick up the necklace Dion gave me, running my fingers across the gem's smooth surface. It's more of a pink color tonight. What color will it turn into when I step into the ballroom? Dion told me it would burn red when I was in danger, and so far, the necklace had stayed true to that promise.

"Where did you get that necklace?" Sofia asks, helping me fasten it. "It's stunning."

"It was a gift from a friend." My words choke in my throat as the Dragon Seer's words haunt me. *Perhaps you'd wish to be reunited with your lost love?*

Is Dion truly my lost love? A strangely familiar ache pulls at me, but how am I supposed to know the truth without my memories? This is another reason why I must find Ami and have her take me to the World of Between, whatever that place is. I vaguely remember Tristan talking about it being a place that Conduits went to. Tomorrow, if I'm still here, I'll need to research more about it.

"It is time for you to go," Sofia says, yanking me from my worries. She passes me a silver mask that matches my dress. It's studded in pearls with the same flowers as are on my bodice rimming the edges. "The Queen has requested you wear this at all times. It will hide your identity until it's time for the King to announce you."

I slip the mask over my face. Somehow it settles my nerves, knowing that I'm hidden and safe for the time being.

"Could you give me a moment to myself before I head to the ball?" I ask.

"Of course." She smiles warmly, and a tug of guilt pings me.

But I shove it aside as she steps out of the room. Quickly, I pull out my dagger, Tidebreaker. Now I'm glad I recharged it the other day. Tristan was right. The moment I'd touched the blade to the Sabian fire, it surged once again with power ebbing across the steel. It shimmers aqua blue. Lifting my skirts, I strap it onto my thigh. I'm not stepping into that ballroom unprepared.

I take a final deep breath and step out of my room, letting my two guards escort me to the ball. I just hope I survive the night.

47
FOOLISH BARGAINS FOR FOOLS IN LOVE
DION

São Paulo, Brazil

"That was a foolish bargain you made with the Eien," Father snaps at me the moment we enter our family mansion. The sunlit white walls, bright Spanish tiles, and star-crested lanterns swaying from the ceiling above always welcome us home no matter the arguments we might be having.

I stiffen at Father's words as we set off down the hall, running my hand through my still-wet hair after traveling through the Water Channels. He'd kept his silence while in Mexico, but now that we were free from curious ears, he was ready to lash out with his disapproval and lectures. I expected this. It has always been this way with him. Nothing I do ever pleases him and I always make the wrong decisions, and yet here I am, desperate to plead my case and prove to him I'm a son that can be worthy of him.

"It had to be done," I say. "They weren't going to make this deal unless we offered them the contract. The Nazco promise doesn't go very far in this world. You should know this."

Father stops in his tracks and faces me. His dark hair hangs over his forehead, wilder than usual, and his sharp chin juts slightly upward, a tell that he's furious. "Don't speak to me of broken promises like you understand the past or what I've done for this family. One thing I've learned over the years is to never make a promise signed with your powers. You have been born with high powers, unlike most immortals. Too many would do anything in their power to get a speck of your visik and yet you sign it away for a girl who is practically a mortal!"

"Her name is Estrella," I retort darkly.

"And not only that, you've signed this contract trusting that Estrella will deliver. You are depending on her when you don't know if she will actually give us this information. She must hate the Empress. Didn't she leave you for that Sabian dog?" He pauses, leaning in closer, and I swallow hard, hating how true his words are. "I can't imagine how she must feel about you after you didn't tell her the truth of who she was. What if she were to find out you were working for the Empress?"

"We're all working for the Empress," I bite back.

"But are we?" He clicks his tongue. "You are foolish, my son. And your infatuation with this girl is going to be your downfall. Just don't make it mine as well."

My whole body shakes, anger surging through my core,

but I keep it firmly locked down inside of me.

"I'm going to the Artifacts Room," I say, changing the subject. "I'd like to take one to help me find this Temple of the Fates."

"Many Tracker artifacts have already attempted that and failed. If they had worked, they would've found the temple already."

Father continues up the stairs, heading toward his office. I don't follow him.

"I'd like to use the Thunder Band," I call up.

He pauses on the stairs as if considering my words. All our artifacts are kept for emergencies in case of attack. They are rare and powerful and highly sought after as few immortals wish to give up their powers to an object for others to use later. What would he think if he knew I'd given Estrella the coveted Ghost Pendant?

"You may use it," Father finally says. He tilts his head but still doesn't turn to look at me. "Do not disappoint me in this."

He continues up the stairs, not bothering to hear my response. Not that I would have one. I spin on my heels and hurry to the Artifacts Room. I prick my finger on the needle, allowing my blood to trickle onto the stone plate for its security recognition.

The Thunder Band is in a carved mahogany box on the back wall. It's designed with lightning and clouds along the edges. Flipping open the lid, I find a bronze band about three inches wide with the large mythical Thunderbird set in the center, its wings outstretched and face fierce as a hurricane. It slips on easily, and I push it to rest on my upper arm. One press on the bird as I call for its power, and I'll be able to create shockwaves along with my lightning.

My phone rings, jolting me out of my reverence for this powerful artifact. I reach for my phone. It's BJ. My heart jolts.

"Tell me you have good news," I answer.

"Do you like parties?"

"No."

"How about dancing?"

"Nope."

"Then I take it you wouldn't be interested in attending a masquerade ball?"

"BJ, stop talking in riddles and tell me what this is about," I demand.

"Get yourself a mask and your best suit," he says. "Because I just got you a ticket into King Julian's Masquerade Ball in honor of his newest Channeler."

My chest squeezes tight. For some reason, it's hard to breathe. I lean against the wall. "When is this ball?"

"Tonight. I got in touch with our spy. He's been in deep cover for years so it's been nearly impossible to get in contact with him. He will notify Estrella of our arrival and then meet us at an underground thermal pool rarely used by the Sabians. I've got the location and am texting it to you now."

"Tell him not to contact Estrella. I don't want to risk anything."

"You got it. I'll meet you there soon."

"No. You stay out of this. If things go wrong, I don't want the Sabians to capture you."

"But what if they capture you?" BJ sounds worried.

"They won't. Good work, my friend. I owe you."

I hang up and hurry out of the Artifacts Room and down the corridor to find a servant. In just a few hours, I'll see Estrella again.

48
GLITTERING BALLGOWNS, DECEPTIVE HEARTS
ESTRELLA

The Castle of Stará, Slovakia

T he Masquerade Ball's entrance blooms like a garden at twilight as I join the line of Sabians eagerly trailing inside. Lilies cling to the arched stone and roses drape from the pillars like an entrance to a secret garden. But the moment I step inside, I pause at the top of the stairs and gasp in awe at the ballroom below me.

Dancers swirl in a tangle of colors. A cascading rainbow-colored waterfall rings three sides of a banquet table piled with food. Silver stars float through the air, illuminating the room in an iridescent glow. King Julian and Queen Kelli sit regally on their golden thrones on a dais overlooking the room. The air smells like spring and tastes like magic. My body shivers as if I've been woken from a sleeping spell.

My legs somehow move, and I descend into the crowd of glittering gowns and masks of raven feathers, dragon scales, and flames of fire. As I squeeze behind a group of ladies gossiping, I feel their powers hovering at the edge of their bodies. One woman wearing a mask with waves curling around her eyes must have the power of the ocean because I can almost taste the sea on my lips as I slip past her.

But then her words stop me short.

"Supposedly the Nazco is here," Ocean Wave Woman says conspiratorially, glancing around. "But I've heard she's powerless as a bird."

I pretend to adjust my shoe as I listen.

The woman with a hawk mask snorts. "You wouldn't know power if you saw it. Still, if she's a Nazco cast-off, she's likely to be a weak little thing. They killed two possible Conduits this century already. What does she look like?"

"Ugly, I'm sure. Aren't all Nazco?" another woman says, and they all titter with laughter.

"Still, my friend Natasha said the Prince is quite taken with her," Ocean Wave Woman says soberly, and the women gasp in horror.

"You are all fools," a startling familiar voice breaks through their gasps. Nina, Tristan's sister's best friend. She's the one who snuck into my room to kill me for vengeance. "I've met her, and she is not so weak and far too dangerous. The Royal Family has been cast under her spell, but tonight, I will free them of the Nazco witch's sorcery."

Anger rises up inside me at her accusations, but fear also twists in my gut. If she realized I was within her grasp, she'd kill me without thinking. Quickly, I dart to the far side of the ballroom like a deer running from its hunter and tuck myself in close to the topiaries lined up along the gilded wall.

I breathe a long sigh of relief that Nina hadn't seen me. But then I shake my head at my stupidity.

Of course she didn't see me, silly! I laugh at myself. *I'm wearing a mask!*

Which is why no one is even glancing in my direction. They are too busy dancing, eating, and chatting. A smile dances across my lips. With my mask, I'm truly hidden. Queen Kelli is wiser than I gave her credit for. These Sabians have no idea I'm the dreadful ex-Nazco Conduit. Boosted by this, I glide out of the shadows and head confidently to the refreshment table. I load up on plump red berries and cream puffs overflowing with chocolate.

"We are the smart ones," a woman with a mask of rain-drop-shaped sapphire tells me. "Get the food first before it's gone."

"I agree," I say, trying to imitate the Slovakian accent. "Everyone seems too busy trying to figure out who this Nazco is."

"Exactly! I'm guessing that's her in the far corner in the pale pink dress standing all alone."

"It does make the most sense," I agree, wondering how long I can keep up my charade. "She won't have any friends."

With full plates, the two of us slip off to the side by a set of flames that twist into the shapes of animals.

"Do you think the King really will make this Nazco his next Conduit?" I dare ask the woman.

"I heard she's worthless. Practically mortal."

"Really?" I take a bite of the cream puff, nonchalantly. "How unfortunate."

"What's unfortunate?" a woman with an ice-crusted mask asks, joining us.

I nearly drop my plate. Her mask may be in place, but I'd recognize that power oozing off her with my eyes closed.

Valeska.

My ribcage holds my racing heart in place. If she recognizes me, she won't hesitate to kill me either. Well, take a number, sister.

"Valeska, you're back from your mission." Sapphire Mask pops a grape in her mouth. "We were talking about the Nazco Conduit being powerless, but I don't think the King cares. He's hoping to make the Empress think he's got a Conduit so she doesn't attack us."

"I don't care what the King wants to do with that Nazco," Valeska half-growls. "I want her dead."

Fear shoots up my spine.

"You're not the only one." Sapphire Mask laughs.

Valeska and I join in. Thankfully, the quartet of violins masks my laughter, which sounds more like choking. Despite my terror, I can't miss this opportunity for information.

"You were on that team that recovered the tablet from the museum," I dare ask. "Congratulations on your success."

"Thank you." Valeska sips from her champagne flute. "Though I won't feel the victory until we find the Temple of the Fates."

"So Mexico was a dead-end?" Sapphire Mask asks. "You had such high hopes the temple would be there."

"An utter flop."

So that was why the Sabians—and apparently me before I lost my memory—were after that tablet. They were searching for the Fates' Temple.

"Unfortunate." I decide to press my luck a little more. "I'm surprised we've yet to decrypt the tablet's message."

"Actually," Valeska grins, glacier-blue eyes glittering, "I got news today that the linguistics team finally deciphered it."

Lazily, I nibble on my canape, but my heart is desperate to learn what she discovered. "Really? What did it say?"

"It's classified."

"If anyone deserves to know, it's you," I feed into her ego.

"Exactly!" Valeska sighs and empties her glass with a single gulp.

She starts telling us about how hard it's been, losing first her teammate and then having to deal with the impossible demands of the King. While she rants, I wave down the server holding a tray of champagne glasses. I press another glass into Valeska's hand.

"With such dedication and commitment," I say, "I hope you'll be chosen for the next mission."

"You're looking at its leader!" Valeska gloats.

"Congrats!" I squeal in delight. "When do you leave?"

"I leave for Africa tomorrow."

"Africa?" Sapphire's lips dip. "Isn't it dreadfully hot there?"

"Quite, and since the clue is so vague, I don't imagine we'll ever find this temple. I've got the poem right here." She pats a pouch at her side. "Maybe the answer will just pop into my head."

She laughs, and so I do, too. But my hand itches to get a hold of that poem. I just don't know how to get it without revealing who I am.

I wonder if Tristan knows about this. I need to talk to him and show him the message I got, but I haven't seen him yet tonight. I excuse myself from the two and scan the crowd. With everyone wearing masks, it's hard to find him. My eyes drift up to the balcony where couples have cloistered in the shadows, but then one man catches my eye because his gaze is pinned to mine. There's something familiar about his swooping black hair and those dark eyes beneath a midnight mask. They seem to swallow me whole. For a heartbeat, I'm sure it's Dion. But that's impossible. There's no way he could be here.

I jerk my gaze away from him, and that's when I find Tristan. He's standing by the tall glass doors that open to a garden. Those wild curls have been tamed behind a mask of flames, and his muscular frame is striking in a black suit with swooping tails. A red cravat hangs slightly loose as if he's been tugging at it.

I give him a pointed glance at the garden doors and that devious smile curls on his lips. An ache tugs at my chest, but I rein it firmly in check. Reading my gesture correctly, he slips outside. As nonchalantly as possible, I weave through the guests, my gown swishing across the marble floor.

A pair of Fire Wielders steps onto the stage and starts performing for the King and Queen sitting on their thrones, breathing out visions of dragons and sea creatures that send the audience into gasps and cheers.

The air is as cool as a spring night when I step outside into the gardens. A glass roof arches overhead. I follow the tiled path around beds of peonies and forget-me-nots, ducking through rose-rimmed arches until I find Tristan standing by a stone railing, silhouetted by the starlit sky.

My steps slow as I move to stand at his side where he's staring through the glass wall, overlooking the ice-crusted edge that plunges into the valley below. His mask hangs between his fingers.

"This ball is incredible," I say, breaking the silence. "It's like magic."

His gaze rips from the view to stare at me. I pull off my mask and feel relief at the cool air.

"You look like magic," he whispers back, his voice pained. His fingers brush across my cheeks, sending a trail of fire across my skin. "You wanted to talk to me?"

"I was talking to Valeska. She said the tablets have been deciphered. Apparently, she and her team are leaving for Africa tomorrow."

His eyebrows lift. "Really? I've not heard of this."

"She has some sort of note about it in her pocket. Has Katka gotten any information on who this Ami is?"

"She's still working on it." He takes my hands, and I feel the heat of his visik ebb and flow through me. "But we will get you answers."

"And what if we don't?" I break away from him to pace back and forth. "I feel like I'm just sitting here waiting for answers, and every moment puts myself and my friends in greater danger. I need to leave and find her myself."

"And how would you do that?" He runs a palm over his face. "I don't think my father will ever let you leave."

"So I'm trapped here forever?"

A pained expression crosses his eyes. "Is this place really

so bad?"

I look away. "I'll find a way to escape."

"Even if you figured out where this Ami was, how would you even get there?"

"Will you help me?" I step closer to him.

"You don't know what you ask."

But I do, which is why guilt tinges my mouth like sour grapes. "At least help give me a head start."

"It would be impossible. You'd never get past the guards."

"Remember the artifact in the Artifacts Room called Timebender that you said manipulates time?" He nods warily, and I brace myself for what I'm about to ask of him. "We could borrow it, and you could use it so I could slip away."

His jaw muscles flex as his eyes study mine. "When?"

"Tonight. It's only a matter of time before someone kills me. Valeska is here looking for me, and I overheard Nina say she's going to kill me the moment she sees me."

"Blast it all," he mutters. "My father has set up a death trap here for you. I'll get the Timebender. Father's planning on introducing you tonight. Promise me you'll wait and see how that goes before you try to escape."

"Okay. Thank you for trusting me, protecting me, and helping me. I hope I can make it up to you and your people someday."

He nods, his gaze latching onto mine, and my heart aches. For what we have and what we don't.

"Save me a dance, will you?" he asks.

My breath shudders. "Of course."

I know I shouldn't, but I reach up and wrap my arms

around the back of his neck. I expect him to pull away, but instead, his head dips, and his lips press against mine. Warm sunsets and beach-lit fires. His hands cord around my body, pulling me to him like he never wants to let me go, claiming me as if he knows I'll never be his.

I'm lost in the fever of his passion. The heat of his caress washes away all my fears and worries.

Someone clears their throat. We break apart like we're on fire. Katka stands before us, dressed in a form-fitting emerald-green gown that accentuates the curves her work clothes have been hiding. A mask of gears and emeralds is pulled up on the top of her head like she went to take it off but forgot to finish the task. Her breasts heave in and out as if she's been running. Or holding in her emotions.

"You said there's nothing going on between the two of you." Her voice is strangled, angry. "You lied to me."

"Katka." Tristan runs both his hands through his hair. "I'm sorry. I don't know why..."

"This is my fault," I quickly say. "I kissed him. It was a mistake."

"Of course, it's your fault," Katka clips, sending a dagger-tipped gaze at me. "I came here to tell you the news because I thought you'd like to know."

Tristan stills. "What news?"

"It's Conrad," she says, and now tears fill her eyes. I think back to the photo in Tristan's room of the three of them. She must have been close to Conrad as well.

"What about Conrad?" Tristan's tone lowers with urgency.

"He's been captured by the Nazco. And they've taken your friend, Lexi, too."

49
WHEN THINGS GO FROM BAD TO WORSE
ESTRELLA

The Castle of Stará, Slovakia

U pon hearing the news of Lexi's capture, I gasp and reach for Tristan's arm for support, which only darkens Katka's glare. Quickly, I pull away from him.

"Where did they take them?" Tristan demands.

"To the Midnight Kingdom," Katka says like they've been dragged to Hell. "The Empress sent a message just moments ago. Said she's imprisoning them until we release Estrella to her."

"No!" I cry out, clamping my hands over my mouth to stifle the sob escaping me. The thought of Lexi being imprisoned is like being stabbed in the heart. "It was bad enough knowing Lexi was at Nadia's, but this is so much worse. I need to turn myself in."

"As much as it pains me to say this because Conrad is my best friend," Tristan heaves a deep breath, "if you turn yourself in, it's exactly what the Empress would want. Conrad knew what he was getting himself into. He's a trained warrior. And Lexi is strong and smart. We need to be smarter about this. We need to stick with the plan."

"But that plan was made before we knew this," I argue, wringing my hands.

"Estrella, you need to turn yourself in," Katka says. "There is no other option."

"The Empress wants you weak and untrained," Tristan tells me, ignoring Katka's response. "Do you think for a moment that she will stay true to her word?"

"I don't know the Empress," my heart sinks through quicksand, "but my gut tells me no."

"Conrad and Lexi are pawns," Tristan says, "and as long as the Empress thinks they're useful, their lives are safe. So we find a way to make sure it stays that way until we can get your powers back."

His eyes find mine, and an unspoken agreement flits between us.

Katka huffs. "I knew neither of you would see reason."

"Katka," Tristan says, "I need you to find everything you can about why they were taken and where they might be."

"This time I'm doing this for Conrad," she says through gritted teeth. She spins on her sharp heels and storms back down the path.

My knees threaten to buckle. "I can't stand the thought of Lexi being in a Nazco prison because of me."

"We'll get her out," Tristan reassures me. "Now more

than ever, you need to get your powers back. I'm going to go to the Artifacts Room. I'll meet you at the ball when I return."

He takes off in a run while I retrace my steps back to the ballroom. My mind whirls as I try to figure out the best path for saving Lexi. The ball is in full swing when I reenter. I blink a few times, readjusting to the glittering lights, music, and laughter. Everyone looks so happy and carefree, eating and drinking, while I feel so lost and confused.

To my right, Nina is standing off to the side, studying the room like a hawk, hunting its prey. Her head swivels in my direction and abruptly stops, eyes narrowing. My heart kicks up a notch. I look suspicious, standing here off to the side, alone like I'm a foreigner who doesn't belong. A server strolls past with a tray of drinks. Quickly, I snatch one up and cast about for a small group to latch myself onto.

"Could I have this dance?" a deep voice says behind me.

I turn to find the same man I saw on the balcony, dark eyes shadowed beneath his mask. Nina starts moving in my direction, and worry chases up my spine. I set my drink on a side table and say, "I'd love to."

We step out onto the dance floor, and I slip one hand in his and the other on his shoulder. Electricity sparks across my palms, and I gasp in shock. I go to pull away, but he draws me closer, leaning in so his lips are brushed against my ear.

"Estrella," the familiar voice whispers, shivering down my spine.

"Dion." I gasp. "Is it really you?"

"Indeed. You look beautiful. You rival the stars tonight."

Our bodies press against each other as we sway to the

music. His solid frame is hard against my curves. The scent of him drifts over me, and I'm tempted to lean into the fantasy that he's the guy I fell in love with in the hallways of a high school. I used to dream of this possibility while lying all alone in Nadia's house, scared and unsure who I was.

My heart patters against my ribcage as the reality sinks in at how familiar it feels to be in his arms. Desperately I try to pull up the memory, but it's just out of my reach. The music surges around us and he twirls me around, my dress whirling out like peonies under the summer sun.

But that life in Florida was a lie that had been planted in my mind. A way to keep me imprisoned and bonded. Why am I feeling these emotions for two guys?

When I spin back into his arms, I ask, "What are you doing here? How is this possible?" I have so many questions, and it doesn't help that my emotions are fighting against my mind.

"A friend got me an invitation." His dark eyes glitter under the shimmering lights. "I've never attended a Sabian ball. Quite the party."

"If they discover you, they'll kill you."

"Most definitely. But it has been worth every second to see you again."

"How are you alive?" I ask, and wariness curls through me. Could he be working for the Empress? Sent to kidnap me and take me to her kingdom? "How did you survive all those people who were chasing us at the pond?"

"Perhaps it was pure will, perhaps it was the fact that I couldn't stand to be away from you."

"You're not here for a dance and drinks. What is it that you want?"

He cups a hand to my cheek, and his eyes darken. Electrifying sparks sizzle dangerously across my skin.

"I made a deal with a powerful immortal. She's agreed to train you and help you get your powers back."

A sharp gasp escapes me. "How is this possible?"

He glances around. "We must leave now. My friend has a way for us to escape."

"I can't go with you." I break contact with him, stepping back.

He closes the gap. "Why?"

"I don't trust you anymore."

Pain lashes across his eyes. "What can I do to prove myself?"

"The Empress has imprisoned my friend, Lexi. I need to get my powers back so I can rescue her. Your offer is tempting, but you're a Nazco immortal. And a powerful one from what I've heard."

"Have you forgotten that you are, too?" He takes my hand. "You can trust me, Estrella. Your mind may not remember, but an immortal heart never truly forgets. Search your heart. It will tell you that all I've ever wanted is for your happiness. Let me take you to this woman. She can help you."

My eyes search his face, and I wish I had the powers of a Truth Seeker. "Who is this person?" I ask skeptically. "How can I know that she really can help?"

"I think when you meet her, you'll understand. Her name is Ami."

I stumble in my dance step. That is the same name the Dragon Seer gave me. A trumpet blares across the room.

Everyone silences and turns to face the dais where the King and Queen sit.

"Come," Dion says urgently, "we must go now. Our window to escape is closing."

Indecision yanks at me, and I hesitate.

King Julian rises and holds up his hands. "As you all know, this celebration is in honor of the ex-Nazco Conduit who has defected to join us."

Whispers rush across the crowd. My gaze flickers to Dion's. His eyes widen, and even his dark mask can't disguise the hurt in them.

"I'm sorry," I whisper to Dion.

"I have wonderful news for my people," the King continues. "She has been training and survived a visit with the Dragon Seer. It is only a matter of time that her powers will rise and she will be able to enter the World of Between and reignite our people's powers once again."

A round of cheers and clapping fills the ballroom, but as I study the crowd, only about half of the partiers are celebrating. *I have many enemies here*, I realize.

"And now it's time for me to introduce her to you all." King Julian focuses on me and holds out a hand. "Come, Estrella. Greet your new family and show them your powers."

A servant pulls aside a metal cage that was covering the top of the pedestal. A blazing red ball of fire hovers above it. *Sabian visik from the World of Between.* This is what Tristan showed me in the training room.

Every eye in the crowd turns to stare at me. Those around me step away as if I'm poison. I begin my walk to the dais, which isn't hard as the bodies move like a parting sea. I feel exposed, naked among this crowd. Will Nina and Valeska use this moment when my back is turned to kill me? Is their vengeance stronger than their allegiance to their King?

My foot takes the first step to the dais when a scream erupts through the quiet hall.

"She will never be one of us!" a voice cries. "The blood of our fallen seek her death."

I whirl around just as a sharp-tipped ice spear hurtles through the air, aimed directly at me.

50
AMBUSHES CAN REALLY MESS UP DINNER PLANS
ESTRELLA

The Castle of Stará, Slovakia

I duck before it slices through my throat. The room erupts into chaos. People start screaming, some scattering away. The powers in this room are intensifying, surging through the air around me. But my focus is on Valeska, advancing toward me. Her glittering pale gown sweeps across the floor. Her hair juts out like icy sharp knives. Two more spears form from her palms as she prepares for another onslaught.

My powers might not be at capacity, yet I feel trickles of both Tristan's and Dion's visik surging through my veins. But how do I use their powers? I've only channeled it back into them. A second spear sails my way. I leap off the steps and dive out of the way, except it's like the spear is following me.

As I land, I swipe at the air, desperately trying to draw up Tristan's fire. A wave of flames gushes out of my palm. It melts the spear enough that when it hits me, its razor tip is already melted off. It slams against my shoulder, jolting me backward, but it's not sharp enough to pierce through my skin.

"Bring the Nullifier!" King Julian calls out.

"Guards, capture the rebel," General Sage orders.

But Valeska isn't alone. Others slip to her side, faces hidden by masks. The glittering globes floating above us explode. Sparkles rain from above, thrusting the ballroom into shadows. More screams ring out as partiers push to escape. One of the men advancing on me waves his hands, and the vines on the wall start creeping toward me. Another woman lifts her hand, causing the waterfall by the wall to slither across the ground like a snake ready for attack.

Terror fills me. I need to get out of here. I race for the exit.

Hands reach to stop me, but General Sage warns, "Don't touch her! She's dangerous. Get the King and Queen to safety!"

I break free once again, following the crowd surging toward the exit. I duck down a dark hallway and race toward the door at the end. I'm nearly there when a hand closes around my arm. I whirl around to face Dion, his black suit shrouded perfectly with the shadows.

"Don't go that way. The hall is full of guards. General Sage has ordered them to kill you if you resist."

"You should run," I tell him. "Being with me only means death."

"I know a way out," he says. "This way."

The last thing I want to do right now is follow Dion, but he's right. General Sage has always been suspicious of me from the moment I stepped through the castle's front gates. The fact that he allowed Valeska to attack is proof he wants me dead. I certainly don't have time to wait around for Tristan.

Dion leads me up the back stairs into the balcony. "There's a secret door that my contact showed me up here."

We scamper along, hugging the back wall until he stops at a golden panel in the wall. He presses against one corner, and it swings inward. He steps through and turns, holding a hand out to me. I hate that I'm trusting him, but my other choice is to put myself at the mercy of the Sabians. I take his hand and enter a narrow corridor. It twists and turns until we reach another door that spits us out into an outer courtyard of the castle.

"We're almost there," Dion says, leading me around the corner. "It's just this—"

His words die on his tongue, and we both stumble to a halt. Standing before us are at least ten immortals, waiting by the back wall as if they were expecting us.

"I'm sorry, Dion," a tall man calls out from where he's wrapped up in vines. "I messed up."

"This is what happens to Nazco spies," Nina says from where she stands in the center of the group. Then she nods, and one of the men slices off the guy's head.

A gasp snaps from me. "How could you?"

"We'll be sending all of your heads back to the Empress

as a payment for her actions," she continues, her blood-red lips curling. "From what I've heard, you're quite the catch, Dion."

I pull out my dagger from the strap on my thigh and hold it before me. The blade shimmers ocean blue, ready to come to my aid. I crouch and prepare to defend myself.

A low growl erupts from Dion. He throws off his mask and jacket. The veins on his face turn silver as rage courses across his body. He throws up a hand and a sharp bolt of electricity shudders across the courtyard, aimed directly at the man who killed the spy. It hits him in the chest, sending him flying through the air and smashing into the wall.

One of the Sabians opens his mouth, and an earth-shattering scream erupts. My dagger clatters to the ground as I'm forced to slam the heels of my palms to my ears. Pain lances through my head, and I fall to my knees.

The moment he stops screaming, a whirlwind of sand sweeps over us, stinging my eyes and coating my mouth. I clamp my eyes shut against the onslaught. They were prepared. They knew exactly what they were doing.

The crackle of electricity fills the air. Dion must be attacking despite the sandstorm. I rise to my feet and blindly rush forward with my dagger. If I can just get ahold of one of the immortals, I can pull their power from them like I did battling Quadril and Chandra.

I only get a few steps when a vine wraps around my ankle and yanks me forward, throwing me to the ground. I'm dragged across the courtyard on my back. Sand burns my eyes, but I slice my blade through the vine, freeing myself. I scramble to my feet, but more vines wrap around me once again, tossing me back to the ground and cocooning me like a mummy.

I'm hauled closer to the group. Abruptly, the sand stops, and the screaming is gone. I blink away the sand to find that I'm lying on the ground before Valeska. She looms over me with a snarl. Her group circles me like vultures eager to consume their prey. Dion is throwing bolt after bolt of electricity, but it's not hitting us.

One of the Sabians with me must be making the shield that surrounds us. I spot him. He's kneeling on the ground in front of the Sabian group, his arms opened wide and feet spread out, head back. How much longer can he hold that shield?

"You think you can waltz in here and take over our kingdom?" Valeska asks.

"No!" I struggle against the Vine Immortal's hold. "That's not true!"

Water slams against my face, gushing down my throat. I sputter and cough.

"Who else is working with you?" Valeska demands. "You're here with others. Admit it!"

"I'm not." I twist my dagger, trying to break myself free.

"In that case, she's no longer needed," Valeska says darkly. She hefts up an ice dagger, preparing to slice my head off.

"Wait!" I yell desperately. "There is actually someone else."

She pauses, white brows lifting. "Who?"

"I can't remember his name, but he works at the front gate," I say, but all my concentration is focused on cutting through the vines. "I was supposed to meet him and let others in."

"What is his name?!" Valeska screams. "Tell me now!"

My dagger breaks through the vines, freeing my arms. I twist my coiled body and stab her in the foot with the dagger. She howls, dropping to the ground in agony. I secretly slide my hand into her pouch and snatch out the scrap of paper inside, tucking it between my breasts. Then I yank my dagger out of her leg. I'm climbing to my feet, but whoever has power of the vines quickly wraps me back up, this time tighter. I grunt, wiggling in desperation to get free.

"Kill her now," one of the Sabians says. "Patrick won't be able to hold the shield for much longer."

One of the bolts of electricity smashes into the wall behind us, sending chunks of stone hurtling through the air. I roll over, trying to protect myself from the barrage. The sandstorm and screaming come to a halt.

"Kill her now!" Valeska screams.

"No!" a voice booms across the courtyard. I lift my head to see Tristan, leaping down from one of the walls. "By order of the King, she must remain alive."

Someone grabs my vine-mummified body, rolls me over, and holds me tight. The guy who had been screaming steps up to me, lifts his ax, and lets it fall.

But it freezes mid-air. I'm in shock. What just happened? I try to move, but it's as if I'm frozen in time.

That's it. Time is on hold. Tristan must have used the Timebender artifact, which means only he has the ability to move through time within this area.

Tristan appears above me. He snatches the ax from the guy and chops me free from the vine. Then he scoops me up in his arms. I want to say something, but my voice is lost in the crystalized world around me.

Next, he runs over to Dion, who's standing still as stone, hands outstretched. Tristan ducks low enough to heft Dion onto his shoulder and then we are all off once again. I'm trying to process everything, but it's like my thoughts and words are stretched apart, unable to connect.

Tristan is running through a warren of corridors when suddenly a rushing wind hurtles through me. The world slams back into sharp colors, and sounds rush back to my ears. Even my thoughts jumble back to me in a hurricane of words.

"What in the blistering stars are you doing?" Dion exclaims. He twists off Tristan and stumbles against the wall.

"Unfortunately, saving you," Tristan pants. "Man, you're heavier than I expected."

"I can walk," I tell Tristan, who promptly puts me down. "Thank you for saving us."

"We're not out of the woods yet," Tristan says. "Thanks to this Nazco, some of my people are dead."

"They're the ones who started it," Dion says.

Tristan focuses on me. "If we tell my father that Valeska trapped you in the north quadrant and you were trying to save yourself, he will protect you. My mother will, too. She knows you mean no harm. But you," he turns to Dion, "they'll kill you on the spot. The only reason why I haven't is my thanks for saving Estrella's life. Valeska had placed two Shield Immortals at that court-yard's entrance. None of General Sage's men could get through."

"I can't stay." I clench my dagger tighter. "I need to go find Ami."

"We need more time. We don't even know who she is."

"He does." I nod to Dion.

Tristan's eyes widen, and he gives Dion a scathing look. "You trust this guy?"

"I'm alive because of him."

Dion crosses his arms with a smug smile. "Guess I'm sticking around."

"Every exit is heavily guarded." Tristan runs a hand over his face. "There's no way any of us are leaving this castle."

"I know a way out," I say. "A lost, secret passageway."

51
I'M GOING TO NEED YOU TO GET ALONG
ESTRELLA

The Mountain of the Dragon, Slovakia

I lead the two guys through the warren of corridors until we reach the back of the castle. All the torches and lanterns have been lit, so it's going to be trickier to escape, but we need to take the risk.

"Follow me and don't talk," I warn them both.

Dion nods grimly while Tristan sheaths his sword and the glow from his blade fades, drenching us in inky darkness.

It's weird to have them both here, standing with me, and a little confusing, too. They're two parts of my life, my old and new. But despite everything, having them beside me is my best chance of survival. I turn the door handle and step out into the night. I wish I had time to change out of this gown, but there's nothing to do about it. I lift up the skirts and step out into the cold. I make sure to tuck myself into the shadows of the walls as best as I can until I reach the Queen's Garden. Once there, I pluck off one of the torches and scurry to the vine-infested fountain. I pause and scan the area to make sure we're not being followed.

"Why are we here?" Dion shifts his feet and casts his gaze around like a trapped animal. "We're too exposed."

"I can't believe I'm agreeing with him," Tristan mutters. "We need to find shelter."

"Don't worry," I crouch to the ground in search of the lever, "we'll be hidden soon. Let me know if someone sees us."

Finally, my fingers scrape along the metal surface. It's ice-cold as I yank it back. The secret entrance grinds open.

"What in the blazes is this?" Tristan asks.

"A secret tunnel." I slip inside and wave for them to follow. "Hurry!"

The two trail after me into the darkness. The moment they're both through, I close the door behind us. The fire from my torch dances across our faces.

"How did you know this was here?" Tristan asks, taking it all in.

"I might have found a map in the library with this on it." I shrug. "It's how I was able to find the Dragon Seer. According to the map, this tunnel goes all the way to the lake at the base of the mountain."

"I'm surprised I didn't know about this," Tristan says, taking in the roughly hewn mountain stone.

"Dion," I say. "Are you really able to take us to Ami?"

"Us?" His gaze darkens. "I'm here to take you. I don't know what he has to do with the recovery of powers."

"He has a point, Tristan. You don't have to come with us."

"I told you I'll do everything in my power to help you," Tristan says. "If you don't want me to come, I won't, but I am here to offer protection."

His gaze cuts pointedly to Dion.

"She doesn't need protection from me," Dion snaps roughly.

"Also, I know the entrance to the Water Channels below," Tristan adds. "Where are we headed?"

"To Eien territory," Dion says.

Tristan's brow lifts, clearly shocked. "Well, this is quite the surprise."

"These Eien." My gaze flickers between the two of them. "Do you trust them?"

"No," they say simultaneously.

"Well, then there's our answer," I decide firmly. "You're both coming. And I'm going to need you to try to get along once we get there. We must arrive as a united front."

"United?" Dion scoffs. "I don't see that happening."

"For once, I'm in agreement," Tristan adds with a snort.

"Then it sounds like you're both staying here." I glare at them and turn and take off down the tunnel.

"But I'm always up for impossible tasks," Tristan says, hurrying after me.

"It appears as if you both forgot that you need me to take you there." Dion joins my other side. "I am the only one who knows the way."

Hours later, we step out of the tunnel at the base of the

mountain. The air is sweet and tastes like freedom. The grass tickles my ankles, and hope flutters in my chest. If this Ami can help me, I can learn how to use my powers and perhaps even train to fight. Then I'll be able to rescue Lexi from the Nazco prison and my friends from Nadia's. As I stride toward the water's edge, I leave behind my fear and doubts of who I am.

Because now it's time for me to become a warrior.

Did you enjoy the story?
If you enjoyed this story, I'd appreciate your time and effort if you'd leave a review and share with other readers what you loved about the book.

Bonus Fun!
Would you like a little more? Head over to my website and get a special bonus scene with Estrella and Tristan. https://christinafarley.com/the-immortal-bound-series/

Don't want the story to end?
I've got you covered! You can read the next book in the series, THE IMMORTAL WARRIOR, and join Estrella on her journey to finding her powers and true love.

Continue the adventure

THE
IMMORTAL
WARRIOR

The Immortal Bound Series
Book 3

YOUR NEXT ADVENTURE

The Immortal Warrior (Book 3): Continue Estrella's journey!

The Dreamscape Series: A thrilling near-future adventure where your dreams are no longer safe.

The Gilded Series: A contemporary fantasy set in Korea.

The Princess and the Page: Get enchanted in this magical, fairytale mash-up set in France.

The Thief of Time: A magical school for librarians.

Fairy Tale Road: Choose your fairy tale ending in this adult romance.

About the Author

CHRISTINA FARLEY writes romantic fantasy and thrilling adventures inspired by her travels. When not wandering the world or creating imaginary ones, she spends time with her family in Florida where they are busy preparing for the next World Cup, baking cheesecakes, and raising a pet dragon in disguise as a very furry cat.

Visit her online:
ChristinaFarley.com
Instagram: @ChristinaLFarley
Facebook: @ChristinaFarleyAuthor
YouTube: @ChristinaFarley
TikTok: @ChristinaFarleyAuthor

Join Christina's Newsletter, the Travelogue: Exclusive access to videos, book updates, giveaways:
https://tinyurl.com/ypb9pm9a

STAY IN TOUCH

I hope you'll stay in touch by joining my newsletter group, The Travelogue, or VIP Reader Group so we can continue to take more adventures together. If you sign up, you'll receive a free book as my way of saying you're awesome.

Christina's Newsletter: Reader news, writing tips, giveaways, and book updates: https://tinyurl.com/ypb9pm9a

Christina's VIP Reader Club: Weekly update with insider news, exclusive content, and exclusive giveaways: https://tinyurl.com/mryncvmf

ACKNOWLEDGMENTS

It is a joy and a gift to sit down and write each day. I owe every word that spills onto the page to my Heavenly Father. Thank you for listening to my heart and being there for me in the darkest times.

Each book I write is like sharing a piece of my heart with my readers. I'm so grateful to all the readers, booksellers, librarians, and reviewers who help me spread a little bit of magic into the world we live in. I'm so grateful to be a part of your life and for you to be a part of mine.

A special thanks goes out to my VIP Reader Group: Christy S, Laura P, Mila C, Beth G, Andrea M, Ava M, Kendra P, Laziz T, Ana B, Amanda F, Jennifer A, Aziza E, Marisela Z, Eva M, Jenny H, Christina V, Amber J, Shana D, Kelli J, Bert B, Dianna B, Tez M, Bri L, Candi M, Julianne J, Amy P, Kris D, Sheree W, Jamie G, Jan W, Stephanie B, Ells, Heath W, Willa Z, Jerry N, Kate H, Joyce K, Tiffany L, Vivi B, Alison R, Callie T, Sarah W, Sunny B, Finely T, Margaret T, Billy F, Jocelyn M, Laziza T, Merry M, Megan B, Susan L, Emily I, Yvonne V, JB, Theresa L, Adalyn B, Megan B, Mitsy P, Skylere K, and Jami. You all are the best!

A huge gasp of awe to Paul at Trif Book Design for creating a cover that I never want to stop staring at. The beautiful map is thanks to Veronika Wunder.

Thank you to my copyeditor, Sarah Ward, for making this manuscript shine despite the quick turnaround.

To Amy and Vivi for all the late-night messages, long road trips, and ideation sessions. I can't wait to see where the next ten years take us.

To Julianne, the best sister I could ever have. Thank you for believing in me.

Always, always to my two loving and beautiful sons, Caleb and Luke. Thank you for your encouragement and being the sounding board for my world-building ideas.

Finally, to my husband, Doug. You are my love, my heart, my everything.

Made in United States
Orlando, FL
08 November 2024

53587357R00228